EDENS

GATE

AN EPIC HARD SCI FI ADVENTURE

HIGH CONCEPT SCIENCE FICTION AT
ITS THRILLING BEST

BOOK ONE OF THE ARCADIA SERIES

IAN FRASER

The Arcadia Series

Eden's Gate

An Epic Hard Sci Fi Adventure
High Concept Science Fiction at its Thrilling Best

Book One of
The Arcadia Series

This is a work of fiction. Names, characters, places, and incidents either are the product of the author's imagination or are used fictitiously. Any resemblance to actual persons, living or dead, events, or locales is entirely coincidental.

Copyright © 2020 by Ian Fraser

All rights reserved. No part of this book may be reproduced or used in any manner without written permission of the copyright owner except for the use of quotations in a book review. For more information, email:

ianfraserpublishing@gmail.com

ISBN: 9798657665116

Cover design by Ian Fraser

Eden's Gate

ALSO BY IAN FRASER

THE ARCADIA SERIES

Trinary Code
Exodus Seven
The Arcadia Series Boxed Set

COMING IN 2022

Creda's Labyrinth

CONTEMPORARY THRILLERS

The Tin Kicker
The Spirit Road

The Arcadia Series

Eden's Gate

— Prologue —

'She is a thing of beauty,' Malachy said. 'As graceful as a dolphin; powerful as thunder.' Luana smiled at her old mentor as the great starliner slipped from her moorings at the Lagrange Two Shipyards. Umbilicals were released to swing languidly away as the sleek vessel eased out of her cradle. A kilometre and a half of gleaming metal was free to embark on a month-long shakedown cruise, before heading out to the Lunar Transit Station to collect her first paying passengers.

The Aurora was one of his, a craft that boasted luxury unparalleled in all the spaceways. Soon, her sister ship, Nebula, would follow, but for now she alone would cater for the pampered super-rich.

On her first voyage, Luana had been so thrilled to be a part of this great endeavour. Four years on and the excitement had dimmed, just a little. Yes, she had now been promoted from fourth lieutenant to third, but the life of an officer aboard ship was largely one of mundane tedium that generally involved endlessly monitoring ship's systems and dealing with a constant stream of complaints, queries and requests from the vessel's four hundred wealthy passengers.

However, Luana had never lost her sense of wonder as she gazed out at the stars. She never failed to appreciate their beauty, and the wondrous adventure that still lay ahead for humanity.

And she never lost the hope that one day, somehow, she would have the opportunity to venture out to visit those stars.

Malachy's days of plying the space lanes were behind him now. While Luana still had this great adventure ahead of her, he was relaxing in the gentle, forgiving gravity of Jupiter's moon Ganymede. There was nothing quite as soothing on frail old bones as a sixth of one Earth gravity.

He would drop her a line every now and then, but their letters were more infrequent now. However, she would make the effort to visit him this time. Luana owed him at least that much.

The Aurora was due to spend two months at Thebe Dock when she arrived at the Jovian system, so she would have plenty of time for social calls then.

Unless, of course, something unexpected occurred on the voyage to Jupiter.

But things like that never happened.

Eden's Gate

— One —

Luana didn't look around. She didn't need to. She knew they were talking about her. She knew they were watching her, in that way young men do. Whisper, whisper, whisper. If stares were laser beams, she would have two pairs of holes burned through her by now. As always, she would wait for one of them to come to her.

'You haven't got a prayer, my friend,' Lester said. 'You couldn't be more dead if I threw you out that airlock.' He gestured toward the hatch in what passed for a ceiling in this topsy-turvy place. He shook his head wistfully, his hair swishing like grass wafted in the breeze. Zero gravity was never kind to unruly hairstyles. 'Seriously bud, this is not going to end well. For you, I mean. I'll be fine. I'll be back here trying not to wet myself from laughing too hard.'

Brent shook his head, a wry grin dragging the corners of his mouth up. 'Watch and learn, my young friend,' he said. 'Watch and learn.'

'Young friend? Oh bite me, I'm two years older than you. You're totally screwed and I'm here to see it. She'll kill you. She'll kill you like a cat ripping the head off a mouse. You want me to inform your next-of-kin now, or go through the formality of watching you die of humiliation first?'

Brent looked across the bridge at his quarry, her back to him, body illuminated in the soft blue of the bridge running lights. He gave Lester a wink and with two fingertips, deftly propelled himself from the seat and glided across the bridge of the ESS Aurora until he reached the environmental control station - which just happened to be right next to Luana Lee's shipboard operations station. She barely registered his arrival, although he did think he detected a faint whisper of a sigh.

'Hey Luana,' he said with a touch more enthusiasm than he'd intended, and noticed a twitch of Captain Johannsen's head in front of them. He continued in a more hushed tone. 'What you doing?'

'Booking my vacation,' she replied distractedly.

'Really?'

She turned to look at him for the first time, her huge brown eyes fixing him with a stare that would freeze lava. 'No. Not really.' She turned back to the console and continued to study water reclamation figures.

'Well I was wondering. If you're not too busy after our shift ends—'

'Whether I'd like to go for a drink?'

'Well I was going to suggest mountain climbing

followed by a hot tub and bagels, but I guess a drink would be okay. A bit unadventurous but I could make allowances.'

She chuckled lightly, seeming relaxed now and Brent took this as an encouraging sign.

'Do you happen to know of any mountains on board the Aurora?' she asked with a raised eyebrow.

'No, but there's a tricky stairwell between decks eight and nine that I'd been planning to tackle. I'll bring a picnic. You just bring your bikini and we'll see how things go. Deal?'

From ahead of them, there was a quiet, but distinctive clearing of the throat. 'Does anyone want to deal with the giant Martian war machine off the port bow?' Captain Alvaro Johannsen growled. It wasn't really a rebuke, just his way of reminding the bridge crew who was in command.

'Sorry Captain,' Luana said, trying to keep the giggle that begged for release in check. She turned to Brent and put a finger to her lips, silently shushing him.

From his own console, Lester just stared in open mouthed amazement. Literally open mouthed, which required a special effort in zero gravity. 'I don't believe it,' he muttered to himself. 'I think that fluky bastard is actually getting somewhere.'

From just in front of him, a warning began to sound. It wasn't too insistent, just a quiet ping-ping-ping, but it was designed to discreetly attract the operator's attention.

Lester frowned as the winking light on the console

drew his eye. Barely an hour would go by without some kind of alarm requiring some human intervention, even out in the empty space between planets. But this one was unusual.

'Proximity warning, Captain,' he said, loud enough for the whole bridge to hear. 'Another ship just entered our sector.'

Captain Alvaro Johannsen looked round, his weathered old faced creased with a frown, white hair that matched his elegant beard swept back and held in place with a generous spray of lacquer.

'Confirmed,' Luana said, the amorous advances of Brent swept aside.

'Distance and course?' Johannsen asked in his sing-song Scandinavian accent.

Luana brought up a fresh screen in front of her, numbers scrolling and dancing in the air. 'Distance ten thousand kilometres and closing. Course converging but not terminal. It should miss us by over a thousand kilometres.'

She glanced up and saw her captain's shoulders drop, just a fraction.

'Still too close for comfort. How long before it reaches its closest approach?'

'Twenty-four minutes, sir,' Lester said, his screens now matching Luana's. He always seemed to be just one step behind her; a fact that niggled.

'What is it?' the captain asked. 'An automated transport?'

Eden's Gate

Negative, sir,' Luana said. 'I've IDed the ship. It's a Martian high-speed personnel transport. The MMV Korolev. Up to thirty passengers and five crew.'

'Send out a greeting.'

'Aye, sir.' She wordlessly gestured to Brent, who immediately propelled himself over to the sensor console on the opposite wall.

'How did it get so close without being spotted?' Johannsen asked, failing to hide the irritation in his voice. 'What happened to the long-range sensors?'

Luana opened and closed screen after screen, images appearing before her in a blur as she sought some answers.

'I'm sorry, Captain. Unknown. No response to standard greeting. It's possible the ship is unpiloted.'

Brent scanned the screens at his station, his eyes darting over each readout, trying to get a general picture. 'Long range sensors show no contacts. No. Wait. I'm locked out.'

Johannsen looked around sharply. 'What?'

'The system is locked down.'

Luana brought up the same display as Brent at her own station. In the top corner were the words "NO CONTACTS". But in the centre, flashing in angry red was the unequivocal phrase "ACCESS DENIED". She input her own command codes and tried again. The computer took almost half a second to process and consider this new information before the screen came to life again. "ACCESS DENIED".

'Damn it,' she cursed quietly. 'Sir, it's not accepting my command codes. It should. It's a low security system. I don't get it.'

Johannsen unbuckled his seatbelt and flew gracefully over to her position, his movements as fluid as a dolphin after decades of shipboard service. He slipped easily into the seat next to Luana, straps automatically snaking around his waist and holding him in place.

'It could be your code that's become corrupted,' he murmured to her, even though he doubted two ID codes would become corrupted at the same time. He tapped in his own code, and was rewarded with the now uncomfortably familiar "ACCESS DENIED" blinking at him. 'Damn.' He typed in another code. Again, all he achieved was another "ACCESS DENIED" notice. 'That is not possible.'

'What was that?' Luana asked.

'Command code override. That should unlock any system on the ship. Who was the last person to use this station?'

She quickly brought up the station history screen, elegant fingers moving nimbly over the virtual keyboard. 'Paska, sir. Second Lieutenant Grant Paska.'

'Where is he now?'

Brent spoke up from the other console. 'He said he was going to do some maintenance on the communications array.'

Johannsen nodded. 'Luana, get him on the radio.'

'Yes sir.' She switched to the communications display. 'Bridge to Lieutenant Paska. Paska, please respond.' She paused as she awaited a response, avoiding the urge to tap her fingernails on the console. 'Bridge to Lieutenant Paska. Paska, please respond. No response, Captain.'

There was an inevitability to the statement that reinforced the feeling of dread that sat at the pit of his stomach like an unyielding ball of lead.

'Very well. Locate his communicator and we will find him that way.

'Yes sir.' Luana ran a scan. Every member of the crew carried their own communicator, and each unit emitted its own unique location code in case he or she were injured and were unable to respond.

'Well?' Johannsen demanded a little impatiently.

'Tracking it now, sir,' she said, moving from the crew list to a virtual, 3D map of the ship. It showed a blinking signal just aft of the gravity rings. She scanned in closer, and closer, until the exact location could be identified. 'The system is showing Lieutenant Paska to be in the communications array, sir. Just as he said he would be.'

'Get down to the array and bring him up here. Now.'
'Yes sir.'

Luana released the clasp holding her securely to the seat and eased herself away. With a small flick against the chair back, she soared to the rear of the bridge and into the travel tube. A second later, she was gone.

Johannsen continued to stare at the monitor in front of him for several seconds before glancing up at the troubled face of Brent, the young officer looking as uneasy as he himself had the first time he had travelled into space, all those years before.

'Has the Korolev changed its course at all?'

'Negative Captain. It should still miss us by over a thousand kilometres.'

'And still no communication from Paska?'

This time it was Lester who spoke up. 'No sir. I'm sending a hail to him on a repeating loop. If he pipes up, we'll know about it.'

'Good.' He offered a reassuring smile to the two young men, but was all too aware that it would be only partially successful. He shook his head as he quietly mumbled: 'What the hell is he up to?'

— Two —

It wasn't a bad way to spend an afternoon, Ben Floyd thought as he extricated himself from the tangle of the woman's arms and legs. He lay back onto the bed, sweat glistening on his forehead, breathless. He looked across at Claudia, who smiled back at him, tongue toying with lips painted a luscious rouge, breasts rising and falling quickly in snatched breaths.

She reached across and ran a single, elegant finger through the matt of hair on his chest. 'You have to go so soon, *tesoro*?' Her voice was deep, heavily accented in an exotic Mediterranean dialect. Floyd happened to know that her ancestry was Italian, but it could have been French, Greek, Croatian, Spanish or any of a dozen other languages from the region.

The finger ran lightly through the carpet of fur in extravagant swirls, moving slowly down to trace a ring around his navel. He clapped his hand over hers and halted its inevitable path.

'No,' he sighed, 'not now.'

Floyd swung his legs over the side of the bed and felt the soft pile of the carpet snake between his toes. The thwarted finger ran down his back and he stifled a shiver, which elicited a mischievous giggle from the woman.

'Haven't you had enough?' he asked as he reached for his shirt and slung it around his shoulders.

'You know me, Benjamin. I have never had enough. I am an insatiable animal that must be constantly indulged. I thought you realised that by now.' She roused herself from the bed and began to button the shirt for him.

'I'm getting the idea. But I need to go. Got an appointment that I don't want to miss.' He pushed her back onto the bed and she giggled like a naughty child, and this time used a toe to stroke his leg.

Floyd glanced at the clock on the wall, just above the window. The monitor gave a perfect three-dimensional representation of stars drifting languidly by, but unlike a real window, these stars moved in a comfortingly linear fashion. In reality, a real view from this point would be an uncomfortable reminder that they were pressed against the outer wall of a giant centrifuge that did an adequate, but not quite perfect job of mimicking gravity. The stateroom was within the outermost ring of the Aurora's gravity section and generated a force close to one g. The innermost rings produced less than half this, but were perfectly suited to the requirements of Martian residents, who were accustomed to a little over a third Earth gravity.

Claudia sighed, realising that even her prodigious charms could delay him no further. She rolled off the bed and pulled his face toward hers, planting a perfect soft kiss on his lips.

'Have it your way then, *amante*. There is always tonight. I need to go take a shower.'

Floyd watched her as she made the few steps to the shower cubicle, taking the time to appreciate her curves one more time, before she disappeared behind the translucent screen.

With the sound of tinkling water in the background, he finished dressing, pulling on a pair of slacks and black, faux-leather shoes.

He glanced at the clock again. He really didn't want to be late for this meeting. The entire six-week voyage had led to this point, not to mention two months careful preparations prior to that on Earth.

Checking he had all he needed – comm-pad, credit card, watch – he took a last, longing look at the slender figure in the shower. He could only see her silhouette, but that was enough. That was enough to tell him not to be late tonight.

'I'm going,' he shouted to her. 'Meet me at the Euphoria Bar at eight. You can let yourself out.'

'Okay, *tesoro*. I will catch you tonight.'

With a final, yearning glance, he left, the door swishing closed behind him.

A few seconds later, the shower was switched off and Claudia reached for a towel, which she wrapped around her sopping hair. She stepped out of the cubicle and went to the desk. Rivulets of water trickled down her body to be lost in the carpet.

She reached into her bag and removed a small, slender communicator. She activated the device, which snaked out to form an elegant crescent. She scanned for the contact she sought and called the number.

'Mr. Landry?' she said as she reached detachedly for a swimsuit, enjoying the feel of the slinky material on her fingertips. 'He is on his way.'

There was a pause as the man at the other end of the line spoke.

'No,' she smiled, 'he doesn't suspect a thing. And I gave him a send-off he will remember for the rest of his life. However long that might be.'

Another pause, and this time the response made her smile.

'Oh no, it was my pleasure. And his, but mostly mine. And after all, it is what you pay me for. *Ciao signore.*'

She hung up and smiled again, tapping the commpad gently against her teeth. She had done her job, had performed the role well. Not that it had been a terrible hardship. Under different circumstances, who knew where this relationship might have led? But she was an actor performing a part. And good actors were well paid for their art.

Eden's Gate

Claudia felt a chill and remembered that her body was still soaking wet from the shower, cooling droplets clinging to her skin.

She dried herself quickly and slipped into the swimsuit. She had one more little surprise for poor Benjamin Floyd.

The glass doors, as ephemeral as the wings of a bumblebee, slid aside with an almost melodic tinkle. Floyd was immediately engulfed in warm, humid air that wrapped its steamy arms around him. Accompanying the heat and sultry atmosphere was the splashing of water and light laughter of people at play. It seemed incongruous that, within what his brain told him was a glorified tin can floating in space, such a place should exist.

The pool area spanned the entire width of the outer gravity ring. It was as idyllic as any jungle paradise on Earth, with a waterfall at the far end, rocks that glistened in the light from the overhead lamps, trees that seemed to go on forever. None were real, of course. A luxury interplanetary starliner was no place for burrowing roots. But they were indistinguishable from the real thing, and that was all that mattered to the wealthy travellers on the ship.

People happily frolicked in the water, some splashing each other gaily, others bouncing a ball around.

But there was one thing that set this scene apart from any similar pool on Earth. The water curved upwards, following the arc of the centrifuge. This was something to which Floyd would never grow accustomed, although it didn't seem to spoil the enjoyment of most.

On either side of this pool and its unnaturally cerulean water, there were individual areas where couples or groups could lounge in relaxed comfort, away from the frivolity of the pool.

He scanned the area, feeling the unrelenting heat from the overhead lamps burn into his scalp. The lamps did a fair job of mimicking genuine sunlight, solar collectors on the exterior of the hull absorbing as much solar radiation as they could, and channelling it into a concentrated stream of heat and light.

Floyd tried to look past the mass of glistening bodies, but without a lot of success. At this time of day, a significant proportion of passengers tended to descend upon the pool area; those that weren't out shopping, taking in an afternoon zero gravity cabaret, or eating a late lunch.

A hover shoe-wearing waitress glided up to him and came to an abrupt stop, the tray of drinks she held in one hand miraculously remaining upright. Like most of the passengers in this play area, her attire was casual in the extreme: an imitation grass skirt and tube top that did little to conceal her flawless ebony body. The only other thing she wore was a smile, painted on and worn assiduously from the beginning of her shift until the end.

Eden's Gate

'You looking for a drink, sailor?' she asked in a broad, midwestern accent.

'No, I'm looking for someone.'

'Lots of unattached someones here, handsome. What's your preference?'

He smiled and shook his head. After two hours with Claudia, that was the last thing he needed. 'No, someone in particular. Max Landry. You know him?'

The smile wavered for a moment. Everyone knew Max Landry. At least, everyone knew him by reputation. 'Yeah, I know Mr. Landry.' She pointed with her free hand to a clearing in the trees to the left of the pool. 'Mr. Landry's party is just over there.'

Floyd squinted in the glare of the "sunshine". He could see five individuals. Three men in garish shirts leant against trees, watching women playing under the waterfall. A woman in a light, flowery summer dress was relaxed in a lounger reading a book. The fifth individual was sat at a wicker table, reading a tablet. This was Max Landry, looking like the most relaxed man in the Solar System in khaki shorts and a hideous Hawaiian shirt that looked like the result of an explosion in a crayon factory. Floyd would know Landry anywhere. The man was stocky, his muscular arms straining the sleeves of his migraine-inducing shirt.

Floyd thanked the waitress, who whizzed away to deliver the tray of drinks. He strolled up to the clearing, easing past kissing couples and snoozing sun worshippers. The three men saw him approaching and each stiffened, smiles frozen on their faces. Floyd wasn't bothered by these... he tried to think of a word other than henchmen. Stooges or goons didn't sound a whole lot less cheesy. Whatever he called them, they were none of his concern.

He ambled up to the table. The goons didn't exactly react, but they were fully alert and ready to pounce if he tried anything.

'Mr. Landry? Max Landry?' he asked. The man looked up from his tablet.

'Can I help you, mate? You're blocking the sunshine.'

The woman peered over the top of her book, her eyes concealed behind an enormous pair of sunglasses. The three men looked at one another, the stooge in the middle holding up a finger to prevent either of the other two from doing anything stupid.

'My name is Floyd, Mr. Landry. Ben Floyd. I'm a detective with—'

'Oh don't worry, mate, I know exactly who you are: Ben Floyd, special investigator with Sub Rosa Security, subcontracted by EarthPol to investigate my affairs. Take a seat, Mr. Floyd. Drink? They mix a pretty fine margarita here.'

Landry had a thick cockney accent, but fortunately did not pepper his speech with too much stereotypical rhyming slang. If asked to guess, Floyd would have said he was in his early fifties. However, he didn't have to guess. He knew that Landry was fifty-three years old, one point seven two meters tall and the owner of a sizeable legitimate business empire. It was his non-legitimate business interests that concerned Floyd.

Landry clicked his fingers and a waitress – by chance, the same one Floyd had just spoken to – came gliding up to the clearing.

'Yes, Mr. Landry?' she asked, looking a little nervous, Floyd thought.

'Margaritas for me and my guest, and another of whatever the lady's having.' He tilted his head in the direction of the woman in the sunlounger, but she had already returned to reading her book. He made no effort to supply his goons with drinks. They presumably could either buy their own or go thirsty.

'Of course, sir.' She zipped away quickly.

'I see you've done your homework. Do you know what I've found?' Floyd asked.

'Now, let's see,' Landry began. 'You've tried all the usual searches, bank accounts, tax records, employee files etc. and come up blank, just as EarthPol had. So, you infiltrated my organization and *still* found nothing. Fancy that, eh? Then you tried the old favourite: you embarked on a torrid relationship with one of my female business associates to see if you could get anything out of her. Amongst other little titbits of pillow talk, she told you about a new and highly illegal operation on Ganymede, and that I was taking this cruise out to Jupiter to oversee things. Is that about right?'

The Arcadia Series

The waitress chose that moment to scoot back to the table where she placed three cocktail glasses. 'Will there be anything else, sir?'

'Nah darlin'. That'll be it for now. Maybe later, though?' His eyes flicked quickly up and down her body and he grinned the smug grin of a man who could have just about whatever he wanted, whenever he wanted.

The girl smiled, but shot away before Landry could elaborate.

'Not bad,' Floyd said. 'Just out of interest, how did you find out?'

'That lawyer you were banging in San Diego?' Landry said.

'Yes?'

Landry glanced across at the woman in the lounger. 'I made her a better offer. Ain't that right, Celeste?'

She lowered the book and for the first time, Floyd got a good look at her face, cocooned in a mop of long, wavy blond hair.

'You better believe it, Max,' she grinned as she took the glass and sipped the margarita. 'Hi Benny. You okay honey?'

'So, you've come here today to arrest me, right?' Landry said. 'You sent a message to your contacts in San Diego and on Ganymede, and now it's time to finish the operation so you and your buddies at Sub Rosa can get paid.'

Floyd said nothing, as the realisation began to reveal that he had been played by an expert. He also became aware of a lump forming at the pit of his stomach. This was liable to turn ugly real quick.

'Well I hate to tell you this,' Landry said, 'but that ain't going to happen today. Those messages never got sent, and just for good measure, your contacts have by now run into nasty little accidents. As you're about to.'

He chuckled as he swilled the cocktail around in the glass.

Floyd finished his own drink, the sweet and sour of lime and salt making him feel more alive than he ever had before. Or perhaps it was the thought that he could be dead in the next five minutes that was responsible.

'Well played,' Floyd said. 'But please don't think that this is over. Oh no, I'm taking you in, Mr. Landry. One way or another.'

'I wouldn't bet on it, and to be honest, if I were you, I'd be more worried about my own situation.' Landry glanced round at the three men and, right on cue, each revealed a hand laser nestling snugly under each man's shirt.

'I see what you mean,' Floyd said with a wry smile, his mouth now feeling very dry, tongue rubbing like sandpaper on the roof of his mouth. He wished he hadn't already finished his drink.

'Ah!' Landry said, looking toward the double glass doors. 'And here comes the other reason for your downfall.'

Floyd looked round and forced himself not to curse aloud. Walking slowly toward him was Claudia, dressed in an aquamarine swimsuit and translucent sarong that did nothing to hide her exquisite legs. He thought back to the last time he had seen her, and the perfect silhouette in the shower.

When she reached the table, Claudia leant over to kiss Landry on the lips, an action that turned Floyd's stomach.

'Hello again, Benjamin. Surprised to see me so soon?'

Landry chuckled again. 'Oh, deary me. Hoodwinked by not one but two exotic femme fatales. And they're both here to see the look on your face. Ain't that nice?'

Floyd couldn't speak. He had been set up. All the time he had thought he was covertly working to bring this crook – this gangster – to justice, Landry had just been laughing in his face as he manipulated the people around him. It was a terrible thing to feel so totally, utterly beaten.

Landry turned and spoke to the three men who still lounged against the trees. 'Let him get out of here and do it quietly. Nice and private like. And make sure no one finds the body. Chuck it out an airlock if you can. If not, bury it in with the rest of the organic waste. Sorry Mr. Floyd. It's just business you see. I can't leave any loose ends lying around. The door's that way if you want to start running.'

Landry beckoned to the waitress again as Floyd stood and walked stiffly toward the exit.

— Three —

The Martian Merchant Vessel Korolev drifted languidly through open space, the only nearby object being the bright point of light ahead. A point of light that was growing brighter, and beginning to exhibit a recognizable shape.

The onboard AI had noted this object and identified it as the ESS Aurora, an Earth registered starliner six weeks out from Earth, bound for Jupiter, but had not altered course to avoid it. Sensors indicated that there was no collision threat, so a course correction was not necessary. Ordinarily, the AI would query this with the crew, but this would not be possible. Sensors showed that there was no crew to question. It ran another sensor sweep, but it just confirmed what it already knew: that there was no living crew aboard.

'Prepare for course correction.'

The instruction confused the AI for a moment. It scanned the ship again, yet still found no trace of a living person. It responded to the message. **'My sensors do not register any lifeforms on board. Please identify.'**

The reply that came back was virtually immediate, indicating that the intelligence, whatever it might be, was probably aboard the ship.

'Command override Alpha 1: epsilon delta 6-6-9-4-2-7 omicron alpha omega theta.'

The AI did the computer version of slouching back in its chair and relaxing. This was the correct command code and it could follow its instructions without resorting to emergency procedures. **'Thank you. Please input your instructions for course correction.'**

The code may have been correct, but the ship's AI was still troubled by the source of the transmission. However, this concern was secondary. It was about to be given new instructions, and brought the manoeuvring thrusters online.

'Initiate a 3.2 second maximum thrust burn. Vector 0-0-3 mark 0-1-6. Firing to begin in thirty seconds – mark.'

'Acknowledged,' the ship's AI confirmed to its mysterious interlocutor. **'Firing will commence in 29.993 seconds.'**

On the outer hull of the transport ship, the manoeuvring thrusters realigned themselves, angling the exhaust jets to give the most efficient use of fuel. However, the AI noted a problem.

Eden's Gate

'The course correction will put the Korolev in conflict with the ESS Aurora. I am pausing the countdown.'

'Negative. Countdown must continue. Command override: epsilon delta 6-6-9-4-2-7 omicron alpha omega theta.'

The AI had never received such an order before, and spent almost a microsecond to evaluate the situation. Preservation of human life superseded all commands – except an alpha 1 command override. The orders were clear and unambiguous, leaving it with no choice but to comply, but that did not mean it couldn't raise an objection. **'Countdown continuing. My records indicate the ESS Aurora to be carrying 450 passengers and crew. Course correction will result in a collision.'**

'Negative. Updated information indicates no lifeforms aboard the ESS Aurora. Command override alpha 1: epsilon delta 6-6-9-4-2-7 omicron alpha omega theta. Compliance is mandatory.'

'Acknowledged,' the AI responded evenly. **'Countdown continues.'**

The orders were unequivocal, and no matter how the AI felt (if its rudimentary algorithms could mimic anything that might be described as feelings), it could not disobey an Alpha 1 command override.

'Three, two, one. Course correction in progress.'

For three-point-two seconds the manoeuvring thrusters burst into life, easing the transport around. If anyone were alive in the pilots' seat, they would have seen the bright, star-like object move to occupy the centre of the viewscreen.

'Course correction complete.' The AI received no more instructions, although its limited intelligence believed that if it had any further questions or requests for clarification, the mysterious entity would instantly respond.

Since it had had its memory wiped almost two weeks earlier by a man named Luther Kane Lynch, it had no way of knowing that it had already had a similar conversation. The ship's internal sensors were showing no life signs for a very good reason: the entire crew had died soon after leaving the docking station on Phobos. The instruction had seemed odd at the time, the AI thought, but it had dutifully blown the airlock when the controlling intelligence that Lynch had installed instructed it to.

It was oblivious to the screams from the crew and passengers, those not still buckled in being blasted out into space.

Following its murder of the crew and subsequent memory wipe, the ship and its AI controller had continued on out into the depths of space.

The only witnesses now were the cold, dead eyes of what remained of the crew.

— Four —

Zero gravity or no, the trek from the bridge of the Aurora to the communications array would have been a long, arduous and even hazardous journey for the unwary. The array was located two thirds of the way along the main hull, just aft of the gravity cylinders that dominated the central area of the ship, but still far enough away from the nuclear propulsion system at the rear. Even in a weightless state, that was over a kilometre of seemingly endless corridors and ladders.

Fortunately, there was a shortcut. Four travel tubes ran the length of the ship, mag-lev generators sending cars hurtling along at fifty kilometres per hour between stations. Within five minutes of leaving the bridge, Lieutenant Luana Lee arrived at the communications array.

She hadn't been sure what to expect. This was so far outside her experience, she couldn't even guess what might await her. As she glided down the vertical access tube, she was relieved to find the array's control centre was devoid of life. Whatever Grant Paska had been doing, he had already left.

Just what *was* he doing? It made no sense. She had thought of nothing else since leaving the bridge, but had come up with no reasonable explanations. She wondered idly whether Malachy had ever had a similar experience. She was fairly sure that he must have. There wasn't a lot that *could* happen aboard a starliner that he hadn't had to deal with at some point.

Luana propelled herself over to the main control panel and activated the unit. It immediately sprung to life, indicator lights flashing, screens and keypads illuminated. She brought up the activity log and frowned. She verified the result and it checked out. Just another odd thing on a very odd day.

'Lieutenant Lee to Captain Johannsen.'

'Go ahead,' came the immediate reply.

'Captain, I'm at the communications array and there's no sign of Lieutenant Paska. The system indicates there's been no activity here for nearly two days. Which seems to suggest…'

'That either he didn't make it, or he was lying,' growled Johannsen.

'Captain!' Lester, the young officer cried. 'The Korolev just changed course and is heading directly for us.'

Johannsen's eyes went wide and nearly a second elapsed before he responded. 'Go to red alert. Evasive manoeuvres. Bring her around, hard turn to starboard. Bring the defence array online.'

'Aye, Captain,' Lester and Brent said in unison.

The normal warm blue bridge lighting was replaced by blood red, enveloping the officers in its crimson glow. It was probably best that the captain couldn't see how ashen the two young officers looked as they took their positions at the helm and weapons stations.

'Luana,' Johannsen said into the communicator, 'alert the crew. Possible collision. But printout only, I don't want to alarm the passengers just yet.'

'Aye, sir,' she replied, and heard the quaver in her own voice, which made her swear silently. She typed out a brief message and hit send. Every crewmember would feel a buzz on their wrist, alerting them to a priority command communication.

On the bridge, Lester looked up at the captain, his eyes wide with terror. 'Captain, manoeuvring thrusters are offline!'

'What?'

Brent looked across. 'Defence array offline as well, sir.'

'Go to auxiliaries,' Johannsen ordered.

'No response,' Brent said.

'Same here,' echoed Lester.

'Override.'

'Negative response.'

'Negative response.'

Hearing the events unfolding on the bridge, Luana quickly downloaded all the data she could from the console, including personnel records on Grant Paska. She had a feeling she knew what order she would receive next.

On the bridge, Johannsen's body suddenly went limp. It was impossible. It could not be happening. It was just inconceivable that every system could suddenly die. Sabotage. It had to be sabotage.

'Time to impact?' he demanded.

Brent had already made the calculation. 'Five minutes, forty seconds.'

Johannsen shook his head. There just wasn't time, but he had one more thing to try. 'Luana, you're the closest. Get down to Defence Auxiliary Control and try to manually override.'

'Aye, sir. I'll try.' She somersaulted in mid-air and shot toward the access hatch.

'And God help us all,' Captain Alvaro Johannsen muttered.

Ben Floyd walked briskly along the corridor that sloped upward with the curvature of the cylinder. It was busy in this area, with bustling crowds heading to and from the pool area. On the one hand, this was a good thing; it meant he had some cover and was protected to some degree from the three henchmen who followed him. On the other, if they decided to start shooting, there were a lot of innocent people who were liable to get hurt.

He chanced a fleeting glance behind. Sure enough, there they were, like a wolf pack hunting a defenceless prey. If he could just stay a little way ahead of them.

The corridor opened out into a wide-open atrium. Shops lined the walls while balconies looked down on the scene. Crowds of shoppers moved as crowds of shoppers always do when one is in a hurry. They sauntered along aimlessly, stood in groups and generally got in everybody's way.

Floyd barged past people, apologizing as he did so. There was one thing in which he was interested; one goal that could be his salvation. At the centre of the atrium were four elevators that surrounded an ornate spiral staircase, running all the way down to the central nexus. He circled the elevators, pressing the call button on each, praying that one would arrive quickly.

On this day, Ben Floyd was in luck. A two-tone chime announced the arrival of an elevator car, and the doors swished open. He leapt inside and punched the up button.

He could see the three men charging through the crowd, hurling people out of the way. But fortunately, they weren't quite stupid enough to start shooting people at random.

The leader, a stocky character with multiple slash scars on his face, lunged forward just as the elevator doors started to slide closed. Sensing an object blocking the way, they opened again. Floyd kicked him hard in the side of the head. His cranium cracked against the edge of the door and he grunted in pain. Floyd kicked again and the man's head snapped back, his body crumpling to the floor outside the elevator. Now that they sensed the path was clear, the doors swished shut and the car began to rise.

The car itself was transparent, as was the cylinder it travelled through, and Floyd saw the three men below him disappearing as he ascended. The spacecraft's designers must have thought that it would be a neat innovation to make the travel tubes transparent, however it was more than a little disconcerting to find oneself suddenly ejected out into space as the car moved from ring to ring, with nothing but three centimetres of clear organic composite between the car's interior and the frozen vacuum of space.

Floyd stood gasping for breath for a few moments. The outer ring, containing decks eleven and twelve, slipped away beneath him and the next ring, containing decks nine and ten, was rapidly approaching.

'Level nine,' he said aloud and the car dutifully came to a stop. Looking down through the glass floor, he could see the three men ascending in another car.

'Time for some hide and seek,' he mumbled to himself as the doors slid open.

This atrium was similar to the one he had just left, but unlike that level, this had no shops, no balconies and no people. Level nine was a residential level, and clearly most of the inhabitants were elsewhere aboard the great liner. There were four corridors leading away from the central staircase and elevator tubes. Two would follow the arc of the ring and would eventually lead back to this spot. The other two went off to the side and went who knew where.

Floyd decided to take his chances and chose one of these. Time was not on his side as the second car was approaching. He couldn't let the men see which path he had chosen, and began to run.

The three men burst from the elevator the instant the doors slid aside, but came to an abrupt halt as they were met with a completely empty atrium. No one moved and the only sound was the constant hum of the ship's systems.

'Where'd he go?' the tall man with blond hair demanded.

'Quiet, Drago,' the leader ordered as he tried to listen for footsteps, but any sound was lost in the ambience of the ship. There were four corridors and three of them. 'We'll split up. I'll take this one. Devan, you take the east corridor. Drago, you take the west. If he took the south, then that's just bad luck. Now move.'

The three men set off. Tor, the leader of the squad, moved cautiously, as an experienced hunter stalks its prey. He knew that the other two would be swaggering along full of confidence, bravado and hunger for blood. Killing was part of their job; he knew that better than anyone. You didn't work security for a man like Max Landry if you didn't have a strong stomach. But what Tor did was necessary. A lot of the time it was a case of kill or be killed, with no room for compromise. The difference between them was that Devan and Drago liked it. They both enjoyed inflicting pain and suffering. The more agony and terror they could squeeze from their victims, the happier they were. Especially Drago. He was a borderline psychopath, and ambitious as well. He would make a play for Tor's job one day, he was sure. But he'd be ready for him. What Drago didn't realise was that he could be just as ruthless – it's just that he would do it as a necessity, not for enjoyment.

In the west corridor, Drago strode along with as much arrogant swagger as Tor had predicted. He was keen to make a name for himself in the organization, willing to do whatever it took. Tor was just the "big man" because he had the ear of Landry. That would all change once his boss saw what he was capable of. And Drago was not the squeamish type. He was looking forward to making his prey suffer.

He heard a noise up ahead and froze, his fingers tightening around the butt of the laser blaster nestled inside his shirt. The sound was high pitched. A laugh. A woman's laugh. He relaxed a little and in a few moments, as he made his way around the cylinder, two pairs of legs came into view; then two torsos and finally two heads. It was a pair of young teenagers. Probably sneaking a few minutes away from their families, Drago thought. The girl shrieked as she was tickled, laughing with joyous, carefree abandon. The boy pulled her tightly to him as he planted his lips over hers and they kissed with unabashed passion. Finally, the pair came up for air and that was when the girl saw Drago. She giggled again and thumped on her boyfriend's arm to get his attention.

'Sorry,' the boy said. 'We were just... uh...'

'Looking for the elevator,' the girl finished improvising for him. She tugged at the hem of her dress, bringing it back down to cover at least a little flesh.

Drago looked her up and down. 'Has anyone else been through here? I am looking for a man. He is a friend of mine.'

'A man?' she said, as if unfamiliar with the breed. 'No, no man has come through here. Just us.'

'You're sure? It's really important I find him.'

'She just told you, didn't she?' the boy said, with far more bravado than was healthy when confronted with a vicious killer.

The girl giggled again, pawing at his chest. 'My hero.'

Drago grunted an acknowledgement and continued on past the couple, his fists clenched hard as he heard the pair of them laughing. Laughing at him. Just as they had when he was a kid growing up in Belgrade. He might make them pay for that before this voyage was over. He would beat the boy so hard that even his own mother wouldn't recognize him. Pretty girls would look away in horror at the sight of him. Yeah, that was what he would do. You wouldn't be laughing then, would you my foolish young friend? And as for the girl, well, he would show her what it felt like to have a real man show her some attention. She wouldn't be laughing at him then, would she? Yeah, that was what he would—

The radio clipped to his belt beeped once. 'Drago, Devan, anything yet?' demanded the voice of Tor.

'Negative. Not a soul,' he heard Devan reply.

'Same here. Just some snotty kid and his slutty bitch,' Drago mumbled.

'Okay, keep looking.'

'You got it,' Devan said, and the radio beeped again to close the channel.

'Damn stupid thing to say,' Drago cursed, and kept mumbling profanities as he approached the next intersection.

— Five —

Floyd knew he would have to turn and fight at some point. He didn't want to. Hand to hand combat was a vicious, violent exercise and best avoided if at all possible. Never start a fight with a superior opponent; that's what they taught him back in his EarthPol Security days. But that was a long time ago, and he was a long way from EarthPol Security's San Diego field office.

He heard the voices, the giggles from the girl, the foolhardy belligerence from the boy and the deep tones of the big blond-haired man.

Damn, thought Floyd. He had assumed correctly that the trio of would-be assassins would split up to try and find him. From what he had seen, his preference would have been to face the dark-haired man, Devan. He thought he would stand a good chance of prevailing against him.

But Drago was tall, stout and looked particularly aggressive, like some bare-knuckle, Eastern European prize-fighter. So much for not starting a fight with a superior opponent. That left just one stratagem: if you are forced to fight someone bigger and meaner than you, do it on your own terms.

Now that was something he might be able to engineer.

He swirled around, taking in the entire intersection, looking for anything, anything at all that might give him an advantage, no matter how small. Unfortunately, on a luxury starliner like this, crew members were not in the habit of carelessly leaving toolboxes or equipment just lying around. All he wanted was a nice, hefty wrench. In fact, anything that would make a handy club, but he was out of luck. There was nothing in the area except an access panel in the wall.

Access panel, he thought. I wonder… The panel was a metal sheet, around thirty centimetres squared.

The girl laughed again.

Floyd tugged at the panel. Nothing happened.

Another giggle, followed by footsteps approaching – the lumbering footfalls of a beast that's not quite worked out the purpose of opposable thumbs. But something big. And dangerous.

He tugged at the panel harder and it came away from the wall. Inside the hatch was an electrical junction box. It seemed that local power distribution was controlled from here.

The footsteps grew louder, and Floyd could hear the man grumbling, each utterance punctuated by heavy breathing. He couldn't have been more than a couple of meters away.

There was no time left. Floyd pressed himself against the wall and waited, heart pounding beneath his ribcage. He felt sure the other man would hear it hammering away inside his chest. Another second.

The instant the tall blond-haired man came into view, Floyd swung the panel around. It smashed into the Serbian's face with all the force that Floyd could muster. The man's nose exploded in a violent spurt of blood and he went flying backwards to land in a crumpled heap on the floor.

Floyd stood there looking from the man on the ground to the distorted metal panel. As weapons go, it had proven quite effective.

But then the man stirred, and an instant later he was back on his feet. Floyd had no choice. He launched himself at him and, as he flew through the air, swung his fist around to crack into the side of the man's head. It should have cracked his skull. It should have laid him out cold. It should have been a decisive, fight winning move, but the man's head barely moved. Even worse, he seemed to be ready for Floyd this time, and at the last instant batted the flying figure away with almost inhuman strength.

Floyd smashed into the wall with a crunch, searing pain shooting through his shoulder. Before he was able to gather himself, the enraged Drago had picked him up and threw him back into the intersection. He landed on his back, the wind knocked out of him. Through blurred vision he saw the massive man looming over him, about to drag him from the floor once more.

Ascertaining that the man's skull was impervious to attack, he decided that he would try a different strategy. It wasn't really a strategy; more like an act of utter desperation.

He kicked upwards. Hard. His booted foot arced through the air between the man's legs until it connected with his groin.

Drago doubled over, eyes screwed tightly shut as the unimaginable pain coursed through him. Through the blinding agony he could not see his opponent get up.

Floyd grabbed the man from behind and, using every last bit of strength he possessed, drove him headfirst into the open access panel. It exploded in sparks and Drago's body jerked in spasm for several tortuous seconds, before he slumped to the ground.

Gasping for breath, Floyd slumped to his knees next to the inert Serbian. He held two fingers to the man's neck. Miraculously, he was still alive. But, crucially, he would not move again until Floyd was long gone.

Floyd felt beneath Drago's shirt and found the blaster, pocketing the weapon. He also retrieved the radio from his belt.

He got up and staggered along the corridor, back in the direction of the atrium. As he passed the young couple he grinned.

'Thanks, I owe you guys one,' he said with a wink.

'Any time,' the young man said.

Floyd lurched on down the corridor.

After staring at the unconscious man for a few seconds, the amorous young couple continued to do what amorous young couples do best.

Captain Alvaro Johannsen's face was bathed in the crimson glow of the bridge emergency alert lighting, although even without it his face would have glowed an angry red as he broiled in impotent rage. Outwardly, his face was set in a visage of grim determination. But within, a fire burned like no fury ever had before.

Paska. This was Paska's doing, was all he could think. The bastard had sabotaged his ship. There was little hope left now. Soon, anyone who could not reach one of the lifepods would be dead. Four hundred people. Four hundred innocent, ignorant people as helpless as he was.

And it was Paska's fault.

No, he thought. He was the captain. Paska may have caused this, but it was his responsibility. He should have stopped him. He should have foreseen this situation. He had never liked Paska, and had never trusted him. He had always put this down to an innate mistrust of Martians. It was an intolerance he had always fought to suppress, but he could not ignore it completely. Perhaps he should have listened to that little voice in his head. The voice that urged caution and vigilance.

This was his fault. No one would blame him. They would, naturally, blame the one directly responsible. Especially when it became known that he was a Martian.

But this was Johannsen's ship, and the responsibility was his.

'Time to impact?' he asked, without the usual strength the young officers had come to expect.

'Just coming up to one minute, thirty seconds, sir,' Brent said.

Johannsen nodded. He was a good lad, young Brent. He had kept his calm and professionalism all through this most appalling of times. He would have made a fine senior officer one day. Maybe even a fine captain.

If he ever had the chance.

Johannsen switched on the communicator. 'Lieutenant Lee, are you at Defence Auxiliary Control yet?'

There was a crackle of static before Luana's breathless voice responded. 'Negative sir. I… I don't think I can make it. Even if… Even if I do, there's no time to bring the array online.'

Johannsen shook his head sadly. That had been his last hope. It had never really been a possibility, but condemned men will always cling to a last hope, regardless of how unlikely its success might be. There was just one course of action left to him.

'Understood,' he said. 'Luana, get yourself to a lifepod. As soon as it's filled, launch.'

'But Captain—'

'That is an order. Good luck Lieutenant. Johannsen out.'

Johannsen sighed, realising that he would never speak to Third Lieutenant Luana Lee again. She had been the finest of his officers. He just wished he'd had the chance to tell her so. He wished he had been able to tell her how much she had come to mean to him. How much he had relied on her. How much he valued her advice and input. Now she was gone. But perhaps she would survive this calamity. He turned to Brent.

'Would you sound the collision alarm for me, please?'

'Aye, sir.'

All around the ship, the collision warning sounded. It would lead to panic, of that Johannsen was sure, but that was unavoidable.

'Mr. Lester, please send out a general distress signal.'

'Aye sir,' Lester said, and his hand moved shakily over the console.

Johannsen unbuckled his harness and assumed something approaching a standing position as he floated a few centimetres above the floor.

'There's nothing more we can do. Gentlemen, it's been a privilege serving with you. Now get yourselves to the lifepods.'

The Arcadia Series

The two younger men shared a glance.

'Thank you, Captain,' Lester said, his eyes glistening in the stark red lighting, his chin visibly trembling.

'Good luck, Captain,' Brent said, his voice stronger, his jaw jutting out in defiance of death.

Lester was the first down the access tunnel, immediately followed by Brent, who took one valuable second to salute his captain.

Once he was alone, Johannsen settled back down in his seat and brought up an external camera view. It showed the MMV Korolev heading directly toward them. It was nothing like as big as the Aurora, but it didn't need to be. It was designed to be efficient, but that maxim precluded any aesthetic considerations. Behind the angular cockpit were four detachable pods – in this case, passenger modules. Above these were a quartet of fuel spheres. There would be a lot of propellant in those. He stared at the squat, ugly transport ship with hatred. That was to be his assassin. He loathed that ship as it began to fill the screen. The only thing he loathed more was Grant Paska.

He switched the image off and plucked a small tablet from his breast pocket. It immediately sprang to life, showing a three-dimensional image of an attractive woman in latter middle age, and two vibrant teenage boys. She smiled at him warmly and gave one of those happy little waves that she reserved for him and their boys. He would stare at this image until the end.

But in the corner of his eye he could see the numbers counting down on the screen: twenty-nine, twenty-eight, twenty-seven, twenty-six, twenty-five…'

The level nine atrium looked nothing like Floyd had remembered it from just a few minutes before. The warm, soft white lighting had been replaced by red emergency lights. A two-tone alarm accompanied the lighting, along with an audible message in a disturbingly calm female voice.

'Warning. Collision alert. Emergency evacuation in progress. All passengers must make their way to the lifepods on deck twelve immediately.'

He stood there, paralyzed as he tried to figure out what the hell was going on. As if his life weren't complicated enough right now.

A laser blast hit the elevator closest to Floyd's head and he spun round, holding his own weapon up. Tor stood at the entrance to the south corridor, his gun pointing directly at Floyd's head.

The two men stood there for a few moments with guns aimed at each other. But Tor was clearly as baffled as he was by the noise and the warning lights.

'Warning. Collision alert. Emergency evacuation in progress. All passengers must make their way to the lifepods on deck twelve immediately.'

'What's happening?' the man with the scarred face demanded.

'I don't know,' Floyd said, his eyes darting around. 'But whatever it is, I'll take it. I'd say this is a stand-off, pal.'

'Only until my guys arrive.'

Floyd looked up, suddenly sensing something, some imminent danger.

'I don't think we have that much time.'

On the bridge of the Aurora, Captain Johannsen stared with grim acceptance at the animated picture of his wife and sons as he listened to that calm, measured voice.

'Warning. Collision alert. Emergency evacuation in progress. All passengers must make their way to the lifepods on deck twelve immediately.'

It wouldn't be long now, he estimated.

'Collision in five, four, three, two, one.'

— Six —

The MMV Korolev smashed into the outer gravity ring at a little over thirty kilometres per second. The cockpit, with the long dead remains of the pilots, was crushed into oblivion, but the sheer mass of the spacecraft tore through the Aurora's gravity decks like a hammer through a matchstick village.

The first of the fuel tanks was ruptured, and an instant later it was ignited. The escaping oxygen from the Aurora allowed it to develop into an expanding sphere of burning hell.

The fireball lived and died swiftly, igniting the few individuals within its radius. Those unfortunate souls screamed in unimaginable agony as the flesh was roasted on their bones. But, as quickly as it was born, the fireball was extinguished by the uncompromising vacuum of space.

The Arcadia Series

Max Landry sat, looking. Listening. Around him, a hundred others did the same. None could quite fathom what was happening as the warm sunlight was replaced by an ominous crimson glow.

'Warning. Collision alert. Emergency evacuation in progress. All passengers must make their way to the lifepods on deck twelve immediately.'

Collision alert? What was there to collide with all the way out here, thought Landry. No, it must be an equipment malfunction. Or a joke. Someone in the crew thinking it would add a little excitement to a humdrum voyage.

'Collision in five, four, three, two, one.'

No, it had to be a joke. It just *had* to be.

The rocks and trees on the far side of the pool were suddenly wrenched apart, and a huge chunk of twisted, burning metal burst into the pool area.

Some people were immediately pulverized by the invading craft, their bloodied remains smeared over the ceiling. Others were impaled on bent, shattered metal.

Max Landry watched in detached horror as men and women were suddenly wrenched from the pool to be carried screaming toward the mangled craft as it continued to carve its way through the gravity ring. One thing of which he was sure: he had to get out. Now.

Clawing his way along the rocks, he dragged himself toward the doors, toward safety. He wasn't far away when the wreckage of the ship disappeared, leaving a gaping hole in the area. Water, rocks and people were instantly plucked away and hurled out into open space.

Landry clung to a handrail, feeling the biting wind tearing at his body. All he could do was hang on.

Around him were the screams of the dying. He saw the pretty young waitress fly past, still clutching the drinks tray and letting out a long, unbroken wail until she disappeared into the blackness of space.

Something caught hold of his ankle and he looked down. Claudia was clinging to him, her eyes wide with terror. The sarong she wore rippled in the gale before being snatched away to follow the waitress.

'Max, help me!' she screamed, her words barely audible in the cacophony.

He could feel himself losing his grip on the handrail, sweating fingers sliding along its length. Claudia's extra weight was dragging him to oblivion.

'Sorry honey,' he yelled, and kicked at her hand with his free foot.

'Max! No!' she yelled.

The fingers slipped away one at a time. Her legs flailed wildly, trying to find something to save her.

Nothing did.

With a final, violent kick, she lost her grip completely and fell, screaming through the air.

Landry watched her go, saw her arms and legs thrashing in terrified desperation. A moment later, she was through the rent and clutching her throat as air was wrenched from her lungs. He lost sight of her as flying debris obscured his view.

There were so many bodies, thrashing and screaming as they were enveloped by the cold, merciless expanse of darkness.

Max Landry dragged himself along the railing, his muscles complaining in agonized protest. One hand over the other, dragging himself along. He was a survivor. He always had been. He wasn't going to join all those other hapless souls. But the main entrance was twenty meters away. He would never make it. A loose rock smashed into the side of his head, almost dislodging his grip.

And then he saw it. Not more than two meters away was a door. It wasn't generally meant for the use of passengers, but right now he would take anything. With renewed strength, he dragged himself toward it and punched the access control. It slid easily open and he was just about to haul himself through when he felt something grab his wrist. He looked round, ready to send another poor soul to their doom but stopped. Celeste clung to his arm, her eyes pleading with him. He would get only one chance, he knew. If this didn't work, he would toss her aside as he had Claudia.

With all the strength he could muster, he yanked Celeste's slim, light body around and with a roar, hurled her through the doorway. She rolled twice, before the raging wind started to drag her back again. But by now Landry had dragged his own body through and slammed the palm of his hand against the control, and the door slid shut.

The silence was instantaneous, and it took a few moments for them to realise that there was still noise, just muffled now.

They both lay on the floor, gasping for breath, unable to comprehend what had happened, and how they were still alive.

Landry dragged himself up and punched a fist into the door control, smashing it in a shower of sparks. 'Don't want anyone else opening it now, do we?' He collapsed against the now blocked door.

'Thanks,' Celeste panted. Her hair was a crazy mess that covered most of her face, but aside from a few scrapes and bruises, she seemed to be okay.

'Don't mention it, darlin'. Never know when you might need a good lawyer.'

Although every muscle in his body screamed for respite, he knew they didn't have time to rest. He was no astro-engineer, but knew enough to realise the Aurora was doomed. He dragged himself up and pulled Celeste to her feet as well, her body still feeling weak as he clutched her to his side.

'Come on,' he said, still fighting for breath. 'We need to get out of here.'

It sounded like the end of the world, and in a sense, that was precisely what it was. The Korolev had blasted its way through all six gravity rings. By the time it had carved a path of death through the last ring, it had largely broken up, but that was of little comfort to the survivors on board the Aurora. The mass was just the same, but was now spread out.

Entire modules smashed into the main hull, exploding, ripping great holes in the superstructure.

Once it had done that, the end was inevitable. The Aurora would now tear herself apart in an anguished, tortuous act of self-destruction.

They had married the day before the ESS Aurora had set sail from Earth. It had been a beautiful wedding, everything that Tamara had ever wanted. Conor hadn't been bothered about getting married, but if it made her happy, then that was fine with him. She had looked so beautiful in that pearly dress, almost pure and angelic.

But he knew all too well how wrong that impression would be.

It truly had been a blissful six weeks, with neither of them having a care in the world, just enjoying being together, indulging one another and taking pleasure whenever they wanted.

Until the thunder came.

Conor and Tamara had been asleep in their cabin when it struck, like the most violent storm ever experienced on Earth. Tamara screamed involuntarily at the sound. And then the earthquake followed it. The ship lurched violently, shaking as if in the clutches of a petulant child.

'What is it?' Tamara screamed, her eyes filled with terror.

'I don't know,' Conor yelled back, and staggered over to the door, which slid aside with a squeak of metal against metal that had not been there before. Outside, people ran. It was bedlam, without order and without reason. Some ran one way; others ran the other.

Conor caught the eye of a woman as she ran past.

'What's happened?' he shouted above the melee.

'A collision,' she screamed as her eyes darted around in near madness, her fingers tearing at her hair as she was engulfed by hysteria.

'A what? What did we hit?'

'I don't know. I... I have to find my partner. Have you seen her?'

Conor had no idea who this woman was, let alone who her partner might be. But before he could offer any sort of response, she was gone, screaming down the hall for someone to find her partner.

He turned back to look at the terror-stricken face of his new wife.

'Did you hear that?' he asked.

She nodded. 'The ship's collided with something.'

'I don't know what to do,' Conor said hopelessly.

'We need to find one of the lifepods,' she said, her fearful mind finding some clarity.

'Of course,' he said, shaking his head. His abused mind should have thought of that. 'They're on deck twelve. Come on.' He reached out a hand to take hers.

'No,' she said. 'I need my trousseau.'

'What?' he asked incredulously. 'No, we need to go.'

'But it has all my—'

'Leave it and come on!'

Conor grabbed her wrist and dragged her from the room. They ran, dodging people going the opposite way.

'Is this the right way?' Conor shouted.

'Yes,' Tamara yelled back. 'The staircase is this way.'

A panicked man ran headlong into Conor and knocked him heavily against the wall where he dropped to the ground.

'Come on!' Tamara yelled, and dragged Conor to his feet before he was crushed underfoot by the crowd, driven insane by fear.

The sound of screeching metal filled the hall as the gravity rings tore themselves apart, metal and silicone panels twisting and bending, contorted until they reached the limit of molecular cohesion. Emergency bulkheads could be heard clanging into place. They could smell the acrid smoke that hung in the air, and the scent of burnt meat.

They reached the spiral staircase, flanked by four elevator shafts. It writhed like a tormented snake, clanking and screaming like a living thing in its final throes of agonized death.

They looked around.

'Where are all the people?' she shouted above the wailing cry of tortured metal.

'I don't know. They all went the wrong way!'

'Then they're all going to die,' she said, and he could see that she wanted to go back and warn them.

'This is our last chance, babe.'

'I know,' she said, tears streaming down her cheeks. 'Should we chance the elevator?'

'No way,' he said. 'It's only one floor. Hopefully the stairs will hold.'

They ran down the staircase, praying that it would hold together and not hurl them out into the frigid void of space.

An almighty, deafening crash rang through the level nine atrium, like the sound of an ocean liner dropped from fifty meters to hit the ground.

'Uh-oh,' Ben Floyd mumbled. 'That can't be good.'

The Arcadia Series

The clanging cacophony was swiftly followed by a rising wind, a gale that tore at his skin, and within a second it felt like he was having his eyeballs sucked out.

Floyd grabbed the nearest thing he could reach, which happened to be the elevator control panel. A second later his body was lifted by the ferocious tempest. He clung on, praying that the small box would support him. The clean and tiny atrium was suddenly a whirling mass of debris and loose detritus, churning and broiling in a nightmare maelstrom.

Through blurred vision, he saw his antagonist, Tor, clinging desperately to one of the stairwell supports.

'Help me!' the man cried, his words almost inaudible over the roaring turmoil. His scarred face did not look like it showed fear often, but now it did. It showed an unimaginable terror. He clawed at the post, his fingers slipping on the shiny metal.

Floyd reached out his free hand, fingers stretching to grab the other man's hand. They touched, fingertips to fingertips.

An object flew past and from the colour of the dress, he recognized it as the girl in the corridor. He could do nothing for her. She was already gone and had disappeared, screaming, into the next passage. The boy was next and he somehow managed to claw at Tor's leg. It wasn't much, but was enough to dislodge the man's hand from the post and he followed the boy toward the tunnel.

Floyd watched as the man's legs smashed into the wall, shattering them, bending them in unnatural angles.

Eden's Gate

Tor disappeared to follow the others, but his anguished cries of agony and fear lingered.

Floyd turned away. There was nothing he could do. All three were lost, as were dozens of others, most probably. He looked up and saw an elevator car approaching. He had to stop it. That car was his only hope.

He heaved his body forward and hit the call button. Two seconds later and he would have been too late, but just when he thought the car was about to go sailing past, it slowed and came to a juddering stop.

The doors slid aside and before he knew what was happening, a figure came flying out. A woman. A small part of his brain identified the clothing as that of an Aurora crewmember. He shot his free hand out to grab her, and just managed to snag her wrist. He clung one-handed to the edge of the elevator, his other hand holding the woman. He had to find some strength, some hidden reserve of energy.

Floyd began to bend his arm, heaving the woman toward him. Thankfully, she had the presence of mind to help the process and once he had lifted her as far as he could, she clawed her way up his body. She manhandled herself into the elevator car and once she had secured herself, worked with Floyd to haul him inside. Both grunted and cursed and heaved, dragging his weight, which seemed to have quadrupled, until his entire body was inside.

The door squeaked shut, the fit not quite as perfect as it normally was, but Floyd wasn't about to complain.

The Arcadia Series

As soon as the doors had made a successful seal, the wind and noise dropped. Mangled crashes and explosions could still be heard, but they were far off now, muffled by the thin organic composite of the car's body.

'Thanks,' Floyd gasped as he allowed himself a few blissful moments to relax his body.

'Likewise,' she replied, propping herself against the wall of the car. 'Level twelve,' she instructed to the computer and the car began to descend.

'What happened?' Floyd asked, getting some of his breath back.

Levels nine and ten disappeared, and both stared slack jawed as they emerged into open space, the transparent tube giving a panoramic view of the indiscriminate destruction. Floyd wasn't sure that was a good idea. Perhaps ignorance really was bliss.

The Aurora was in tatters, its main hull twisted and crushed, the gravity rings relentlessly turning, mangling the ship still further. The central body of the craft was writhing like some hideous alien serpent, explosions erupting from its surface. Hull plating exploded outward, great chunks of debris flung out to crash into the gravity rings.

Floyd was amazed they had lived this long.

'We were hit by another ship,' she said quickly, trying to regain some composure.

'Holy God. Must've been something big. The name's Floyd, by the way. Ben Floyd.' He held out his hand and she dutifully shook it.

'Lieutenant Luana Lee, third officer.'

'Pleased to meet you. So, what are our chances?'

The hellish scene slipped away and they entered the enclosed structure of the outmost gravity ring.

'Depends on whether we can get to a lifepod. They're all on Level 12. Here we go. Get ready.'

When the doors opened, it was clear that this was scarcely better than the nightmare they had just left. These were the final death throes of the great starliner. It only had minutes, perhaps seconds to live.

A young couple emerged from one corridor, clutching each other tightly. From another corridor a man emerged, screaming like a banshee, all reason lost. Floyd watched him tear past and run into a restroom.

At that moment, a massive chunk of debris, a dozen times the size of the elevator car, crashed into the side of the ring. Floyd and Luana held their breath, expecting it to come crashing down on top of them. But it didn't. By some miracle, it stayed there, suspended above them. However, it did dislodge one of the overlooking balconies, which crashed down onto the toilet cubicle, obliterating it and crushing its hapless occupant to mush.

A group of a dozen women came running from another corridor, all dressed in identical scarlet bodices and tutus.

'Chorus line dancers,' Floyd said dully, as if that was perfectly normal in this situation. Of course, why wouldn't you have chorus line dancers in all of this?

The twelve girls ran straight past them and into another corridor. Another woman emerged from the same direction, in a flowing scarlet dress, sequins glimmering in the light, tassels flapping wildly like a nest of angry snakes.

'This is nuts,' he murmured.

Luana pointed to the corridor where the twelve girls had just disappeared. 'Lifepod 10 is just down there. It's the closest lifepod to this position.'

The woman in scarlet ran up to Floyd and grabbed him by the collar. 'Where did they go? Tell me! Where did they go?'

'The dancers? Same way as we're going. Lifepod 10.' As gently as he could under the circumstances, he pulled her hands away from his collar.

Floyd turned and fist bumped Luana, and the two of them set off at a run for the lifepod.

'Wait, is that where we're supposed to go?'

The dancer turned to see a girl, maybe a year or two younger than she was, and a young man. They clutched each other tightly, as if letting go for just an instant would risk them losing each other forever.

'Yes, that's what the—'

At that moment, one of the loose passenger modules from the Korolev smashed through the corridor that Floyd and Luana were running towards. In the blink of an eye, salvation turned to despair as an entire three-meter section of tunnel was torn into shreds.

Eden's Gate

Floyd and Luana both tried to stop, but were immediately swept away by a fierce tornado, plucking them from the ground and hurling them through the air.

In delirious confusion, Floyd saw all twelve dancers sucked from further down the corridor and hurled, screaming and flailing, into open space. More deaths. More pointless, stupid deaths. But not quite instant deaths. Most lost consciousness within an agonized fifteen or twenty seconds. But some poor souls had been known to last over two minutes, feeling their fingers and toes freeze, eyeballs expand and splinter and heart finally give up the uneven struggle to sustain a ravaged body.

It was not a good way to die.

Ben Floyd thought of these things as he was hurled through the air. This was to be his fate. He thought it curious that, in just a couple of seconds, he had contemplated all of this. Time was such a sluggish beast sometimes. He wondered—

When they were just four scant meters from the entrance to the corridor – and the huge, jagged rent in the tube – something unexpected happened. A wall of metal slammed down: an emergency bulkhead, suddenly blocking the gaping hole.

Floyd was so surprised, it took him a moment to realise that he and Luana were now hurtling toward a solid metal door at an uncomfortably high speed. There was no time to turn, to find a comfortable position. All he could do was hold out his arms at the last instant to slightly cushion the impact.

He slammed into the door hard, hearing his own pained grunt as he did so. Half a second later, Luana joined him, although she had gotten herself into a more favourable position. He learned then that she had a cat-like agility and could twist her body easily.

They both slumped to the floor groaning, and quite incredulous at their luck.

The woman in the scarlet dress had also been picked up and tossed like a rag doll, as had the young couple, Tamara and Conor. But their distance had helped them, and the three found themselves skidding along the floor and coming to a more graceful stop.

'Okay, lifepod 11 it is, then,' Luana said, staggering to her feet and helping Floyd up.

'Lifepod 11 works for me.'

— Seven —

A small corridor led off from the main thoroughfare of level twelve. There should have been illuminated arrows directing people to the lifepod, but power to this section had been cut off. If it weren't for Luana and her familiarity with the ship, they never would have found it. It was no more than five meters long, and ended in an open hatch. Luana breathed a heartfelt sigh of relief when she saw that open, beckoning hatch. It represented salvation; a chance for life.

She and Floyd led the way and when they reached the end of the shaft, peered down into the cylindrical tube that led to lifepod 11. The interior of the pod, three meters below, was illuminated in crimson.

And it was clear that they weren't the first to arrive. At the bottom of the shaft, lying on the floor, was a body. It lay on its front, limbs spread out.

They shared a glance, before looking back into that suddenly unnerving place.

'Who's that?' Floyd asked.

Luana shrugged. 'No idea, but he's hurt, that's for sure.'

Floyd noticed a small pool of blood near the man's head.

There was another huge shunt – more debris striking the gravity ring – and they were all slammed against the bulkhead.

'Really had enough of this now,' Floyd cursed.

'Okay,' Luana said, ignoring him. 'Time to get in. Who's first? Quick as you like.'

Floyd moved aside to let Tamara go first. She stepped daintily onto the ladder and gingerly descended, gripping it tightly. Conor followed her, equally cautious.

'Come on, come on,' Floyd whispered, anxiously looking at the walls twisting and deforming. Even if they got everyone inside, would this damage affect the docking clamps that held the lifepod securely to the ship? Would the clamps even last that long? He had a sudden vision of the lifepod breaking loose and spiralling away, and he and Luana ejected into the void.

The woman in the red dress was next, and she seemed just as uncomfortable descending a vertical ladder as the previous two, but she was soon down and into the body of the lifepod.

Next was an unfamiliar face and Floyd frowned, wondering if he'd seen this man before.

Eden's Gate

'Hold up you guys; room for one more?'

'Sure,' said Luana. 'More the merrier.' There was another crash from some other part of the gravity ring and she looked anxiously along the corridor.

'Cheers. Dane Jefferson.' The amiable black man grinned a full pearly white graveyard of immaculate teeth. His hair was long, but coiled into a bun with dreadlocks that looked like they could inadvertently pluck out an eyeball for the unwary.

'Get your ass in there, buddy,' Floyd said.

'You got it, boss.' The man did as he was told, sliding down the ladder.

That's more like it, Floyd thought.

Then Floyd looked up and saw who was next, his face dropping.

'Oh no,' he groaned.

'What?' asked Luana in confusion.

'Of all the…'

'Bet you never expected to see me again, Mr. Floyd,' Max Landry greeted him with an unabashed smile.

'Max, I ought to—'

'Please Benny,' Celeste begged, clutching her shoulders as she shivered with cold and fear. 'I don't want to die out here.'

From the far end of the corridor, just a few meters away, the floor began to split as it warped and buckled.

'Can we all do this later?' Luana said. 'We're kinda pressed for time here.'

Floyd waved with resignation, and Celeste stepped forward, lowering herself down the ladder. Floyd grabbed Landry by the collar of his garish Hawaiian shirt and all but tossed the Englishman down the access tube.

'You next, Floyd,' Luana said, but at that moment the rip in the floor became a gaping rent, and they felt an all too familiar wind seize them.

Floyd was ready this time.

Luana was not.

She was plucked from the floor and propelled down the shaft. Floyd, with one hand firmly gripping the ladder, snatched her hand and dragged her back, and she was able to claw her way down the ladder. He was right behind her and the moment his head was clear, punched the control to the iris hatch, sealing them inside.

Luana wasted two valuable seconds to hug him, before jumping down to the floor and making for the cockpit. Floyd was a little slower, taking the time to secure the inner hatch, before following her.

He didn't have a lot of time to orientate himself, and quickly scanned the layout of the vessel. This was clearly more than just a "pod". It seemed to consist of a cylinder at the centre, stretching from bow to stern. At the rear was a storage hold; ahead was the cockpit. In separate nacelles either side were the passenger compartments.

Ahead, Luana eased into the pilot's seat and buckled herself in. She flicked half a dozen switches, and the red light was replaced by a stark white light throughout the

Eden's Gate

ship. She donned the headset and flicked on the cockpit to cabin intercom.

'Everyone, buckle yourselves in tight and secure that injured man.'

Checking the cabin camera as she activated ship's systems, she noted that Conor and Dane were manhandling the limp figure into the port nacelle while Tamara protected his head. Reaching overhead, she flicked another dozen switches and environmental systems hummed into life.

'Hold tight everyone,' she said into the intercom. 'This is going to be a rough ride.'

As if to reinforce the point, the lifepod was rocked by another collision.

Floyd stumbled into the cockpit. 'Do you need any help?'

'Are you a starpilot?'

'Atmospheric only.'

'Close enough,' she grinned back at him, and tossed the co-pilot's headset at him. 'Strap yourself in, flyboy.'

Luana punched four prominent buttons on the forward console, and Floyd heard the engines whine into life.

'You in, Floyd?'

He snapped the buckle into place, securing him in the seat. 'Copy that.'

'Okay, hang on tight.' She keyed the cabin mike again. 'Everyone in? Okay, as soon as we disengage, we're going to lose gravity, so make sure you're strapped in tight. Launching in five, four, three…'

There came the sound of restraining latches springing back, and a deep rumble from the main engines.

'…two, one, launching.'

The last of the latches released the little ship and it was flung away from the disintegrating wreck of the Aurora. The centrifugal force of the gravity rings' rotation ensured the lifepod was propelled away with considerable energy.

Between the two seats were four throttles, which Luana gently eased forward.

Floyd felt a deep, slightly unsettling rumble in his seat as Luana unleashed the full power of the main engines. He was compressed into his seat as the ship was blasted forwards. Pieces of spaceship were everywhere, objects large and small littering the observation window. The scanner in front of him was all but useless, the view ahead an unbroken field of debris.

It sounded like rain all around them, tiny and not so tiny fragments bouncing off the hull.

The lifepod dipped and weaved, Luana caressing the controls with tender dexterity. A large chunk of the Aurora spun into view just ahead of them and she guided the ship beneath it, rolling away and guiding them to safety.

The debris field seemed to be clearing, the smashed fragments of starliner becoming smaller.

'That was a little bit close,' Floyd said, wiping sweat from his forehead and realising his heart was pounding like a bass drum. 'Several times back there I thought we were—'

There was no warning, no collision alarm. It was a stray piece of the Korolev that hit them. It impacted from above, exploding in a hail of sparks. The roar from within the ship was deafening, and the explosion sent them spinning away and completely out of control. Emergency bulkheads snapped into place.

Inside the cockpit, Floyd could only see the stars spinning, the Aurora briefly coming into view, then disappearing again. Multiple alarms sounded, creating a discordant cacophony.

'Hull breach, section five. Area sealed off,' Luana shouted, and Floyd grabbed the co-pilot's control column. Both fought with the controls, desperately trying to cancel the barrelling spin.

'Did we lose anybody?' he shouted.

'Negative. Section five is the aft cargo bay.'

Floyd grunted in acknowledgement as he tried to regain some control of the ship. The rolling slowed, stopped momentarily, then completed several revolutions in the other direction before they had the ship under some semblance of control.

Floyd and Luana shared a don't-want-to-do-that-again-soon look, and grinned.

'We've got to put some distance between us and the Aurora,' she said, easing the throttle controls forward until they were at maximum power.

The little ship was finally free of the debris field, most of the wreckage coming from the gravity rings and being flung out laterally. It scurried away like a mouse trying to escape a cat.

Then the cat erupted as its nuclear reactors went critical, the reactions uncontrolled. An expanding sphere of white-hot radiation blasted out from the propulsion section at the rear of the doomed ship. It raced along the main hull, tearing it apart and incinerating vast sections. The pathetic remains of the gravity rings were engulfed and vaporized. The final area to feel its pitiless destructive touch was the bridge, where Captain Alvaro Johannsen sat staring unblinkingly at his family. He heard nothing, saw nothing as his body sizzled for the briefest of instants, before its atoms were brushed away.

The blast wave quickly caught up with the lifepod as it ran for its life, and tossed it aside. It tumbled through space, again out of control, until its two pilots finally managed to steady it.

Against the vast, empty backdrop of space, the small, insignificant little ship trod its lonely path.

— Eight —

Luana eased the throttles back to the ion engine equivalent of idling, and the rumbling in the cockpit eased back to a barely perceivable vibration.

'I'm cutting power,' she told Floyd. 'We don't know which direction to head in yet, so there's no point wasting our xenon fuel reserves. The nav-com should lock onto the most promising target but I'd like to see what it comes up with for myself. We should be far enough away from the blast zone to avoid debris. Probably.'

'Makes sense,' Floyd acknowledged as he brought the navigational display up on his console. 'One thing's for sure.'

'What's that?'

'I'm writing a strongly worded letter of complaint to the management.'

'You and me both,' she laughed. 'Right, try scanning for emergency beacons and heat signatures. Find out how many other pods got away so we can link up.'

'I'm on it. Give me a minute; I'm new to this system.'

Floyd scrolled down the menu. He assumed that local area scanning would be a sub-menu of the navigational screen. And he was right, smiling to himself. Not a lot had gone right today, so he assumed it was about time for a change of luck. He found the screen he was looking for quite quickly, once he had ascertained how the system was set up.

'Let's see, local contacts, local contacts...' He frowned, and went back a step to make sure he was on the right screen. He checked again, just to make sure he had it calibrated correctly. He did. He was scanning an area of a hundred thousand square kilometres, but the message on the screen seemed unequivocal: there were no contacts registering within a hundred-thousand-kilometre scanning sphere. In the corner of the screen was an option to run a system diagnostic, which he began.

'This can't be right,' he muttered.

'What is it?'

The diagnostic result came back and, with a sickening inevitability, the result was as Floyd had feared. The instrumentation was functioning perfectly. 'No signatures. Nothing.'

'That can't be right,' she said, looking over to his screen. 'Have you tried running a diagnostic?'

'Yep, and checked calibration.' He turned to her and said gravely: 'We're the only lifepod to make it away.'

Luana's face took on a haunted expression, her skin ashen. 'Oh my God, those poor souls.' She thought of her captain and of Brent. She was going to go out on a date with him. They were going to have a picnic between decks. She thought of poor, luckless Lester.

Floyd saw her eyes glistening, and she quickly blinked the tears away. This was not the time. She had to remain strong.

'We can't think about that right now. There'll be plenty of time to grieve later. I need to check on the damage to the ship. It's not looking good.'

Her screen displayed two lists: primary and secondary systems. A disturbing number of items were flashing red.

'Propulsion and life support are both good,' she said. 'Aft retro thrusters offline. Oxygen is okay. We lost two O_2 tanks but eight are intact. This lifepod is designed to hold twenty-six people, and there are only nine of us, so the loss of two tanks won't be a problem.'

'Maybe just eight if that guy we found doesn't wake up.'

She nodded ruefully. 'Good point. I've just sent the emergency signal. We should hear from Earth within the hour.'

Floyd scanned the two lists on Luana's screen and noted one of the primary systems flashing red. 'What's that?'

She sighed. 'That's the really bad news. Section five: the aft storage bay. It was compromised by the collision. There was a hull breach and it's currently open to space.

That means we've lost most of our food reserves, so it looks like we'll starve long before we suffocate.'

'That's a cheery thought. Anything else critical we need to worry about?'

'It doesn't look like it at the moment. Several non-critical systems are down. I'll have to do a manual inspection to make sure.' She unbuckled her harness and floated free of the seat.

'You're going outside?' he asked, suddenly concerned. It seemed ludicrous to him, after all the times they had both come close to death as they tried to escape the doomed starliner, that he should be worried about a simple external inspection of the ship. He was under no illusions: Luana was the best asset they had and to lose her would be devastating to their chances.

'These things are pretty basic,' she said, giving the bulkhead a couple of slaps. 'They don't come with maintenance bots. Now eyes forward, soldier.'

For a second he was confused, until he saw her unzip her tunic.

'Oh,' he said, and looked away quickly. The spacesuits that the lifepod carried were designed to be worn without anything underneath, except underwear, and even that was optional. Two minutes later, she was ready. The skin-tight suits were quick to put on, as they may be required in a hurry. They really were a marvel of modern design, possessing incredible thermal efficiency. This was why they were so body hugging. Air circulating was an inefficient waste. A single suit also contained enough air to last the occupant six hours easily. Seven or eight if relaxed or sleeping.

'How do I look?' Luana said.

He was confused for a second as he heard the voice in his headphones. He looked round.

'Er... very... silver?' An electronic laugh sounded in his ear.

Luana checked the systems display on her sleeve. No leaks, temperature nominal, air supply 100% (79% nitrogen, 21% oxygen), humidity level 50% and stable, thrusters at full capacity, electromagnets working and a dozen other parameters checked out okay.

The lifepod contained two airlocks. One was in the ceiling, toward the rear, just forward of the unusable storage bay. The other exited through the floor of the ship, just aft of the cockpit. Luana opted for the forward airlock. Admittedly, it would mean taking a longer journey to get to the aft retro thrusters, but it meant she could bypass the passengers. She wasn't quite ready to face them yet.

'Break a leg,' Floyd said as she opened the hatch at the rear of the cockpit.

'Piece of cake,' she said as she disappeared, closing the cockpit hatch behind her. Fortunately, the suit allowed considerable freedom of movement, so she had no trouble in the zero-gravity environment operating the airlock alone. It was a two-meter wide cylinder that projected out of the bottom of the pod.

With the inner hatch securely sealed, she opened the outer hatch. The last few whispers of air were blown out into space, gently tugging at her body.

'Okay, I'm outside,' she radioed to Floyd.

'Roger that. Let me know if you need any help.'

'Will do, but I know what I'm doing out here and you don't.'

'Fair point,' Floyd said. 'Let's see where we are.'

As Luana slowly jetted her way around the ship and toward the rear, Floyd brought up the local area maps, replacing the depressing list of damaged systems.

There was a quiet beep as Luana made contact again. 'We were right in the middle of the asteroid belt, about as far from anything useful as we could possibly be.'

'I'm looking at the charts now, and it appears that you're right. There are a few asteroids that are so small, they're barely worthy of the name. No passing ships, no way stations. Just a whole lot of nothing.'

'Ceres isn't far,' she said, 'but it's in the wrong direction. It would take our ion engines weeks to bring us to a dead stop, and a couple weeks more to bring us back up to speed and heading where we want to go.'

'That's annoying, to say the least. I can see it on the chart. I'll check to see what *is* in range.'

'I've reached the impact zone,' Luana said as she came to a stop, activating the magnets in her boots and coming to rest. 'It's a real mess out here. That lump of whatever it was carved a slash in the storage bay half a meter wide and two meters long.'

Eden's Gate

'Not really a surprise. Anything salvageable?'

She shone a flashlight into the gaping hole, being careful not to snag her suit on the jagged metal. All she could see was empty storage units, doors ripped open, restraining straps torn and hanging uselessly. 'Not a thing. Looks like everything was sucked out into space.'

'Okay, are you coming back in now?'

She ran a finger along the slash in the hull, being careful not to puncture the glove. The organic polyamide was incredibly strong, but the was no point in taking any chances. She had wondered whether there was any chance the hole could be sealed, but it was too irregular, the dents in the metal making the surface too uneven.

'No, not just yet,' she said wiping her hands as she always did when getting them dirty, then realising how absurd that notion was in her present situation. She decided not to radio this one in. 'There's damage to the dorsal retro thrusters. They need to be fixed if we're ever going to land this thing somewhere. I might as well do it now.'

'Okay, take your time. Don't rush anything.' Ben Floyd would have been much happier if he could have been out there instead of her. But Luana was right, she was experienced at this type of work and he wasn't.

'Afraid that if I don't make it, you'll have to fly this thing yourself?' she said, and he could hear the grin in her voice.

'I can fly anything, but the paperwork would be a bitch.'

'You're all heart, Floyd.'

He flicked the current screen away and brought up another, displaying the most reasonable projected course for them to take.

'This is odd,' he said, scratching his chin. 'My screen is showing that asteroid 349 Dembowska is within range.'

At that moment, Luana was cranking open a damaged access panel to the retro thrusters. She was sure that if there had been an atmosphere, it would have emitted a loud, tortured squeak.

Inside, there was some clear damage to the optical cabling, and a diagnostic scan confirmed this. It wasn't serious; she would just have to replace the cabling between the two adjacent junctions.

She talked as she worked. 'The lifepod is programmed to lock onto the nearest power source. There could be a mining operation there. I'm hoping there is. Our only realistic hope is to find asteroid miners.'

'But according to this, there's nothing there. It's just a lump of rock a hundred and forty klicks across. And under the asteroid notation it says in big, scary, don't-screw-with-us letters: "C1 EXPLORATION PROHIBITED".'

'You're right, that is odd. Exploration prohibited is usually intended to warn off prospectors on safety or security grounds. But this is a Class 1 exclusion you say? That means no human exploration, no robot landers and no orbiting probes. Nothing is permitted within ten thousand kilometres. Interesting.'

'And we're headed there?'

'It appears so,' Luana said, locking the new units in place.

'Well there must be something on that asteroid. If not, then this lifepod is taking us a hell of a long way just to find a lump of barren rock.'

'Now who's being cheery?' Luana asked, with a strong hint of mockery. 'Anyway, I've replaced the damaged cabling in the aft retro thrusters. Could you run a diagnostic for me?'

'Sure thing. Stand-by.' Floyd leaned across to the diagnostic panel and typed in the instruction to the computer. The aft retro thruster screen came up, and each red light flicked over to green. 'Looks good from here. All showing green.'

'Great, I'll secure everything here and head back in.'

— Nine —

Once they were absolutely sure that systems to the two nacelles were functioning perfectly, Luana decided it was time to give their guests some gravity to make things more comfortable.

At least space sickness wasn't a problem. Everyone on board the Aurora had had a dose of medication administered before they had left Earth, just to make sure there were no unpleasant incidents. While watching a spectacle of exotic, zero-gravity dancing, there were few things that could do more to spoil the mood than having someone projectile vomit nearby. This was why such medication was mandatory, and a single dose would protect someone for at least five years.

'Cockpit to cabin,' she began. 'We've finished running system checks up here and completed repairs. We're in pretty good shape, considering. So, I'm going to fire up the centrifuge. It'll take approximately one minute to spool up to full seventy-five percent gravity. Any objects that are not secured will land on your heads when they are subject to gravity. Actually, they'll just slide down the wall, but best secure them just in case. And make sure you're strapped in until it's up to full gravity. Cockpit out.'

Luana switched off the intercom and exhaled deeply. She looked across to Floyd.

He shrugged and tapped his knuckles to his temple. 'Knock on wood.'

She smiled and reached for the switch, flipped up its safety cover, and pressed it. The button lit up in green. That was it. All they could do now was wait and see if it worked – or tore the ship apart because of unseen damage.

Fortunately, the latter event did not happen. There was a whirring, a hum and a faint clank of machinery starting up. The nacelles began, ever so slowly, to rotate around the central axis of the ship. It was a crude imitation of the Aurora's gravity rings, using centrifugal force to simulate gravity, but was better than nothing.

A minute later, they were up to full strength, spinning without any issues and both Luana and Floyd breathed sighs of relief, fist bumping each other to celebrate this minor victory.

'Time to go talk to the passengers,' Floyd said without much enthusiasm. 'Unless you want to go do it?'

'Oh no, I wouldn't want to deprive you,' she said.

'It's no trouble, really.'

'I'll bet. But I'm captain of this vessel, and as captain I'm giving you a field commission of lieutenant. Now get out there, Lieutenant, or I'll have you up on charges.'

'Yes sir!' Floyd said with a salute and a grin. 'But it's your turn next time.'

'Deal. I'll be down in a few minutes; I just want to run some diagnostics on the nacelles, now that they're up and running.'

Acting First Lieutenant Benjamin Floyd glided out of the cockpit and out into the main cylinder. Directly ahead of him was the hatch to the main storage bay – the unfortunate section five. He thought it best not to dwell on the fact that that hatch was all that protected them from the vacuum of space. Every hatch on the ship was designed to withstand far more pressure than it was ever likely to be asked to resist, but it was still a little discomforting to consider that a small metal hatch was all that stood between them, and the minus two-hundred-and-seventy-degree Celsius vacuum of space.

Just in front of the hatch was a pair of small observation windows on either side of the cylinder. They were just fifteen centimetres across, but were one of the only areas on the ship where one could observe the stars. There were no observation windows in the nacelles as the sight of the stars swirling past would lead to severe vertigo, and no amount of preventative medication would stem the tide of vomit that would ensue. Fabric storage compartments lined every wall, only the two airlocks remaining free.

Eden's Gate

But right now, he needed to inspect the two nacelles. They could be reached by access tubes and ladders. This was where Floyd had to be careful. Although conditions at the top of the ladder were weightless, at the bottom – inside one of the nacelles – there was seventy-five percent of Earth gravity. Simply launching from the top could easily result in a broken ankle when he hit the bottom at an alarming thirty kilometres per hour.

He was suitably cautious on this first occasion and hopped the last couple of rungs from the bottom.

There was little privacy in these areas. Seats were self-contained units that could be opened out to form a relatively comfortable bed. They came with their own entertainment units with vast libraries of music and video. Researchers had long since concluded that boredom might be the greatest challenge survivors could face, and great efforts had been made to ensure the passengers were kept occupied. Each nacelle was designed to hold twelve people, and sustain them for up to six weeks. That was how long it was estimated a rescue ship would take to rendezvous with them. In theory. Floyd did not like to think what conditions would be like if the lifepod was home to its full complement of twenty-six people. Having said this, the nacelles demonstrated a masterfully inventive use of space. At one end of each nacelle was a rudimentary bathroom, and at the other was a food preparation area, although their emergency rations would not require very much in the way of preparation.

This nacelle, though, currently only had three occupants – two of whom he would happily toss out of an airlock.

'Are you guys okay?' he asked, because he certainly had nothing against the young woman in the scarlet dress.

'Okay,' she answered hesitantly. 'Do you have any idea what happened to the Aurora? Dane said he thought it was an asteroid impact.'

'No, we collided with another vessel, Ms...?'

'Shaw. Suzy Shaw. I'm a performer in the Starlight Lounge. At least I was until... Are we linking up with the other lifepods?'

Floyd had been dreading this, but was glad to spare Luana the ordeal of being the bearer of such tragic news. He glanced around, and up, noting that everyone, from both nacelles, was listening. With a sigh he sat down next to Suzy and took her hand.

'I'm afraid not,' he said as gently as he could, but loud enough for everyone to hear. 'It appears that we're the only survivors from the Aurora. We've run extensive sensor sweeps and sent wide bandwidth hails, but there's been no response from other surviving ships. There's no getting away from it: we are the last surviving lifepod. I'm... so sorry.'

'It's okay,' she said with a weak smile. 'No, of course it's not okay, but—'

'I understand what you mean. No part of any of this is okay.'

A tear rolled down her cheek. 'I saw most of my friends die, right in front of my eyes. I thought I was going to die as well. I wish I had. I feel so guilty. I should have been with them.'

Floyd recalled the bizarre sight of a dozen chorus girls running through the atrium, only to be sucked out into space. 'None of that was your fault, and nothing would have been gained by your death. You did nothing to let them down.'

He gently placed her hand back on her leg and stood.

'Funny ain't it, Mr. Floyd?' Max Landry said. 'Of all the people who could've ended up on this ship, it had to be you and me. What d'ya say we let bygones be bygones and work together.'

He proffered a hand, but Floyd simply stared at it, his face a swirling mess of emotions, none of them definable; none of them good.

Floyd walked the few paces to where Landry sat, unsure of what he was going to do. He wanted to kill him. He wanted to grab him by the throat and squeeze the life out of him. He wanted to beat him until he was a bloodied pulp. He could think of all manner of unpleasant things that he could do to the gangster.

Instead, he bent over until his face was barely three centimetres from his antagonist's. 'Let me make one thing clear, Max. You are under arrest. You're my prisoner and when this is over, you're going to jail. We are not allies. We are not friends. You're a common crook. Got it?'

The Arcadia Series

He stood again, but did not take his eyes off the shorter man. Landry just smiled, not phased in the least.

'Sooner or later, you're going to need me, Mr. Floyd. You mark my words. You'll need me, and I'll be there to help you. I think you can guess what I'll want in return.'

Floyd said nothing, but turned away. His eyes fell on Suzy once more. She sat there, looking forlorn and lost, a shiver running through her. She still wore the scarlet costume that looked ridiculous in this situation.

'We'll see if we can find you some clothing that's a little more... appropriate, Ms. Shaw.'

She looked up at him, and then down at her body, acting as if she had only just realised she was still dressed as a nightclub entertainer. She smiled again. 'Thank you.'

'What about me?' Celeste said, holding her hands out to draw attention to the fact that she was still wearing a light summer dress, her arms and shoulders uncovered, the material too thin to offer much protection. 'Don't I get anything? Or are you just looking after your girlfriend? Your *new* girlfriend, Benny.'

Floyd tried to conceal his fury, but predictably was only partially successful. She had caught him off guard with this remark, as unfounded as the accusation was. There was a reason Celeste Karlin was one of the best lawyers in San Diego. She could manipulate people with the deftest of touches, uncovering their weaknesses and exploiting them to the full. She was brutal in the courtroom, and could easily turn those talents to whatever situation in which she happened to find herself. Suzy

Shaw was an extremely attractive young woman; there was no getting away from that. She was a professional singer and dancer. It was her job to look good. For a heterosexual man to deny this would have been a ludicrous conceit. But acknowledging this did not mean he had any intentions in that regard. An innocent man wrongly accused is the easiest to manipulate. In another situation, he might tip his notional hat to Celeste for such a superbly well executed job. But not here, not now.

'We'll find you something.' He managed to say this without suffixing it with: "you traitorous bitch".

Floyd turned and headed up the ladder, turning a hundred and eighty degrees at the top, and descending into the other nacelle where he dropped lightly.

'Anyone here need some fresh clothing?' he asked, knowing that they had heard every word that had just been spoken.

'I may be needing a change of underwear,' Dane Jefferson said. 'Damn near soiled myself back there on the Aurora.'

'I'm sure you can make do for now,' Floyd replied with a smirk.

'I think we could.' Another man stood, young and dark haired. 'My name's Conor Jax and this is my wife, Tamara.'

To Floyd, neither looked old enough to be married. But then again, this was just a reminder that he was not getting any younger.

'I really could do with something fresh,' Tamara said.

'I'll see what I can do,' Floyd said, but then he turned his attention to the unconscious figure in the far bed. 'What about our friend here?'

'I don't think a clean set of clothes will help him, bud,' Dane said.

'No, I mean, how's he doing?'

Tamara stood and went over to the man. 'He hasn't stirred since we got here. I've hooked him up to an IV and systems monitor. All we can do now is let him sleep. He's breathing okay but he had a nasty bang on the head. I'll keep an eye on him.'

'You seem to know what you're doing,' Floyd commented.

'I spent two years as a med-tech at Johns Hopkins, so I know the basics.'

There was the sound of movement from above, and a second later Luana dropped into the nacelle.

'How're we all doing here?' she asked brightly.

'We're holding up,' Conor said.

'Who do I see about a refund?' Dane asked.

She chuckled, her eyes roaming around the nacelle. 'I'll see what I can do when we get home. How about the…' As her gaze fell upon the unconscious man, the smile froze on her face, before slowly fading away.

Floyd had a sudden feeling of dread. 'What? What is it? Who is he?'

She strode over to the figure and yanked him upright, her face a mask of furious hate. 'Wake up!' She slapped him on both cheeks, the head lolling lazily. 'Wake up you bastard!'

Floyd flung his arms around her and dragged her away, the figure slumping listlessly back down. Tamara rushed over to tend to her patient, checking the IV and respiration monitors were still attached and working.

'Luana, who is he?' Floyd demanded.

She shrugged him away, but did not go back to have another go at the man. However, her gaze did not stray from him, her eyes like lasers piercing him with twin beams of pure, unfiltered hate.

'Paska,' she spat. 'Second Lieutenant Grant Paska.' She looked around at the shocked faces that stared back at her. 'Let me know, the minute he wakes up.'

Without waiting for a response, she turned and was quickly up the ladder and back within the safety of the cockpit.

— Ten —

Hanging at an absurd angle, Floyd began his series of checks. Air supply 100%, temperature normal, humidity level 50% and stable, thrusters at full capacity, electromagnets working. He was singing from the same checklist as Luana had the previous day, but today was different. He would be accompanying her for an EVA.

He looked across the cockpit at her, and then down at himself. The suit fit her like a glove, accentuating her curves as it clung to her body. The suit had to be skin-tight to function properly. On her, this was an advantage. She looked great in hers. He looked terrible, the suit bulging in all the wrong places and, even worse, flattening another area that he really wished would have some kind of presence. Anything at all. But no. Ben Floyd might as well be a eunuch.

'All set?' Luana asked as she finished her checklist. Her voice was electronically modified, and it was disconcerting seeing her two meters away, yet seeming to be speaking into his ear.

'All systems nominal. Suit systems, anyway. I look ridiculous in this thing. You look fantastic, like you were born to wear one of these. I look like a Thanksgiving turkey.'

She chuckled and wiggled her backside at him. 'You don't look so bad. These suits are just not very forgiving. Now, shall we?'

He waved, and she led them out of the cockpit and through to airlock one, set into the ceiling of the cylinder.

Floyd dragged a rolled-up parcel along with him, which was tethered to his belt. This was the important stuff. After surveying the external damage to the storage bay on her previous excursion, they had, after a lot of discussion on the subject, decided that it needed to be sealed, even if only fairly loosely. The parcel contained a large sheet of flexi-steel which was not, despite the name, actual steel, but a laminate of multiple layers of aluminium and organic polyamide. It was as tough as leather. No, tougher than that, even. It was more like a medieval knight's chainmail, but a lot more flexible.

Floyd had voiced his concerns to her about the pressure on the storage bay hatch, and she too had a nagging, possibly irrational worry that it could give way. If it did, then everyone would instantly be flushed out into space, and that would end their adventure there and then. So, they decided that it would make them both feel better if the gaping rent in the hull could be sealed.

Luana opened the inner airlock hatch and the two of them, together with their cargo of flexi-steel, eased themselves up until they were inside the airlock and the hatch could be sealed behind them.

Floyd could hear air being sucked out of the chamber, and as it was, felt the suit adjusting itself around him. The design suddenly made sense to him; it only worked properly once in a vacuum. That didn't explain how Luana managed to look quite so good in hers from the moment she put it on. He concluded that she must be one of those freaks who could effortlessly look good in anything, at any time and in any situation.

Once the air had been completely expelled, they fist-bumped to affirm that both were ready.

'I've got a small confession to make,' Floyd said. 'I've never actually been in space before. Not without a nice, sturdy ship around me.'

'Oh, there's nothing to it,' she said, and sounded genuinely sincere. 'You shouldn't need to adjust your environmental controls at all. They will adapt to changing conditions automatically. Same with the sun visor, so you won't get blinded. The only thing you need to worry about is your thruster controls. It's simple enough to operate. Just remember to use small inputs. Gently does it is the key. Okay?'

'Sure. Let's go.' He surprised himself at how positive he sounded.

Luana opened the outer hatch, and they felt a slight tug as the last vestiges of atmosphere tugged at them. It was a sobering reminder that if the airlock hadn't been decompressed, they'd have been shot out into space like a pair of cannon shells.

They gently eased themselves outside, and Ben Floyd finally knew what it felt like to fly in space. For an instant, he felt a giddy elation as he spun around and could see three hundred and sixty degrees in any axis. He had only been focusing on the technical aspects of extra vehicular activity, and had not stopped to think how wonderful it would feel to be out here, a part of space itself, at one with the stars.

'It's amazing,' he mumbled, and Luana smiled at his joy.

'It sure is.'

'I recognize these stars,' he said, pointing up. 'But… they're not twinkling.'

'They don't twinkle from inside the lifepod, either,' she pointed out.

'True, but out here it just seems more real. More immediate. The whole universe is just spread out in front of us.'

'You don't have to tell me,' she said, feeling the infectiousness of his words and becoming caught up in his enthusiasm. 'You wouldn't believe how many hours I've put in doing EVAs, just so I can experience this.'

Every few seconds, one of the nacelles would swoop past as they cartwheeled perpetually. Even this seemed to have a kind of beauty to it, an elegance that he was sure had long been lost on the ship's designers.

'I don't blame you. It feels like… I don't know, like the universe has texture now, whereas before it was a flat canvas.'

'Okay, time to get to work, Buzz.'

'Aldrin?'

'No, Lightyear.'

And that brought him back to reality. He spent a couple of seconds more to marvel at the galaxy, before concentrating on what he should be doing.

'I'm going to experiment with the manoeuvring jets,' he said. 'I'll try not to go shooting off into space, but be ready, just in case I overcook it.'

'Okay, off you go.'

The two of them hung there, a meter above the ship, thrown into shadow with each pass of the nacelles. Floyd very tentatively touched the control to propel him up and away from the airlock. It worked. Sort of. He was now moving away from the ship at around a meter every couple of minutes. He tried two more quick bursts, and that had more of an effect. He was now moving away at a much more respectable one meter every couple of seconds. A couple of bursts in the other direction, and his ascent slowed almost to nothing. He brought himself back down until he was back in front of Luana.

'So easy, a kid could do it,' he said.

'Yeah, because going up and down is all there is to it. Come on, Buzz, let's get this sheet unfurled.'

They got to work, unwrapping the flexi-steel like a picnic blanket and laying it over the huge hole in the top of the ship. It was safe to leave it there. The sheet was hardly likely to blow away in a breeze.

'We need to secure this thing,' Luana said.

'I know. I'm thinking the dorsal retro supports would be ideal.'

'That's what I was thinking. There are twenty-four bolts securing each one, and four mounting blocks on each side, which should give us—'

'A hundred and ninety-two bolts in all,' he interrupted, determined he wasn't about to be out-mathed. 'Hope you haven't got a hot date tonight, because this is going to take us a while.'

'Well, nothing I can't cancel,' she sighed, and the two of them settled down to attaching the first ninety-six bolts.

'What's he like?' Floyd asked after a couple of minutes of silence.

'Who, my hot date?'

'No, your buddy. Grant Paska.'

'Oh,' she said, suddenly deflating. 'I don't know, really. We've served on two full cruises together. Well, one and a half. There's something off about him.'

'Off?'

'Yeah, as in he's not quite there. Not that he's insane or anything like that, just distant. Aloof. I put a lot of that down to him being Martian. They can be a bit strange.'

'But you didn't like him.'

'Not really. I mean I never said anything. When you're an officer on a starliner, you try to make sure you can get on with anybody. Not him, though. He made me feel uncomfortable.'

'But I take it you never thought he would do something like sabotage the ship.'

'Oh no. Why would I? Why would someone do something like that? It's crazy.'

'It's mass murder, and he's clearly found a way to rationalize it. Somehow, killing four hundred people makes sense to him. It serves a purpose.'

'Maybe he was jealous of the wealthy passengers. Your guess is as good as mine,' she said, securing another bolt. 'He's a Martian, and you know how weird they can be. Or maybe it's his size. He's short, by anybody's standards, and particularly so for a Mars born.'

They were making good progress, and pretty soon, they had secured most of the bolts on one side of the ship, holding the flexi-steel sheet nice and tightly.

Luana took hold of the other side of the sheet and gave a quick burst from her jets, propelling her backwards.

'At this rate,' Floyd said, 'we should be done in the next half hour.'

'With luck, yeah. It's lucky—'

That was the moment disaster chose to strike.

It seemed to happen in slow motion. Luana had gone to give another short burst of her jets, but instead of being pushed backward, toward the starboard side of the ship, she went straight down into the jagged fissure in the

Eden's Gate

hull. The instant she made contact, she knew she was in trouble. Serious trouble.

Her backside – which Floyd had found so appealing when first seeing her in the cockpit – snagged on a sawtooth sliver of metal. It sliced through the organic polyamide like a scalpel, cutting a rough line four centimetres long.

'Floyd!' she cried as she realised what was happening.

Before the suit had time to react to the sudden pressure drop, air burst from the hole and she was catapulted from the ship, like an inflated balloon that has been released to fly around a room.

Floyd watched her go with horror, her body tumbling and rolling, her direction random. He fired his own jets. Not with gentle bursts this time, but with one long, concentrated thrust. He shot after her, executing a ninety-degree roll so he could see where she was.

He was way off, Luana shooting away in a thirty-degree different direction. He could see her attitude jets trying to get control, attempting to stabilize her rate of roll, reduce her momentum. But everything she tried just sent her off in a new direction, her body tumbling so fast that she could only see the universe as a blur.

'Luana, cut your thrusters!' he shouted.

'But I need to get control,' she shouted back. 'I can't—'

'Do it! Now!'

She did as she was told.

With her streaking away still, but in a roughly straight line, he accelerated after her.

'I'm fifty meters from you,' he said. 'Keep calm and hold steady.'

There was no response.

'Forty, thirty, twenty, ten.'

Floyd reached out to grab her, his hand touching her arm, fingers sliding along it. In an instant, he was past and moving away from her again.

'Damn it,' he cursed, and fired his reverse jets to try and make it back to her. He found that using the thrusters for lengthy, sustained bursts caused severe vibration, and it was difficult to even see Luana through blurred vision.

He eased off on the power again. Ahead, he could see Luana's figure flailing wildly as she tried to get a hand on the breach in her suit. At least she was still conscious, he thought. They were approaching one another at a frightening rate, their combined speed probably thirty meters per second. He hit his braking thrusters, feeling his eyeballs compressed into his skull. Blurred vision was almost impossible to deal with, but now he faced blacking out, his vision gone altogether.

Floyd's mind swirled as he tried to make impossible calculations. Luana was probably a hundred meters away at the point he was blinded. He estimated they had been closing at thirty meters per second. That meant they would hit each other in around three seconds. But his braking thrusters were decelerating him at an unknown rate, which would increase that time to maybe five or six seconds. How long had elapsed? Four or five seconds?

He cut power and flung out his arms and legs wildly. He was still effectively blind, only able to roughly make out light from dark and only caught sight of the figure at the last instant. There was no time to react, no time to move. He clenched his fist and through some miracle that he was never going to question, caught hold of something. It slipped through his fingers, sliding along until he touched a hand. Luana's hand.

They clung onto one another like a drowning man clings onto a piece of driftwood.

'Floyd?' Luana asked, sounding exhausted.

His vision was clearing, the spacesuited figure resolving into a recognizable shape. He dragged her to him and they embraced, clinging to one another like long-separated lovers.

'Yeah, let me… Let me try and get that leak.'

He felt around the back, down to wear he thought the tear was. It had opened up into a flap, frozen flesh protruding from the torn polyamide.

'How's your air?' he asked as he reached into his belt and retrieved a patch and spray adhesive.

'Bad. Down to under ten percent and dropping, but not too quickly.'

Her voice sounded edgy, like she was talking through clenched teeth. He sprayed all around the tear and slapped the patch over it. The adhesive would only stick to the organic polyamide of the suit, and not her exposed skin. The adhesive that came into contact with her flesh instantly became an anaesthetic, a liniment and moisturizer, all rolled into one.

'There,' he said, 'that should see you right until we get back to the ship.'

'You enjoyed slapping that patch on my ass way too much, Floyd,' she said, but still sounded tired and in some pain.

'What can I say? A man's gotta do what a man's gotta do.'

Floyd looked around them and finally caught sight of the lifepod, hanging in the sky above them. Or below. He really couldn't get his head around this arbitrary realm where up and down were merely a subjective point of view. The ship was three or four hundred meters away.

'Right, leave your thrusters alone for now, Luana. Hold onto me tightly. I'm going to fire my jets now.'

'Got it.'

He vectored the jet upwards and fired it.

Nothing happened.

He tried again, and again nothing.

'Er, I might have a problem here,' he said.

'What's your propellent tank reading,' she asked.

Floyd checked and sure enough, it was reading a big, fat zero.

'You're right. I'm empty. What've you got?'

Luana checked her own gauge. 'Not good. Propellent is down to under five percent. Not enough for a sustained burst.'

'But maybe enough to intercept the ship. The problem is, we're aiming at a moving target. Can you estimate a vector and burn duration that'll intersect with the ship?'

'I can try, but it'll be little more than guesswork.'

'Do it. I'll hang on to you, then.'

'Okay, here goes.'

Luana gave a brief burst from her thrusters and the pair of them began to drift ponderously toward a tiny point in space where she estimated the lifepod would be when they got there.

'That's all I want to use for now,' she said. 'Whatever's left we may be able to use for a course correction or deceleration.'

'Well, we'll find out in good time,' Floyd said. 'Well done. How's your air now?'

'About six percent. I'm not sure it'll be enough to get me back to the ship. You may need to operate my thrusters to get you home.' She said this in a matter-of-fact tone, unemotionally acknowledging that she could well be dead before they got to within range of the lifepod.

'Don't worry, I'll get us home. Tell me, did he strike you as the jealous type?'

'What?' she said. 'Who?'

'Paska. You said you thought he might be jealous of the wealthy passengers.'

'Oh, yeah. Seems a long time ago we were talking about that. There was something about him that just wasn't right. It wasn't anything he said, but you just got the feeling there was more going on with him than he let on. But I really had the impression he hated the super-rich, so it seemed a little odd that he would put himself in a position where he was in contact with them for so much of the time.'

As she spoke, Floyd kept a close eye on the lifepod and their speed and direction. Luana's "best guess" was astonishingly good, and from what he could see, there would only need to be a slight course correction.

'Odd, yes, but there probably is some logic to it somewhere,' he said. 'So, you're sure he did it? You're sure he was responsible for destroying the ship?'

'Yeah, he did it. I'm sure of it. He… Sorry, what was I saying?' She sounded more exhausted than ever.

'How's your air, Luana?' he asked, now seriously concerned.

'My what?'

'Your air, Luana. Check your gauge.'

She lifted her arm and held her wrist against the visor of her helmet. 'I can't see very well. I'm just going to…'

'Luana? Luana!' He shouted.

'I'm just gonna have a little sleep. Just for… just for a minute…'

'Luana, you need to stay awake.' Floyd shook her gently, and then again, more forcefully, but she had gone limp. Aside from a low groan, she said nothing else.

In another minute or two, she would be dead, so he had no choice but to act. The lifepod, he estimated, was up to five minutes distant. That delay had to be shortened. He took hold of Luana's arm and checked the readout on the screen. Air was, indeed, down to zero, and her thruster was at three percent. He made a slight change to the vector of the jet, and fired it.

He and Luana shot off in the direction of the ship, accelerating for five full seconds before the thruster spluttered to nothing. They were now flying toward the ship at a dizzying fifteen meters per second. Floyd would have just one chance to make this work. One chance to save them both. If he failed, they would go floating off into outer space forever.

Lifepod 11 loomed before them, its hull still displaying the scorch marks from when it had made its desperate escape from the Aurora. It grew larger in his visor with each passing second, until it filled his field of vision. The nacelles swooped around, and in his head, Floyd was sure he could hear them going whoosh-whoosh-whoosh as he approached.

Luana was a dead weight he clutched in one arm, leaving the other arm free to grab a hold of the ship. As long as they weren't smashed away by the nacelles, like a tennis player hitting a volley, they would hit the lifepod roughly amidships.

He braced himself, his body going tense and Luana feeling even more limp in his grasp. A nacelle swooped past, missing them by less than a meter. Floyd held his breath as it did, willing it to miss them. He had just a heartbeat left to act.

The two of them hit the ship right at the rotating mid-section, the cylinder turning slowly, but Floyd unable to grasp anything. Panicked, he scrabbled on the smooth metal, clutching for anything that would suffice as a handhold, but there was nothing.

They slid back, their own momentum dragging them toward the rear of the craft. In another couple of seconds they would have slipped off the stern and be flying off into space.

And then Floyd saw their salvation.

It shimmered before them, like a victory flag frozen in time. The sheet of flexi-steel hung in space, one side secured to the ship, the other pointing out into the heavens.

Floyd snatched it, feeling the material in his fingers, sliding. He clutched it with every fibre of strength he possessed, and it held firm.

For a second.

There was virtually no elasticity in the material, so as soon as the sheet had gone taut, Floyd and Luana were slammed against the side of the ship again. The impact jarred his whole body, his grip loosening for a moment.

With horror, Floyd felt the material sliding through his fingers again. He tightened his grip, and this time managed to hold on.

Gasping for breath and fighting the exhaustion that threatened to overcome him, Floyd dragged them both toward the airlock and punched the control that opened the outer hatch.

Eden's Gate

He had felt nothing from Luana for over two minutes, her body completely lifeless against his.

Floyd prayed she was still alive, that somehow there were a few molecules of air left to sustain her.

Manhandling the two of them into the airlock wasn't as easy as he would have liked. Luana's long legs, although an aesthetic attribute, seemed disinclined to go into the aperture without some coaxing. Finally, he had them both inside and punched the control to close the outer hatch.

'Computer, repressurize,' he ordered, but nothing happened.

Floyd cursed, remembering that he needed to key the mike first.

'Computer, repressurize!' he shouted again, and this time hearing the blissful sound of air hissing into the small cylinder that held them.

Floyd quickly detached first her helmet, and then his own. Luana's lips were blue, her eyelids half closed. He touched two fingers to her throat, but could find not even a hint of a pulse. Placing one hand behind her neck, he used the other to prize her mouth open. She offered no resistance, so he pushed his mouth against hers and exhaled deeply, pulled away to take another lungful of air, and repeated the action.

Still no response.

Propping her body against the cylindrical wall of the airlock, he began heart massage, pushing the palms of his hands firmly against her chest. Pump-pump-pump-pump-pump.

Nothing.

Pump-pump-pump-pump-pump.

Nothing.

Pump-pump-pump-pump-pump.

Two more breaths.

Pump-pump-pump-pump-pump.

A strangled gasp escaped her mouth and she coughed, spluttered, and breathed a long, deep, glorious breath.

Luana opened her eyes and saw Floyd staring back at her with a look of riotous joy on his face.

'Clurkit,' she croaked, swallowed, and tried again. 'You did it.' Her words were barely more than a whisper, but were the sweetest melody to Floyd's ears.

'Just about. How do you feel?'

'Okay. Better than being dead. A funny tingling in my butt cheek. I get the feeling it's going to hurt like hell when it thaw's out.'

'Yeah, it was exposed to open space for way longer than is healthy. But don't worry, I'm sure Tamara will have you fixed up in no time.'

Luana frowned and looked thoughtful.

'You know,' she said, 'do you think you could do it? I'd rather my ass wasn't the number one topic of conversation for the foreseeable future.'

Floyd felt himself blush. He actually blushed, and cursed himself silently for it. 'Okay, as long as you're sure.'

'I'm not asking you to bear my children or anything.'

He laughed, and almost made it sound genuine, and not the nervous laugh of a teenage boy about to see a girl naked for the first time.

This wasn't how Ben Floyd had seen this day panning out.

— Eleven —

Luana and Floyd floated with their backs to the aft storage area hatch, ensuring they weren't actually touching it. With the storage bay interior still annoyingly open to space, the hatch was frozen, ice covering the small window and spreading out like spiders' legs. Floyd made a mental note to put some insulation over it, before someone fell asleep and found themselves stuck to the hatch. If Luana's experience the previous day had been anything to go by, a frostbitten backside would be a painful episode.

The small observation windows in the cylinder didn't have this problem. They were designed to be exposed to space and were insulated accordingly.

Luana had emerged from their adventure reasonably well, with no long-lasting effects. An enzyme-based regenerative dressing covered the affected cheek, which would remain tender for a few days, but other than that and a few bruises, she was perfectly healthy.

Eden's Gate

Six pairs of expectant eyes stared back at them, their owners all hovering in the central cylinder. An inspection of the ship's supplies had uncovered clothing. It was just uniform pants and shirts, designed to adjust their size to individual requirements, but they served a function. All were a pale grey, but anything would have been an improvement over Max Landry's Hawaiian shirt.

'Here's the situation,' Luana began. 'We have plenty of fuel and oxygen. Water reclamation is near a hundred percent so that's not a problem either. However, our food reserves are critically low. Most of the food was lost in the collision, but the emergency ration packs will keep us alive. Celeste has calculated that the ration packs will last for forty days. Flight time to our destination is forty-two days, so I've decided that we will eat Dane to make up the shortfall.'

All eyes fell on the Jamaican, his dreadlocks flying like the tentacles of a sea anemone in the zero-gravity environment. 'Hey baby, fine by me. And I know just the place you can start.'

Luana's face screwed up as she tried to expunge that mental image from her overactive imagination. 'On second thoughts, it may be better to just go a little hungry.'

'Hey, this is good stuff. Guaranteed no indigestion.'
'Quiet, Dane.'
'You be wanting cream sauce with that?'
'Enough! Shut up and never say anything again. Ever.'

The Arcadia Series

She shook her head, as if trying to rid herself of a particularly annoying insect. 'Now, communications are still a problem. We're receiving background radio chatter from Earth, the Moon, Mars, Jupiter and numerous ships in between. Even the scientific research station on Triton, but no one is responding to our messages. We seem to be transmitting as far as I can tell, but we're just not getting any replies. Which means either no one is answering - unlikely - or there's a fault that I've been unable to detect. I'm not a comms expert, so is there anyone here with any relative experience?'

No one spoke for a few seconds, and just when she was about to move on, Dane put his hand up. Or rather, down. As he was floating upside down at the time, it would be a moot point as to which was accurate.

'I've done a little work on comms systems software before. I could take a look at it for you.'

'Okay, see what you can do with it.'

'That's as long as you haven't eaten my arms off by then.'

'We'll try to be selective and only eat the useless bits. Like your brain.'

'It's no trouble,' Dane continued, undaunted. 'You wouldn't believe the dexterity I have in my toes.'

'Shut up, Dane!' The words were harsh, but the tone anything but. She, like Floyd, recognized the importance of someone like Dane Jefferson to a small group adrift in the cosmos. They were all either going to love him, or he would be found dead somewhere in the next couple of days.

'Your customer service technique could use a little polishing, sweetheart,' he said, his bottom lip thrust out, but he gave her a wink.'

'Now,' she said in a tone that said all too clearly that it was time to move on. 'The computer has located a power source on a small asteroid known as 349 Dembowska. That's what we're heading for. We're hoping that this power source is a crewed mining operation. The lifepod is equipped with an extensive vid library, eBooks and interactive games. We're in pretty good shape, so everyone try to stay positive. Keep focused on that.'

Apart from Dane, no one else had uttered a word, but when there was a question, it came from the unlikeliest of sources.

'What do you think our chances are really?' Tamara Jax asked quietly. 'I mean, how likely is it we'll find a mining base on this asteroid? A mining base with people, not just robots.'

It was a fair question and needed to be addressed. She could give them any number of mollifying platitudes, but they deserved some honest answers. Luana glanced across at Floyd, who just shrugged. That was the most honest answer anyone could give to that question, but she knew that a simple shrug would not suffice.

'I wish I could tell you. I wish we had some way of finding out. An energy signature points to some kind of human presence, and the most likely source is a mining operation. I'm fairly convinced that's what it is. However, we have to be prepared for it being a remotely mined operation, consisting of just robots. It's a possibility we have to consider, but right now, it's our only alternative. At least until we get the radio working.

'But I can tell you that I for one have high hopes, and I'm pinning those hopes on finding what we need, getting home, and having some incredible stories to tell. One thing's for sure: we are all going to be celebrities for a while.'

Five of the group nodded with approval, seemingly appreciating Luana's honesty. Fortunately, everyone on board was of higher than average intelligence, and accepted without further question the difficulty of Luana's position. They realised that if they were all going to die on that lonely asteroid so far away, then no one would be blaming her.

Dane hung there upside down with a wistful expression on his face.

'I could be a hero,' he said. 'Babes love a hero.'

'Keep it real, Dane,' Floyd said. 'There's only so much flapdoodle people would believe.'

'Amen to that,' Luana agreed, making it clear the meeting was over and easing herself past the others as she went back to the cockpit.

'"Dane Jefferson: How I saved the Aurora survivors". Jeez, I'm gonna get me some honeys.'

'Well you got six weeks, buddy, to prepare for the monumental disappointment that's coming your way,' Floyd said as he passed.

'Yeah,' Dane said, still with that wistful look in his eye. 'Wait. What?'

— Twelve —

Life inside the small ship had quickly assumed a routine, and different people had taken on specific roles. It hadn't been planned that way; it was just the way things had worked out.

People had gravitated into small groups of likeminded or almost likeminded cliques. Floyd wasn't surprised. This situation was not like the days of the great liners on Earth. When the Titanic sank, survivors in lifeboats could expect to be rescued within hours. In space, the timeframe was likely to be weeks, and the human brain does not react well to long periods of incarceration.

There was plenty of library material on board, but even so, these people would need watching. It would be all too easy for these loose cliques to become rival gangs, and then they really would have a problem.

However, for the moment, things were going as well as they could expect. Landry and Celeste largely kept to themselves, as did Conor and Tamara. Suzy seemed to have gone quiet, but Dane more than made up for this with his boisterous humour.

Luana and Floyd spent much of their time in the cockpit, monitoring and repairing ship's systems and generally staving off boredom. The zero-gravity of the cockpit was also easier on Luana's sore backside. The enzyme dressings had now been removed, and she was well on the way to being one hundred percent fit again. The only reminder of the injury was soreness when she put weight on it, and a bruise the size of Floyd's fist that was now turning from purple to yellow and green. Yes, Luana was more than happy to spend most of her time hanging loosely a few centimetres above the pilot's seat.

This was where Conor found them on the tenth day of the journey.

'Knock, knock,' he said as he floated into the snug cockpit.

'Hey Conor,' Floyd said, turning to look at their visitor. 'What's up, buddy?'

'He's awake.'

Luana turned to look at Conor Jax, then shared a look with her first lieutenant.

Without a word, both pinged the latches on their harnesses and floated free.

Grant Paska squirmed, the motion strangely organic in the zero gravity. His hands were cuffed behind his back, as were his feet. He was short and stocky, with an expressively large, bushy beard and eyebrows to match that gave him a decidedly Neanderthal appearance.

Floyd had initially been surprised to find restraints on board the small ship, but the designers had foreseen the possibility that they may be necessary on a long and dangerous journey. Even with all the entertainments available, it was easy for psychoses to manifest themselves, which could easily escalate into violent conflicts. It had happened before in similar situations and would no doubt happen again, so preventative precautions were planned for well in advance.

Luana, as captain, would conduct the interrogation. Paska hung in the air just in front of the cockpit hatch, while the others – all of them, for no one was going to miss this – took whatever vantage point they could.

'Grant Paska,' she began, 'you abandoned your post on the bridge a short time before the Aurora was attacked. You claimed to be heading for the communications array, but the logs showed that the station hadn't been touched in two days.'

Paska looked dishevelled, his hair a spiky mess, the cut on his temple red and filled with dried blood.

'Luana,' he said, 'I know what you're getting at, and I can see how easy it would be to jump to that conclusion. But the simple truth is that I was heading for the array, but was stopped by a passenger requiring assistance.

Eden's Gate

Obviously, I needed to attend to that first. There was a problem with the drinks dispenser in her cabin.'

Luana continued, ignoring the explanation. 'Furthermore, your console on the bridge – the console that it just so happens scanned for long range contacts – had been locked down. Even the captain was unable to gain access.'

Paska shrugged. 'I can't explain that. Yes, I agree that there would have to be a saboteur on board, and the logical assumption is that he – or she – was responsible for locking down the console.'

'So,' she said, leaning forward, 'who do you believe the saboteur was?'

'I couldn't say for sure. The most reasonable subject would be one of the bridge crew on duty at the time. There were four people on the bridge when I left, including you.'

'He's guilty,' Max Landry suddenly butted in. 'You can see it written all over his face.'

'Quiet Max,' Floyd rebuked the Englishman.

'I'm not guilty,' Paska protested calmly. 'I've done nothing wrong.'

'If you're not guilty,' Landry persisted, 'then why are you the only one in here sweating?'

'So would you be if you were tied up and being accused of mass murder in this… this kangaroo court.' He was getting flustered, his agitation turning to bluster.

'Thank you, Mr. Landry,' Luana said, holding up a hand to discourage any further interruptions. 'Paska, before we escaped, I did have just enough time to download your personnel records. You were born on Mars, were you not?'

'Yes, but I don't see what that's got to do—'

'And at university became politically active?'

'It's not unusual for students to take an interest in politics. It's a tradition that goes back centuries.'

'Specifically, in the Martian Independence Movement.'

There was a stifled gasp from one of the observers.

'I ended that association a long time ago. The records show that,' Paska said, trying to wipe some of the sweat from his forehead, but with his hands bound behind his back, failing.

'You were also under surveillance by Martian security because of your association with a man named Luther Kane Lynch. Does that name mean anything to you?'

'Not a thing, but I think you're trying to fit me up.'

'Luther Kane Lynch is well known to the security services on Mars and Earth for being active in a number of MIM terrorist atrocities, including the bombing of the Lunar Transit Station, which killed over two hundred innocent people.'

'He is lying,' Landry interrupted again. 'I've seen it enough times before, and I can tell when someone's trying to deceive me.'

'This is a fix!' Paska cried, fidgeting in the air, twisting and contorting, trying to break loose from his restraints. 'I've never had anything to do with anyone like that. And I'm not lying. I'm not guilty.'

'You are lying,' Luana said coldly.

'I'm not! For God's sake, I wasn't the only one on that bridge. You were there as well. So was the captain and so were two others. How do any of us know it wasn't one of you?'

'Trying to shift blame is the oldest trick in the book,' Landry said. 'I say we toss him out the airlock.'

'This is crazy. Where's your proof? All I can see is flimsy circumstantial evidence.'

Luana raised a hand to silence him. 'How did you disable the defence systems on the Aurora?'

'I didn't!'

'Max is right; he is lying,' Celeste said. 'I've seen plenty of his type in court. Guilty as they come.'

'He's a goddamn terrorist?' Dane said, seeming to wake up and come into the conversation late.

'I'm not a terrorist.'

'You are,' Luana pressed.

'You've got nothing,' Paska hissed through clenched teeth, tugging at his restraints.

Luana stared at him coldly for several seconds as she considered her next move. She knew he was guilty. She was sure of it. Circumstantial evidence be damned. He was a mass murderer.

'Get him in the airlock,' she said without a hint of emotion.

'Wait Luana,' Floyd said, suddenly feeling uneasy. 'Are you sure—'

'Do it.'

Floyd wasn't happy about this, and from the disquieted looks on several faces, he wasn't the only one. But, despite his misgivings, Luana was the captain and he couldn't be seen to contradict her. He clicked his fingers at Dane and the two of them moved to take the struggling form of Grant Paska. Floyd tapped the keypad next to the airlock in the floor and the hatch slid open.

'She's the terrorist!' Paska shouted, twisting his body this way and that as he tried to keep from being pushed into the airlock. 'It's her, I tell you!'

His struggles were to no avail, and once his feet had been manhandled into the airlock, the rest of him followed easily. Floyd looked at Dane, who seemed ready to throw up as all manner of emotions churned around in his head. Floyd himself tried to stay stoic, but he could certainly empathize.

Paska was a coldblooded killer; of that he was sure. And as such, he deserved to die. But not like this. Not at the hands of a self-appointed lynch mob.

'Wait, this is crazy,' Paska screamed as he twisted and writhed.

Floyd tapped the keypad again and the inner hatch slid shut. Both the inner and outer hatches had small observation windows set in them. He saw the frantically squirming figure mouthing something but he could not tell what. He switched on the intercom.

Eden's Gate

'Let me out! I'm innocent, don't you see?'

'Prepare to open the outer hatch,' Luana ordered.

'Oh Jesus, please, I didn't do anything!'

'You sure you want to do this?' Floyd said to her.

'He's right,' Dane added. 'Hell of a thing to murder someone in cold blood.'

'Then I'll open the door myself,' she said, and glided over to the airlock, pushing the other two out of the way. Her hand rested on the keypad, ready to open the outer hatch. 'Paska, did you disable the defence array on the Aurora?'

'What? No. I'm innocent!'

'Did you disable the Aurora's manoeuvring capability?'

'This is so unfair,' Paska snivelled. The man sounded wretched.

'I'll give you a count of five. Five…'

'Luana,' Floyd said quietly. 'He's not worth throwing your life away for.'

'…four, three…'

'Yes, yes, I did it,' Paska screamed through desperate tears. 'I'm sorry. I did it. I did it. I disabled the manoeuvring thrusters. And the defence array. And the other lifepods. Yes, I'm guilty but please, please don't kill me. I'm begging you! Begging you!'

'What?' Luana said. 'The lifepods?'

'I guess that'd explain why ours was the only ship to get away,' Floyd said.

Luana paused for a moment as she considered this. She imagined what it must have been like for those poor people. Some of the lifepods must have been full and ready to launch. She imagined what it must have felt like to hit the button to release the docking clamps, and for nothing to happen. Or maybe Paska had found a way to disable the engines. Either way, it was a horrible, cruel way to die. They had survived the crumbling ruins of the Aurora and made it to safety. Then they were just trapped there, unable to free themselves as the ship was destroyed around them.

And if this went to court, a good lawyer could well get him off. Even life imprisonment would still be life, which was more than his victims had been permitted.

No, there was only one way to be sure.

'…two, one.'

Luana lifted the safety cover and touched the button that would release the hatch. The button was cool, and wobbled very slightly when she put a tiny bit of pressure on it. She closed her eyes and—

'Wait!'

This was a different voice. An unexpected voice. Celeste Karlin floated over to Luana and put a hand on her shoulder, turning her just enough for them to face one another.

'A confession obtained under duress would be dismissed by any court in the Solar System. Let him stand trial on Mars or Ganymede. They still have the death penalty, and you won't be tried for murder yourself. If you do this, you will be. I guarantee it.'

'Please,' whimpered Paska.

Luana thought about the other woman's words. They all made sense. There was an inescapable logic to everything she had said. It was just that it was not what Luana wanted to hear. She wanted that man dead. She wanted him to pay. Yes, he would pay, and in the interim he would be made to suffer as he languished in a Martian penal facility.

She eased the pressure on the button and removed her finger from it completely, gently closing the safety cover. 'Keep him in the airlock. I don't want that piece of filth having any luxuries.'

'Oh, don't worry,' Floyd said, feeling like he was deflating as the stress ebbed from his body. 'By the time we reach 349 Dembowska he'll wish you *had* pressed that button.'

'Amen to that, bro,' Dane said. 'Now can I have that change of underwear?'

Luana unzipped her tunic and tossed it aside as she took her position in the cockpit, sinking into the pilots' seat. She didn't bother with the harness. Right now, she needed to feel comfortable, and that was going to be much easier in just her vest and no restraining straps.

Without a word, Floyd floated in and eased into the co-pilots' seat.

'I just nearly killed a man,' she said flatly.

'Yep. In fact, you nearly didn't need to. I think he was about to soil himself to death. Literally poop himself inside out.'

She chuckled lightly at that mental image, and a little of the tension ebbed from her body.'

Floyd reached inside his tunic and retrieved a small, flat, silver flask. 'Special occasion,' he said. 'The finest Kentucky Bourbon you'll find in ten million klicks.'

He took a sniff at the top of the flask and nearly fainted from the heavenly smell. He took a small swig, before passing the flask to Luana.

'Here. I don't care what they say, alcohol *is* the answer.'

She took three healthy gulps and left the flask hanging in the air in front of them. Floyd was right. It tasted good. Really good, and reminded her of the baijiu her uncle used to give her as a girl in Wenzhou.

They didn't say any more. They didn't need to. They just sat there, savouring the taste, savouring the moment.

Luana wondered what Malachy would have done in the same situation. She knew that he had been shipwrecked once before, and spent several days floating in space awaiting rescue. But she doubted he had ever been in a position where he could decide whether or not to end a man's life.

What would he have done? He certainly would not have contemplated murder. Malachy was better than that. He was better than her, and he had taught her better than that.

"There is good in all situations, Luana," Malachy had once told her. "You just have to know where to look for it. Trust me, lass, it'll be there, a twinkling light of good in all the darkness." And he was right. It was always there. No matter how hidden, it was always there.

Luana put thoughts of murder out of her head. It *was* murder; there was no getting away from that. She could dress it up in more genteel language like 'prosecution', 'elimination' or 'justice', but she was in no doubt: it *was* murder, and she could not allow herself to think that way. Celeste was right, of course. True justice would be served on Mars or Ganymede, and Luana would then have the satisfaction that Paska had been put to death, and justice would have been served.

This would be the right thing to do. It was what Malachy would have done. Although she could never envisage Malachi taking any satisfaction from the death of another, even under these extreme circumstances.

She looked across at Floyd and gave him a small smile. They had only known each other ten days, but from the instant they met, he had risked his life to save hers. And he kept on doing it. It was no small thing to have someone with her upon whom she could rely.

Floyd reached out and took Luana's hand in his, holding it gently, his thumb languidly moving back and forth, feeling the contours of the back of her hand.

She leaned in closer, her face close enough for him to feel her breath on his top lip. A little closer still, and her lips parted.

'Are you sure this is a good idea?' he asked softly.

'Probably not,' she replied, and pressed her lips against his.

The kiss was gentle to start with, just a caress as his arms snaked around her waist. They kissed like that forever and for an instant, lips pressed together, parting and pressure increasing. Hands wandered, exploring this new territory, this new forbidden land.

He reached under the vest, feeling her impossibly smooth skin, before pulling his mouth away from hers and lifting the garment over her head. With this barrier cast aside, their tender caresses turned into passionate desperation.

She fumbled with his tunic, his pants. They drifted in the air in a dizzying wave of yearning, kissing, fumbling, stroking, pleasuring…

Dane stayed at the airlock entrance, just watching the man below as he stared back up at him. Was he really the murderer of over four hundred people? If so, and it seemed highly likely that it was, then did he feel no remorse for this? Why did he do it?

Dane Jefferson had a very pragmatic view on life. He enjoyed mysteries, but loathed chaos. He just could not fathom Paska's motivations, or how the deliberate destruction of the Aurora could benefit the people of Mars.

He eventually turned away and made for the cockpit to see if Floyd needed any help with Luana. It was a small miracle that he stopped, finger poised over the hatch release. The window into the cockpit may have been small, but was plenty big enough for Dane to see what was transpiring.

'Damn,' he whispered to himself with a grin. 'Atta boy Floydy.'

He turned away, shaking his head, the mischievous grin plastered over his face not showing any sign of evaporating. He decided that, being the honourable gentleman that he was, he would stand guard and let them have their fun in peace.

— Thirteen —

Night is a subjective concept in space. When the stars can be seen at any time, an artificial system of timekeeping must be adopted. On board the lonely little lifepod 11, they had nominally kept to Aurora's shipboard time, which in turn had kept to Greenwich Mean Time. The monotonous tedium of life on board was surprisingly tiring, and keeping to a regimented schedule was challenging.

But, generally speaking, most of the passengers and crew – plus one suspected mass murderer – tended to turn in around midnight. One or two would privately listen to music and be sung to sleep, but it was rare, as they entered their third week, for people to be awake past one in the morning.

Tonight, though, someone did stir.

Luana sat it the pilot's seat, thinking, brooding, pondering, questioning. She had not spoken to Paska since the night of the interrogation, as it had rather ostentatiously been coined. However, the fact that she hadn't spoken to him did not mean that she did not still have questions.

Perhaps she *should* speak to him. Perhaps he would be more willing to comply after two weeks of misery since he had awakened.

Floyd snoozed next to her. They had made love several times since that first wild and desperate coupling. Subsequent encounters had not been quite as urgent, but were no less enjoyable as a result. She was clearly nowhere near being his first. She had a feeling (although it was not something that she had questioned him on – yet) that he had had a long stream of lovers over the years. But his experience did not make him arrogant, rather he was attentive, and she had not as yet come away feeling disappointed or used as she had done in the past.

She was not exactly a timid virgin herself, she had to admit, and had indulged herself whenever she had felt the need and desire. Being an officer on a starliner was not a career that lent itself toward stable relationships, so most of her sexual escapades had been fleeting, passionate affairs. The company did not prohibit such affairs, but encouraged discretion, which she was happy to abide by. Her academy days were another matter, but everyone experimented at the dawn of adulthood.

The academy was a long way away now, and those days long since passed, but she was enjoying her time with Ben Floyd, even if the circumstances were less than ideal. He had become her rock, and had proven his devotion to her since long before their sexual attachment. If he was willing to risk his life to save hers for no other reason than to just do it without expectation of reward, then that was more than fine with her.

But tonight, this was something she needed to do alone, without him being there as her conscience and voice of reason. He was annoyingly adept at guiding her away from potentially self-inflicted harm.

Luana quietly unbuckled her harness, which had been loosely attached around her waist, eased herself from the seat and glided out to the airlock.

There must have been some ambient lighting coming from the central cylinder, because, as soon as her head appeared at the small window in the airlock hatch, Paska looked up at her.

They stayed staring at one another for over a minute, saying nothing, just contemplating each other. Both questioned the other's motives, feelings, intentions, but neither would reveal any of those things. At least not yet. Luana was the first to break the spell, activating the communicator.

'Why did you do it, Paska?'

'You know why.'

'Explain it to me.'

'What's the point? You just want me dead.'

'You're right. I do. But for now, I just want to know why you did it, and how you can murder four-hundred and forty-one people without a second thought. Without a hint of remorse.'

Eden's Gate

He laughed, but it was not a laugh of humour. It was a mirthless, ironic kind of laugh, and a little unsettling to her.

'I used to watch you Luana, you know that? You remember all those hours we spent on the bridge of the Aurora? I would watch you and wonder what it would be like. With you. You never seemed to realise it. You never seemed to realise what an enchanting figure you presented when you were at your console. Never seemed to realise the effect you had on men. I could stare at you for hours, just wondering how you would feel, how you would taste. I wanted you. Wanted you so badly, but knew I could never have you. You were too aloof. Too unattainable. Others called you a stuck-up bitch, too frigid and too in love with yourself to notice those around you, but not me. I appreciated you, with all your feminine charms.'

'What drove you to do it?' she asked, trying to ignore the lascivious words, trying to suppress the bile that rose in her throat. 'What drove you to destroy the Aurora?'

'I used to spend hours, just wondering what passions simmered beneath the surface. For those few who did catch your eye, I wondered how wild would you get? I still wonder. I still think about you that way. All the time.'

His gaze was disconcerting, as if he were peering into her soul and unveiling her darkest fears, stripping her layer by layer until she stood naked before him.

'Do you seriously think you can change anything through acts of extreme violence?' she asked, ignoring the invasion. 'Or do you just get off on having the power? Is that it, Grant? Is it the power that you get off on?'

'Even in that instant, when you were poised and ready to kill me, I wondered what it would be like with you. To feel your skin against mine, to smell your perfume, to taste you, to lick you from your ears to the tips of your toes.'

She didn't respond. She wanted to, oh, she wanted to. She wanted to tell him what a vile piece of filth he was. She wanted to tell him that she wouldn't let him touch her if he was the last man alive in the universe. She wanted to tell him that she would rather kill herself than let him lay a finger on her. She said none of these things. But she would not be cowed, or humiliated by this creature.

'You are beyond redemption, Paska. You are utterly evil. It would be so easy…'

Her delicate hand strayed to the small control panel, an index finger dancing over the safety cover, gently lifting it and slipping it back in place, over and over again. His eyes flicked in the direction of that hand, just for an instant, but it was enough to satisfy her. He was still afraid. Still feared the death that awaited him on the other side of the outer hatch. And he knew that she still had the power to make it happen.

'I could just flush your worthless body into space, and watch you die.'

'Then why don't you do it?'

He was not on the verge of hysterics this time. His fear was well contained, but she could tell it was still there. He had had time to come to terms with his death. Perhaps he even welcomed it. But she couldn't give him an answer. She wanted to kill him, but Dane had been right: it was a hell of a thing to take another human life. Even a life as abominable as this one.

'I thought so,' Paska said with a smile. 'I'll make a deal with you: you give me what I want, and I'll tell you what you want to know. You show me that fine body of yours, and I'll explain why I destroyed the Aurora.'

That was all. That was all he wanted. It was such a trivial, inanely simple request. It wasn't as if she had ever been shy about exposing her body in the past. But this was different. He was asking her to relinquish her pride and self-respect. How badly did she want to learn his motives? How far would she allow herself to be led?

Not far enough.

Luana stopped toying with the airlock control and turned to head back to the cockpit.

'I don't do deals with terrorists.'

She disappeared, and a moment later, the hatch to the cockpit hissed shut.

In the darkness, with only the stars as his witness, Grant Paska smiled. 'You will.'

— Fourteen —

Floyd took this opportunity to just hang out (or rather, float) and watch the stars roll by. This was rapidly becoming his favourite spot on the ship. Not that there were too many areas to choose from.

Just in front of the storage hold, which had now been covered with several layers of sacking to keep the cold at bay, was one of the few places one could just sit and contemplate the universe. Admittedly, he could have had a more unobstructed view from the cockpit, but, and he knew it was just his own subconscious teasing him, in the cockpit he felt obliged to monitor ship's systems, make minor course corrections, initiate minor repairs etc. In other words, the cockpit represented work. Here, he could relax.

After their previous adventure outside the ship, Floyd and Luana had decided that the storage hatch would be adequate protection on its own and no further attempt would be made to cover the gash in the hull. Beneath the insulating sacking they had attached three layers of flexi-steel, so if the hatch were to fail, there would at least be some protection. As far as he was concerned, they had teased the great space gods enough, and he was in no hurry to incur more of their wrath.

There was a small window on either side from which he could not only watch the stars, but also watch the nacelles as they rotated ceaselessly. He had a palm sized comm-pad with him, just in case the urge to read or watch a vid took him.

'Hey buddy.' It was Dane's voice, the wild haired Jamaican emerging from one of the nacelles. 'Mind if I join you?'

'No, pull up a chaise longue and make yourself comfortable.' For once, he really didn't mind being disturbed. He could always make time for Dane.

'You really taking Max in when we get to Jupiter? Or Earth. Or wherever it is we end up?'

'Damn straight. First chance I get. I'd have him clapped in irons right now if I could, but we're running out of airlocks to keep the criminals.'

'Guy must have really pissed you off,' Dane said, hitching up his sleeve to wipe away a mark on the window. Jupiter was in view at the moment, shining brighter than any of the stars in their sky. They could even make out the four Galilean moons, gleaming in the darkness.

'Yeah, sending his goon squad after me had that effect,' Floyd replied, twirling the comm-pad between his fingertips and letting go, watching it continue its elegant pirouette. There was something supremely, yet disproportionately satisfying about performing such a mundane trick in zero-gravity. 'Dane, you're closer to everyone than Luana or me. How're they coping?'

'Okay, I guess. Max is fine, taking it in his stride. I get the feeling he's been in tight spots before. I'd love to know some of the things he's gotten up to. Seems to have had a pretty colourful career.'

'You can say that again. Likes to think of himself as a cockney Al Capone, but don't let any of his patter fool you.' Floyd made air quotes with his fingers. '"But I'm a legitimate businessman, guv". He's a crook, through and through. Sure, he does have *bona fide* legitimate businesses, but that's just a cover. Prostitution, racketeering, illegal arms trading; there's not a lot that Max Landry won't deal in, if there's a profit to be made.'

'And he didn't take kindly to you approaching him on the Aurora. Not exactly your smartest move there, man.'

Floyd laughed with an accompanying shake of the head. 'Yeah, you're probably right. But I was set up. You know me and Celeste had a thing going back in San Diego?'

'Shut the front door!'

'Yep, I didn't realise it at the time, but she was working for Landry. Still, you live and learn. How's she doing anyway?'

'Celeste is fine as long as she's got Max with her. They make an odd pair but it seems to work between them. I'm guessing she'll go her own way when we get back to civilization.'

Floyd hadn't really considered her in the equation. If they managed to get back to Earth, then she might have to face some charges as well. Although he was fairly sure that she could find a hundred and one legal arguments to get herself off.

'Suzy is a little fragile,' Dane continued. 'She's quite withdrawn now. I think she had a lot of friends on the Aurora. I'd say keep an eye on her. Out of everyone she's the most likely to lose it, which would be a shame as she's a nice lady.'

'Uh-huh. And Conor and Tamara?'

Dane let out an unexpected chuckle, which earned him a pair of raised eyebrows from Floyd.

'They have a much more specific problem. I was talking to Conor. It seems their relationship is… How can I put it? Quite physical. In fact, I'd say it's almost exclusively physical. They haven't had it in three weeks now, and I get the feeling they've never gone three days before. Seriously, I'd bet they'd put a few rabbits to shame. So they're frustrated, to say the least. Very frustrated, if you know what I mean.'

'Yeah, I think I just about managed to crack that code. That's not the kind of problem I considered when we left the Aurora, but I'll see what I can do.'

'I think they'd appreciate it, bud. They're a good couple, just a little… privileged. You know what I mean? I don't think they're used to roughing it. Always had money, rich parents, always done what they want, when they want. Not really my sort of people, but hey, I can get on with anybody if I have to.'

'You're a real hero Dane.'

'Thanks. I try.'

They both had a chuckle. It was a little forced, but there's nothing better than laughter to ease the tension.

'What are you doing out here, Dane?' Floyd asked, the question suddenly popping into his head. He knew the reason for everyone else's presence on board the Aurora. Landry and Celeste were on their way to oversee some nefarious project on Ganymede. Conor and Tamara were on a honeymoon cruise. Suzy was a singer and dancer. But Dane Jefferson remained a mystery.

'You mean what was I doing on the Aurora? I'm on my way to Europa. The company needed an engineering software technician for their mining operation. I was their guy. I guess I'm gonna be a little late for work.'

'Yeah, I'll write you a sicknote. And what about you? Are you doing okay, Dane?'

'Me? Oh, I'm cool. Just counting the days, bro, till I get back to Earth or to Europa. Either would do me right now. Not working out too badly for you though, eh?'

Floyd frowned. 'What do you mean?'

'Hey, don't get me wrong, Luana's a babe. You're lucky I didn't get a chance to turn on the old Jefferson charm first. She wouldn't have stood a chance. So, I'll try not to get too jealous, bud,' he said with a wink.

Floyd suddenly felt very self-conscious. 'You... you know about that?'

'You should try closing the cockpit window when you do the wild thing, bro. But don't worry, I didn't tell anyone else.'

'You've been watching us?'

'Hey, it's not like I was there with opera glasses and a bag of popcorn. Though I am wondering how Luana got that bruise on her butt.'

Floyd decided he'd suffered enough humiliation for one day and caught the tablet, popping it into his pocket. 'I er... I think I'll get to work on Conor and Tamara's little problem.'

Floyd glided into the cockpit. Luana was out of her seat and had a panel off the wall as she continued to work on the recalcitrant communications system.

She glanced up from her work just long enough to give him the briefest of smiles. 'Anything from our friend in airlock two?'

Floyd closed the hatch behind him. 'Not so much as a whisper. It seems the only person he'll speak to is you.'

'Ooh, lucky me. I'll try again when the thought of speaking to him doesn't make me feel physically sick.'

She sighed, frowning at the bank of green lights. If only she could find something in there that wasn't working. She was sure that the communications problem was something so tiny, so insignificant, yet so completely immobilizing. Luana shook her head, knowing that if she didn't take a break, she would end up smashing a wrench into the damned system.

She proffered two packets. 'Brown protein goo or yellow protein goo?'

'Hmm, decisions, decisions. Surprise me.'

He got to sample the delights of yellow protein goo. It could have been banana pudding. It could have been chicken biryani. The flavours seemed to just coalesce into one unidentifiable gloopy sameness after a while.

'Still no luck with the comms?' he asked as he slurped some goo.

She sighed a deep, long sigh. 'No. Diagnostics check out. Visual analysis checks out. Transmitter dish checks out. Dane has run a complete debugging routine and can't find anything wrong with the system either. It's driving me crazy.'

'Oh, I thought that was me doing that.'

She raised an eyebrow at him as she 'enjoyed' some delicious brown slop. 'You're not *that* good,' she said, turning back to the console and running yet more diagnostics.

'On a related subject, Dane just informed me of an impending situation.'

'Hmm?' she said distractedly as she slid an optical circuit board from its cradle.

'Yeah. None of the passengers have had any privacy in the past three weeks, and some people are getting a little frustrated, if you know what I mean,' he said, realising that he was borrowing Dane's phrase.

'Frustrated about what?' she murmured, running a sensor over each of the optical connection points.

It was clear that he didn't have one hundred percent of her attention.

'Conor and Tamara need to bump uglies.'

Luana jumped as if someone had just stuck a two-hundred-volt cable down her pants. Her diagnostic tool went careering into the circuit board and instantly, a dozen green lights suddenly turned red. And to complete the scene, an alarm began to sound in the cockpit. She quickly reset circuit breakers and mercifully, the alarm ceased and the lights returned to green. 'Oh. Rumpy-pumpy?'

'I figured we might be able to rig up a cot in the forward cargo hold,' he said, trying so hard not to laugh. 'If we say it's for the use of everyone and they take it in turns to spend a night in there, it won't sound quite so much like a playboys' passion wagon.'

The forward hold was located just behind the cockpit door, directly above Paska's airlock. As time went by, the stores within were gradually being depleted, so it wouldn't be a huge job to redistribute what was left around the rest of the ship.

'It's a good idea,' Luana conceded. 'Can you organize that?'

'Sure. I just wanted to run it past you first.'

She abandoned the comms panel for a moment to lean across and kiss him. 'Thanks. I'm really glad I've got you here, Floyd.'

'Wouldn't miss it. Three weeks down; three weeks to go.'

— Fifteen —

At a little after one in the morning, Luana slipped from her seat and glided free. She was ready. She was ready to do this. Grant Paska demanded something from her and she was ready to address his demand. It really wasn't that much to relinquish, a little self-respect and dignity, when the reward would be the answers she so desperately sought.

She hovered in the doorway for a few seconds. A few seconds grew to a few minutes, and a few minutes became a quarter of an hour.

It had to be done now. If she put it off any longer, she wouldn't be able to do it at all.

Luana floated forward, clicked the cockpit door closed and took her place over the inner hatch of airlock two. Her head created a shadow that blocked a tiny, but noticeable amount of light. It was enough to garner Paska's attention. He looked up and, seeing who it was, smiled.

'I knew you'd come eventually. Are you ready to give me what I want?'

Luana ignored the question for now. She knew that if she genuinely wanted those answers, she would have to acquiesce to his demands. But she wasn't about to make it easy for him.

'How did you disable so many systems on board the Aurora? Did you have help?'

'First of all, give me what I desire. I don't ask for much. After all, a condemned man has few pleasures. Permit me this one, sweet lady.'

She loathed the vile man. Truly loathed him. And never more than at this moment. However, she would do this. He would own the image of her in his mind, but it was necessary.

Luana reached down and felt the waistband of her pants and ran a thumb around it until she came to the clasp. She did not take her eyes off Paska as she did this. She wanted him to feel her hate. She wanted him to know just how much loathing she felt for him.

Slowly, she unclasped the buckle and slipped the pants down to her thighs. She still wore her vest, and had no plans to remove that, and all that covered her backside was a small pair of white panties. She had worn less while sunbathing on the beach, she told herself. The panties were no less substantial than the bikini bottoms Celeste had been wearing when she first arrived on the ship. But, Luana thought, she was not on the beach to perform for a repellent mass-murdering letch.

Eden's Gate

She eased her body forward until the panties were visible through the small hatch window.

Through the intercom, Paska groaned with approval as he stared up at pure white fabric framed by smooth, pink flesh.

Luana slowly rolled over so that he could have a view of her behind.

What he got to see was two words scrawled onto the fabric: "KISS MY ASS".

Paska let out a whoop and started to laugh heartily. ' Oh, I always liked you, Luana.'

With that over with, she eased her pants back up over her buttocks and fastened them. As is so often the way with these things, the anticipation was far worse than the ordeal itself. It was over now. It hadn't been quite as bad as she had feared, but she would give him no more.

Paska continued to chuckle for over a minute, which seemed to be a little over the top to her, and she wondered if the confinement, and the constant threat of a hideous death, were affecting his sanity. And then she considered that he had just murdered over four hundred people, so his sanity was somewhat in question anyway.

'You wanted to know how I disabled the Aurora's systems?' he said, once he had calmed down sufficiently. 'I had full access to the ship's sensor systems, so the long-range sensors were easy enough to disable. Johannsen was an old fool, and never guarded his security clearances as he should. Locking down the workstations was equally simple. I also placed electromagnetic disruptors at strategic points around the ship to compromise the defence systems. EMDs also worked to fry the launch systems on the lifepods. Except this one, of course. I needed this one intact and functioning.'

'And it was simple bad luck that you fell and were knocked out?' she asked.

'Precisely. I was just at the top of the shaft when the Korolev hit. You have my clumsiness to thank for your being alive. You think me a monster, Luana? An abomination? But as a resident of Earth you have no idea how it feels to have your destiny controlled by an occupying force. That's how it feels to us Martians, you do realise that? We want to govern our own affairs. Does that sound so unreasonable?'

That simple statement confirmed what she had surmised. Grant Paska was nothing more than a crackpot revolutionary. She actually had no issue with Mars achieving independence, but there were diplomatic ways and means.

'You flatter yourself, Paska. You're not a monster or an abomination. You are just a sad little man with sad little dreams. You are a pathetic wretch who is hopeless with women and has to resort to bribery to see one in her underwear. You claim to have political ideals, yet you use the base tactics of a terrorist. You think murdering innocent people will help you achieve your goals? You're nothing but a sad little man trying to act important. A sad, lamentably pathetic little creature that no one could ever love.'

'Perhaps I am, sweet lady, perhaps I am. It's a means to an end. When Mars is free, we can once again become human.'

'But how will this atrocity achieve that? It makes no sense. None at all. Earth won't suddenly give up Mars just because a few snivelling malcontents run around killing people. That has never worked and it never will.'

'There is more at stake here than a few hundred or a few thousand lives. There is a grand design to all this. It will work. There was a reason it happened; a reason it happened just here, in this specific point in space. Luana, there is a greater plan at work here than you can possibly realise or appreciate.'

She leant in closer to the window, her breath fogging the glass for an instant. 'What is it? What is this grand plan?'

He smiled and stretched out with hands clasped behind his head. 'For the answer to that, my dear, you will have to return tomorrow, and give me a little more of what I desire.'

Luana sighed. She really thought she was getting close to an answer, but now she just had more questions. What was this bigger plan? And why had the destruction of the Aurora happened precisely where it did?

'You're so full of it, Paska,' she said, reaching for the button to cut off the intercom.

'Undoubtedly. But if you want the answer to all this, return tomorrow night. I'll be wanting to see a little more of the treasures you have been concealing.'

Grant Paska was more relaxed than he had been since… Well, he couldn't remember the last time he had felt this relaxed. Certainly not since before the Aurora had set sail over ten weeks earlier.

He now had the lovely Luana right where he wanted her. She was a feisty one all right. Oh yes, but that just made the process that much more enticing. What should he get her to show him next? He was thinking it was about time he got to see her breasts in all their voluptuous, feminine glory.

Sadly, the game had to come to an end soon. There were now just two short weeks until they arrived at the asteroid 349 Dembowska.

He had not shifted from his position since she had gone, taking that blissful piece of human contact with her. Day after artificial day he had waited, waited for her to return as he knew she would eventually. That was her fundamental flaw: her curiosity. She just could not help herself.

A shadow fell on him, just as it had when she had visited him an hour or more ago. But this time, it did not remain just a shadow. A flashlight replaced it, a powerful beam that caused him to squint and hold a hand up to his face.

'Who is that?' he asked, unaware whether the intercom was in operation or not.

The light did not move, but kept him locked in its stark beam.

'I demand to know who you are,' he ordered, but there was a hesitancy to his voice.

The flashlight was extinguished, and through vision spotted by after images, he began to make out a face.

'Oh, it's you,' he said in a relieved tone. 'What do you want?'

The figure said nothing, merely stared at him.

'Well, whatever it is, I have nothing to say to you.'

Paska turned away and looked off to one side, ignoring the figure. He wasn't about to be intimidated. He had slain hundreds. He was a legend. At least, he would be when the Solar System learned what he had done. On Mars, they would sing songs in his honour, would chant his name as the great liberator. Through blood and terror, he had shown them the way, and now the path was clear. Nothing could stem the tide of revolution, nothing could hold the Martian people in shackles.

Despite himself, he looked back at the small window above him. The figure was still there, saying nothing, doing nothing. It just stared impassively, as if waiting for him to do something. He decided to play the same game, believing he knew what it was trying to do. It wanted him uneasy, it wanted him scared. But he had faced death. He had been responsible for many, many deaths. He would not allow anyone to intimidate him again. All his life he had felt a small, insignificant man. For many years, he had hidden behind an over the top, bushy beard that he thought made him look stronger, more masculine. But it did neither, merely accentuating his inadequacies.

Paska stared back at the window, his face impassive, but mind churning.

So that was how they stayed, two people, both captives of the other's gaze, both contemplating the other.

The figure moved. It was just a tiny, innocuous action. In another situation, it would be disregarded as irrelevant. But not now.

'No!' he bellowed, the sound barely audible from inside the cabin.

Paska watched as the hand moved inexorably toward the control panel.

'No! No! No!'

He couldn't see it, but he knew what was happening. He thrust his body up until his terrified face was pressed against the glass. He had been prepared for death, had almost expected it. But he had unfinished business now. She was going to show him everything, was about to indulge his fantasies. He was going to make it happen. He was going to own her. He couldn't die now.

'You can't do this!'

The fingers clasped the control panel as the eyes followed the pathetic soul beyond the glass. He was screaming. Spit and bile were smeared over the plexiglass as the man screamed for his life.

A single finger rhythmically tapped lightly on the safety cover.

Tap-tap-tap.

Almost as if the figure were toying with the notion, pondering whether to take that next fatal step.

Tap-tap-tap.

Let the man live, or let him die. That was the question at hand.

Tap-tap-tap.

The decision was made. It had been made long before now. The finger gently, but very deliberately, lifted the safety cover and rested on the button.

'Please! I beg you!' screamed the terrified man, his eyes wide and flecks of spit showering the plexiglass.

Without hesitation, the finger pressed down hard.

There was a dull clunk, and in a swift, pitiless motion, the outer hatch to the airlock opened. The lifepod lurched ever so slightly as air was expelled at a frightening velocity. There was an instantaneous burst of chaotic activity, dust swirling around in the sudden vortex.

The man, his scream lost, was dragged from the window, as if grabbed by some great, invisible space monster, and he shot out into the void like a bullet from a gun.

Grant Paska thrashed and squirmed as the moisture in his lungs boiled and the water in his eyeballs evaporated.

The figure was satisfied to note that the man stayed alive longer than most. It must have taken an agonizing forty-five seconds for consciousness to leave him, his twitching limbs finally becoming still.

A minute later, he was dead, his frozen body free to orbit the sun as just another meteoroid between Mars and Jupiter.

— Sixteen —

The airlock hatch felt cold to Luana's touch. Small crystalline fingers of ice reached out from the window's rim. It was cold now, but how must it have felt for Grant Paska, suddenly being subjected to that? She knew what the effects of a sudden depressurization were, of course. It had been uncomfortable enough for her just to have a few square centimetres of skin exposed to the brutal cold of space. Even now, the affected area was tender to the touch.

Sadly, explosive decompression had happened on numerous occasions since humans had ventured away from the safety of Earth's surface. And there was plenty of video evidence as well. Some of these videos were required viewing for officer training, and she had vivid memories of these accidents, and how the victims had suffered. It was not a subject on which she had ever liked to dwell.

Luana heard a noise from above and looked up. Floyd was dropping down into the airlock to join her.

'Well it was a pretty forlorn hope,' he said, 'but I can categorically say that he isn't anywhere on the ship.'

'I really didn't expect him to be but, you know, we had to check. And the log shows that the hatch was opened from the cabin control, so I don't think he went willingly.'

'That sucks.'

Luana winced.

'Sorry, bad choice of words there. If the door was opened without depressurizing first, he'd have shot out into space like a missile, so there's precious little chance of ever finding his body. What's that?'

Luana glanced down to where he was looking, and held up the small palm-sized tablet for him to see. 'Paska's comm-pad. Thankfully, he'd secured it in the locker. I wonder if he expected something like this to happen?'

Floyd looked uneasy, like there was something playing on his mind that he didn't want to talk about openly. She had a reasonable idea what it might be.

'Go on,' she said. 'Spit it out.'

He grinned nervously. They had only known each other a month, yet could read each other's moods as well as any married couple.

'Luana, are you sure you didn't… I mean everyone saw what you were going to do to him. You came so close to it before. Did he say something to you? Something that made you do it? No one would blame you if you did.'

Eden's Gate

'No. It wasn't me,' she said flatly.

'Look, it's just the two of us here. And I won't tell a soul if you—'

'I'm telling you it wasn't me. I swear.' She could feel the upswelling of anger. It simmered beneath the surface, and it would not take much to make it boil over.

'I woke up last night,' he said, his gaze piercing as he looked at her, searching for any sign that she might be lying. 'You weren't there.'

Luana sighed. 'You're right. I went to speak to him again last night. It's been bugging me ever since the first time we spoke. I needed to know. I needed to know how he did it. I needed to know *why* he did it. I've been grappling with this ever since…'

'Go on,' Floyd urged. His tone was gentle. Soothing. Like her, he just wanted answers.

'He said…' She floundered, unhappy to talk about this to anyone. She didn't even like thinking about it herself, in the privacy of her own head. 'He said he had a thing for me, you know? He said he used to watch me on the bridge of the Aurora, and imagine what it would be like to…' She shivered, feeling bile rise in her throat. 'He wanted me to take my clothes off for him.'

Floyd's eyes went wide.

'That's what he asked me to do that first time. I finally relented last night and showed him… I showed him a little, just to get him talking. He said the attack on the Aurora was part of a greater plan, and there was a reason the collision happened in that precise place.'

'What reason?'

'That's the thing. He wouldn't say! He told me to come back tonight, show him some more and he would tell me. That's why I want you to believe it wasn't me who did this. It's so frustrating! I really think he was going to tell me something useful tonight, and now he's dead. We'll never know what it was.'

Floyd held up both his hands. 'Oh, I believe you! But if it wasn't you, then who the hell was it?'

'I don't know, but whoever it was, I could wring their bloody neck this morning.'

Floyd grinned. 'Agreed. The timing couldn't have been lousier.' He gestured toward the comm-pad again. 'Have you had any luck with that?'

'No, it's password protected. No getting into it without the correct pass code.'

Luana powered the comm-pad up, the screen illuminated in a medium green. The words: "Please input pass code" flashed on and off unequivocally.

'Hmm. Have you tried the obvious ones? Birthdays, anniversaries etc?'

'Yep, those that are on record, in various combinations. Schools, parents' names, siblings.'

'Uh-huh. Including Luther Kane Lynch?'

'Yes, including the esteemed Mr. Luther Kane Lynch. In multiple combinations.'

Floyd thought for a few moments, trying to tease an answer out of his brain. And then an idea began to form.

Eden's Gate

'Wait a minute,' he said. 'You told me you thought he wanted you to know something.'

'Yes.'

'You thought he was going to tell you.'

'Yes, but—'

'Try Luana. L-U-A-N-A.'

She looked at him for a moment, then typed the name into the machine. The pass code message was replaced with a much friendlier, "Welcome back, Grant" greeting.

'Bingo,' Floyd said.

'I'll be damned,' she replied in wonder. 'So he did want to tell me something. There's one open file here.'

She tapped the file to open it and a series of numbers were displayed:

1-58-19-22-7 15-18-12-7-52 2.896 324/092 1930/06-23-2416

'Oh no,' she sighed, crestfallen. 'It's just gibberish.'

Floyd looked at the numbers and frowned. Looking at the numbers as a whole, it did indeed appear unfathomable, but large numbers were almost designed to do that. He had trained himself over the years to break down number sequences into manageable chunks to establish recognizable patterns. His ability to do this had helped to make him a first-class investigator. Something stirred in the back of his mind and he gestured for her to give him the tablet.

'No, wait,' he said, 'these are coordinates.' He rearranged the sequence into something more recognizable.

$$1\text{-}58\text{-}19\text{-}22\text{-}7$$
$$15\text{-}18\text{-}12\text{-}7\text{-}52$$
$$2.896$$
$$324/092$$
$$1930/06\text{-}23\text{-}2416$$

'Of course, I should've seen that,' she grumbled, furious with herself.

'It's okay, not everyone can be as brilliant as me. Hours, minutes, seconds, microseconds and nanoseconds. This third line would be AUs. The fourth line is a trajectory. The fifth is a time in interplanetary standard. It's all there.'

'I don't get it,' Luana said with a frown. All this was starting to give her a headache. 'Was that the point where the Korolev intersected with the Aurora?'

'Beats the hell out of me. We'll need to put these numbers through the nav-com.'

Luana didn't know what this meant, and it might not give them any other clue as to what might be going on, but something was always better than nothing. And there seemed little harm in trying.

Floyd and Luana slipped into their seats in the cockpit, Floyd bringing the navigational computer online. The screen sprang to life, showing current course, start and end points, speed, trajectory, gravitational shift compensation, engine power status and a dozen other parameters. Floyd cleared the display, ready to input a fresh set of figures.

'You got those numbers?' he asked, and Luana sent the comm-pad spinning in his direction to catch, which was a much easier feat in a weightless environment when not having to gauge the effect of gravity. He slotted the device into the nav-com. 'I know there's not much chance of finding who did it, but have you found any indication in this thing of who sent our friend out for a bit of sightseeing?'

With the figures transferred, he popped the comm-pad out again and tossed it back to Luana.

'No,' she said, 'but I don't think anyone's going to lose any sleep over it.'

'No, he was not exactly mister popular. Did the internal cameras show anything?'

'No, the internal cameras had been disabled.'

Floyd stopped working on the nav-com for a few moments as he thought about this. 'That's very interesting. It would need to be someone who knows their way around a technical surveillance system. Let's see: who on board would be capable of doing that? You, me, Landry, Dane. Is that it?'

'I think Conor might have the technical skill. He's a geotechnical engineer, but he'd know too much to be discounted.'

'So that basically means just Celeste, Tamara and Suzy can be discounted.'

'Except Tamara would have knowledge of monitoring systems as a med-tech.'

Floyd started banging his head against the side of the cockpit, eliciting a chuckle from Luana.

'Well, I'm betting it's Landry. I'd stake my reputation on it.'

'You haven't got a reputation.'

'Okay, if I had one, I'd stake it on it,' he said with just a hint of affront.

'But have you got any evidence? Aside from him trying to kill you back on the Aurora, have you got any reason to suspect him over anyone else, other than because you really don't like him?'

Floyd thought about it for a moment. She was right. He had no evidence, but Landry had tried to have him killed, which immediately painted him as a suspect.

'During the interrogation,' Floyd said, 'he was the first one to suggest shoving your pal Paska out of the airlock. Even before you.'

'It doesn't necessarily follow that it was him, though,' Luana said with a sigh. 'Listen, we'll have to go into this in greater depth, of course, but let's just put that aside for the time being. I don't think anyone on board is too bothered that the nasty little twerp is dead. If it was Landry, most of them would give him a medal.'

Floyd wasn't sure whether to laugh or be really depressed at the thought of that. 'Okay, we'll put a pin in the subject and come back to it later.'

'Fine. Now let's see what this message is telling us.'

Floyd turned back to the nav-com and continued setting up the coordinates. He assigned parameters to each of the values and pressed the option for a visual representation. The computer took a couple of seconds to create a three-dimensional image, and once it was done, displayed it on the main screen.

'I'll be damned,' Luana whispered. 'It's instructions for a rendezvous.'

'Sure looks that way.' Floyd flicked the image around, studying it from different angles. 'It's definitely not the collision point for Aurora and the Korolev. Values and positions are all wrong.'

Luana made some quick calculations on her own screen. 'No, nowhere near.' She overlaid their current flight plan onto this new image. 'The rendezvous would be a little out of our way, but I think we could make it okay.'

'What do you think it is? A rescue ship? Hell of a lot of trouble they've gone to, to rescue one man. Somehow, I just don't buy that.'

'I can't think what else it might be,' she said, staring intently at the 3D model.

'A supply ship?' he ventured, then shook his head. 'No, he was expecting to be alone on this lifepod. He'd have had provisions to last years. The only reason we're struggling is because of the impact damage leaving Aurora.'

'If it's not a rescue ship, then I wonder what it can be?' Luana mused, tapping fingernails against her teeth. She made another calculation, combining the two scenarios and working out the most efficient route.

'You're not thinking of making that rendezvous? Luana, if it turns out to be nothing, it'll add a full two days to our trip.'

'We can eke out our food reserves for another couple of days,' she reasoned. 'There's no guarantee we'll find anything on 349 Dembowska anyway. This way, there's a chance we'll find a ship. And supplies. That's got to be worth a gamble, hasn't it?'

Floyd searched for an argument to contradict this proposal, but finding none, just grinned. 'Looks like we're taking a little detour.' He loaded the new flight plan from the nav-com into the helm control system and prepared to make the course adjustments.

'I'm going to tell our passengers what we're doing,' Luana said, clicking on the intercom. 'Cockpit to cabin. We believe there *may* be a supply ship waiting for us. It's two days out of our way but with our prisoner AWOL, we have one less mouth to feed, so it shouldn't mean any more hardship. I believe it's worth the sacrifice, as we still don't know whether we'll find supplies on 349 Dembowska. Cockpit out.'

Floyd began to power up the manoeuvring thrusters. 'You know, we'll probably be blasted out of the sky the moment they realise it's not Paska arriving to meet them. You do know that, don't you?'

'Nothing ventured, nothing gained.'

Floyd smiled and shook his head. 'Right.'

— Seventeen —

Floyd slid down the ladder, keeping his velocity steady until he reached the bottom, where he landed lightly on the soft carpeting. He was getting quite accustomed to doing this now, having made the descent probably a hundred times over the past month.

He turned to look around. Suzy was currently in the central cylinder, gazing out into forever, the stars her only companions. Despite Dane's warnings, she did not seem to have cracked. At least not yet, although Floyd and Luana were monitoring her and were prepared for any 'incidents' that may occur.

Dane himself was in the other nacelle, chatting amiably to Conor and Tamara. They were now, apparently, far more relaxed than they had been. It was amazing just how cathartic regular sex can be, Floyd thought, and could definitely empathize.

Not having to deal with the imminent spectre of death on a minute-to-minute basis also helped in this regard.

There were only two people in this nacelle with him: Max Landry and Celeste Karlin. He wasn't going to waste any time on pleasantries with these two. They were still criminals, and he was going to make damned sure they faced a court over it.

'Landry, a word,' Floyd said, gesturing toward the far end of the nacelle, and the Englishman reluctantly dragged himself from the chair and went to join Floyd.

'I think I can guess what this is all about,' Landry said, not appearing even slightly nervous.

'Why'd you do it?' Floyd demanded.

'I'm guessing you're referring to last night's unfortunate incident?'

'Obviously.'

'And you automatically assumed it was me. Well I'm sorry to break it to you—'

Floyd grabbed him by the lapels and slammed him against the bathroom door, which, sensing pressure against it, obediently opened. Landry stumbled through backwards, Floyd's clenched fists still grasping the shirt, knuckles pressing into his throat.

'Don't try to deny it. Don't you even *attempt* to say it wasn't you.'

Landry gurgled a response as he tried to reply, and Floyd eased off on the pressure, but kept the shirt firmly in his grip.

'You know, Mr. Floyd,' he said haltingly, just able to wheeze a few words out, 'you can knock me into the middle of next week, but it still won't make it true.'

'You have a history, Max,' Floyd said between clenched teeth. 'You're a murderer. You sent your thugs after me on the Aurora. You wanted me dead. You told me you were going to have me killed. And you were the first to suggest throwing Paska out the airlock. It was you, Max, so why try to deny it? It's just us. You can tell me now, can't you?'

'Why…' croaked Landry. He smiled, spittle dribbling down his chin as he spoke. 'Why would I kill a dead man?'

Floyd suddenly felt a little less certain of himself, and slackened his grip a little further. 'What?'

'You say I sent some people after you? Well, a court can decide that. If it gets that far. I trust that little lady back there to make sure it doesn't. You recording this, Celeste?'

'Every word, Max,' came the lawyer's response from behind them.'

Uh-oh.

'And you're right,' Landry continued. 'Paska deserved to die. He was a terrorist and killed all those people on the Aurora. I don't think you'll find many people on this ship that would disagree. But the point is: Grant Paska was going to die soon enough anyway. If someone on this ship didn't do it, then a court would. He was stupid and left too many loose ends. There's no way a court could acquit him. That's why you have to accept that it wasn't me.'

Floyd slowly released him, and backed away into the main area of the nacelle. There was a logic to what Landry said. An inescapable logic that was impossible to ignore.

'Celeste,' Landry said. 'Turn the recorder off.'

'Are you sure, babe?'

'Yeah.'

She did as she was instructed, and pocketed the comm-pad.

'Now we can talk freely, Mr. Floyd.'

'Haven't you said enough?' Floyd replied, with a not insignificant amount of bitterness in his voice.

'Now we're not being recorded, yes, I did send those blokes after you, and I wanted you killed. But, and I can't emphasize this strongly enough, I did not kill Grant Paska. Don't waste your time investigating me, because you won't get anywhere.'

The two men stared at each other for several seconds. Floyd had no doubt now that Landry was telling the truth, and that he had been misdirecting his assumptions of guilt. He was right. There would be no point in killing a man who had been marked for death already, which meant that whoever did kill Paska, he or she hadn't considered this, or didn't believe it.

Floyd turned away and reached for the ladder.

'Don't worry, Mr. Floyd, I'm not naïve enough to expect an apology. But I would like you to stop thinking of me as the enemy. We can help each other, can't we? At least until we get back to civilization.'

Floyd said nothing, and made his way up the ladder. He sank into his seat in the cockpit, feeling deflated and demoralized.

'I'm guessing it didn't go too well with Max?' Luana prompted.

'It wasn't him,' he said flatly. 'I was sure it was him before, but now…'

'Prejudice can be a bitch to rational thought. I'm hardly innocent in that regard myself.'

'Yeah, but he just came up with the most logical argument imaginable. Paska was certainly going to be convicted, and on Mars or Ganymede, or anywhere else apart from Earth and the Moon, he would get the death penalty.'

'And there's no point killing someone who's going to be dead soon anyway.'

'Precisely,' Floyd said, not only annoyed that it wasn't Landry, but also annoyed that he hadn't thought of this himself. His blind loathing of Max Landry had precluded any other possibility. Now he had to look elsewhere. He reluctantly admitted that it didn't say a lot for his powers as an investigator.

'So the question remains,' Luana said, 'if it wasn't Landry, then who was it? Who could it have been?'

'I don't know. It had to be someone with the technical knowledge to disable the cameras, but who thought that Paska might get away with it. One thing I'm sure of – now, at least – is that it wasn't my old friend Max Landry.'

'And what bothers you now is that it is probably someone you know, like and trust. And following this route could well land them in serious trouble, simply for doing something that the court was going to do at some point anyway.'

This was a very valid point, and having it put into plain English crystalized his thoughts perfectly. Now he had to ask himself: do I want to throw one of my friends under the bus simply to see justice done?

This was not the kind of moral ambiguity that he had envisaged when they had escaped the Aurora, but one way or another, he would have to make a decision, sooner or later.

Suzy stared out of the tiny window just forward of the aft storage hold hatch. She liked it here, away from other people, away from gossip and intrigue, away from the judgements people make. All she wanted was to be alone, to be free.

Somewhere out there was Earth, floating alone in the lonely wilderness. She would have to go back there. With no ship to call home, all she could do was return to Earth. Maybe she could find a job as a singer or dancer in Vegas or Reno or Paris. If she was really lucky, she might be able to get on a waiting list to serve on another starliner. The trouble was, there were so few of those and she would be starting from the bottom again.

She may have been setting her sights too high to get a gig on a starliner again, but there were orbiting hotels that might have work, or maybe the Lunar Transit Station outside Clavius City. The least favoured option would be the Lagrange Two shipyards, working the bars and clubs entertaining the construction crews. She had heard stories about the L-Two gigs, and had no wish to subject herself to that if she could possibly avoid it.

It was all so depressing, the thought of starting again from scratch. She was a good singer, and knew how to perform, how to please a crowd. She knew how to single out any in the audience with a playful point of a finger or a wink of an eye, and make them feel like the most special person in the galaxy. She knew precisely where the line was between dazzling cabaret and sleazy strip club. Her performances were exotic, sure, and occasionally bordered on the risqué, but she never strayed too far over the line.

The trouble was, there were a million other pretty girls out there who could do equally well.

She watched the nacelles swoop rhythmically past, obscuring the stars for a couple of seconds each revolution. It was mesmerizing and hypnotic and she felt she could just hang here forever, fading away until she died, just watching those nacelles as they unendingly swooped past. In her mind, her body would have long since turned to dust when those nacelles ceased turning.

A head appeared from the ladder to one of the nacelles, interrupting her dreams. Dane Jefferson grinned and came over, his insane dreadlocks sweeping in all directions like Medusa caught in a hurricane.

'Hey Suze, you doing okay, sweetheart?' He drifted over and rested against the other window, slipping a thumb into one of the fabric handles to stop himself floating away again.

'Yeah, I'm fine,' she said absently, but anyone could tell that she was anything *but* fine.

'Bad business about Paska. It's all anyone can talk about. Have you got any theories?'

'Who can say?' Suzy shrugged. 'It's not as if no one had a motive. He killed all those people. All those people who didn't have a chance. It was all because of him. Anyone could have been responsible for killing him. Luana was going to throw him out of the airlock. Max agreed as well, and if Max wanted it done, then so did Celeste. So, everyone had a motive.'

'Yeah, that's what I thought. It could have been anyone and everyone had a motive. Then I had an idea. You know there were no cameras operating?'

She nodded, but said nothing.

'I remembered the monitor on the airlock hatch is on an independent system. I discovered that while I was working on the comms system. And then I found this.'

Dane plucked a comm-pad from his pocket and switched it on. He turned around so they could both see the video that was playing. It showed the airlock two keypad, and a hand. A hand with long, slender fingers. They moved with the grace and elegance of a dancer. The index finger tapped on the safety cover several times, as if its owner were toying with an idea, contemplating whether to make the next move. The thumb and forefinger lifted the safety cover and the button within was pressed hard, the index finger bent back with the force of the action.

And at the tip of that finger was a scarlet painted nail.

'Now I may be wrong,' Dane said, 'but I can only think of one person on this ship with fingernails that colour.'

Suzy looked down at her hands. She had always been quite proud of her hands, and her elegant fingers. They had an aristocratic look, like the hands of one of those great film noir beauties like Ava Gardner or Hedy Lamarr whom she idolized. She slowly turned them over and ten gleaming scarlet nails stared back at her. She looked up at Dane, a fearful acceptance in her eyes. She knew what this could mean. She wasn't a naïve child. She was an attractive woman and he had something that could ruin her life – should he choose to use it.

'What do you want, Dane?'

'Oh nothing. Don't get me wrong. Sick bastard had it coming to him. There ain't one person on this ship who hadn't thought of doing the same thing.'

'Then why…?'

'I've already deleted the video on the hatch panel. And now…' He wrapped the fingers of one of her hands around the comm-pad, and directed the scarlet nailed index finger of her other hand to hit the delete button. 'There. Now there's no record of it at all. No evidence to link it to you. It's a pity because you really have lovely hands. But, needs must. I just have one question: why did you do it when none of the rest of us did?'

Suzy was too astonished to speak straight away. Men just didn't do things like that. Was it possible that the crazy haired Dane was a gentleman? A true, old-fashioned gentleman with a true gentleman's values.

She turned back to the window. 'He took everything from me, Dane. We were like a family on the Aurora. It was our home. It was my home. Even Luana has a life back on Earth. My whole life was on the Aurora. I was the top billed performer in the Starlight Lounge. I loved it. The crowds loved me. It was just the most wonderful life. And now it's gone. I've lost everything. All my friends: the singers, the dancers, even the lighting technicians and producers. The chorus line singers were like my sisters… It was such a great life. But he took it all away. He murdered them all, and showed no remorse. And there was every possibility that he'd wriggle out of it. You know what the courts are like. Bastards like that never get what they deserve. Innocent people suffer, and the guilty live charmed lives.'

'You won't get any argument from me. Some people don't deserve the luxury of life. You're not one of them. I just didn't want you to get in any trouble.'

Suzy turned back to face him again, taking both his hands in hers. 'Thank you, Dane. Thank you for protecting me.'

She leant forward and pressed her lips against his, the kiss not passionate as lovers' kisses are, but lingering and charged with meaning. She pulled away again and stared into his eyes, before easing past him and disappearing into one of the nacelles.

'Hot damn,' muttered a stunned Dane Jefferson.

— Eighteen —

The lifepod's proximity warning detector began to chime in the cockpit. It wasn't a blaring klaxon designed to induce a sudden, involuntary bowel evacuation, but it was insistent, nonetheless.

Ben Floyd reached above his console to silence the alarm. 'There it is, right where it's supposed to be.' He began the braking manoeuvre as the object – whatever it was – came into range. He hadn't really been serious when he had suggested that the rendezvous ship would blow them to smithereens as soon as they realised it wasn't Paska meeting them, but he did feel a certain trepidation as they approached.

'Any idea what it is yet?' Luana asked.

'Not yet. Too far for a visual and it's not broadcasting any ID signal. Time to bring the scanners online.'

'But if it is an enemy ship, the scans might trigger defences,' she said, biting her lip nervously.

'We're going to be on top of them soon enough anyway. I'd like to have some idea of what we're dealing with before we get there.'

'Okay, here goes.' Luana started scanning the object, several lists gradually becoming populated. 'Well, it's metal. And it's small. Around two meters. Too small to be a rescue ship. It could be a single occupant pod. Or have supplies.'

'I doubt it'd have supplies. This lifepod should've had plenty for one man. I think we're close enough now for a visual.'

'Okay, let's see what it looks like.'

A tiny object appeared on the screen. It was too small to make out any details and could have been a grain of rice, for all they could tell from that distance.

'Magnifying,' Luana said.

The object suddenly became a hundred times larger. It was predominantly cylindrical around half a meter in diameter. At one end was a bulbous section, packed with instruments. At the other were fuel pods and a propulsion system.

'Not going to win any beauty contests is it?' Floyd murmured without a lot of humour. Despite what logic had been suggesting, he was still disappointed not to find a nice, shiny rescue ship packed with delicious supplies.

'Is it me or does it look mean?' Luana asked.

They were now approaching the object rapidly, and Floyd increased power to the braking thrusters.

'Listen,' he said, 'just because it looks like a bomb, doesn't necessarily mean it *is* a bomb.'

'I never said it was a bomb.'

'You implied it.'

'Well you've got to admit, it does look a bit... bombular.'

'Now you're just making up words. It could just as easily be a coffin,' he said.

'Oh, that's *so* much more appealing. Okay,' Luana said, trying to bring the conversation back on track, 'the only way to find out is to rendezvous and see for ourselves. We'll keep the ship at a safe distance and I'll go across in an environment suit.'

'I don't know. It's dangerous. That thing could be rigged to explode as soon as someone touches it.'

'It's doubtful. Paska was expected to get it aboard somehow.' She leaned across and kissed him on the cheek. 'It'll be okay.'

'Just be careful,' he said, the concern plain to see on his face. 'No more repeats of the storage bay incident. Remember, I won't be out there to save your ass this time.'

'You're never going to let me forget that, are you?'

'Absolutely never. I'll be reminding you about it on the day you die. I just don't want it to be today.'

'Yes dad. I'll get suited up. Go no closer than five klicks, just in case it is booby trapped.'

Luana glided across the cockpit and grabbed the environment suit from its locker.

The Arcadia Series

The lone figure of Luana Lee emerged from airlock two, descending below the lifepod. Her tiny form was dwarfed by the ship, which seemed much larger when viewed from the outside than within the cramped confines of the ship.

She ignited her jet pack and scooted away, heading for the bright speck in the distance, although "in the distance" was a misleading term. With no points of reference, it could have been a vast object fifty thousand kilometres away, or a tiny one, just five meters distant.

'Communications check,' came Floyd's voice.

'Roger that; reading you loud and clear, strength five. Are you picking me up on the scanner?'

There was a moment's pause before he responded. 'Yep, got this little green dot moving at ten meters per second. You should reach the object in a little over eight minutes.'

'Eight minutes. Check.'

There was nothing more for her to do except admire the view and hope that this thing, whatever it was, did not have a proximity detector linked to a very powerful explosive charge.

At the one-kilometre mark, the object began to reveal a few details. Luana gave two quick bursts on her attitude jets and rotated a hundred and eighty degrees. There was the lifepod, hanging alone in space, waiting.

She waved at it, wondering how closely Floyd was keeping tabs on her.

'I can see you,' he said. 'You're coming up on it pretty fast. You'd better start your braking manoeuvres.'

'Just checking you were awake, Floyd.' She gave another two bursts on the attitude jets and turned to face the object again. She seemed much closer than she expected, so turned again and gave a long, powerful blast on her main thruster. She turned once more and saw that she was now just fifty meters away and closing slowly. She could now use her smaller manoeuvring jets to cover the last few meters.

'How does it look?' Floyd asked.

'Small and ugly.'

'No need to get personal.'

Luana wondered if he could see her eyes roll from this distance, or whether he could hear them scraping against their sockets.

She was close now. Uncomfortably close. Luana gave another small burst from her braking thrusters and came to a direct halt, relative to the object.

And close up, it didn't look any less bomb-like to her.

'I'm five meters away. If there was a proximity detector, I'd have tripped it by now. Is there any change in the object's power output?'

'Negative. Still showing minimal power signature. It's up to you. You can abort now if you like.'

'Not a chance. I'm going to make contact.'

She gave another tiny burst from her jets and moved forward. Reaching out, as if touching fire, she made contact, feeling the texture of its skin beneath her fingertips. She had no tactile way of estimating its temperature, but her readout said it was colder than ice.

'You still with us Luana?' came Floyd's slightly agitated voice.

'Yes. Sorry, I'm fine.'

She maneuvered her way over the object, being careful not to carelessly trigger something potentially explosive. Built into the device's nose were a number of bulbous nodules that appeared to be sensor devices. Just behind these was a screen, set into the cylindrical main body. The screen was black, with just three words flashing in green in the centre: "system mode: standby".

'There's a control panel here and a screen. It's functioning. Nothing looks out of the ordinary. No red lights, ominous countdown or message saying boom time in ten seconds.'

Luana activated the screen and braced herself, just in case this detonated it. But it didn't. Instead, the screen showed a number of different parameters.

'Okay, whatever it is, it's powered down and awaiting a manual power up. To be honest there's not much I can do from out here.'

'You think we should bring it aboard then?' Floyd asked. The longer they stayed here, the more he just wanted to pick Luana up and get the hell out of there.

'I do. I can't see any immediate danger, but we'll keep it in airlock two and be prepared to eject it at the first sign of trouble.'

'Sounds sensible. Sensiblish.'

'Now who's making up words? Bring the ship in closer.'

'Roger that.'

Floyd fired up the main engines and brought the lifepod in, covering the five kilometres in just a few seconds. He swung her around, retros performing the spaceship equivalent of a handbrake turn.

'Easy, flyboy,' Luana chided.

'Chicks love it when a guy does that. I bet you're quivering at the knees now.'

She shook her head. 'I've never wanted you more. Idiot. No one likes a show-off. Okay, I'm bringing the object aboard now. Keep the ship dead steady. It may be weightless out here, but this thing will have a lot of inertia behind it, and I'd rather it didn't get bounced around too much.'

'Take your time.'

She used small bursts of thrust from her attitude jets to ease the object into a position just below the airlock. It was slow and surprisingly arduous work. On Earth, the object would have weighed at least half a tonne, so was reluctant to move at all, and when it did, was equally reluctant to stop. This was one of the perils of manoeuvring objects with a large mass in space. Zero gravity was all well and good, but it didn't reduce an object's inertia. If it got out of control, it could easily crush her, just as a car would on Earth. Or it could smash into the ship and explode. Neither prospect was appealing, so she followed Floyd's advice and took her time.

The object was bathed in the warm crimson glow from the airlock, the outer hatch open and inviting her in. Once it was lined up, Luana ever so gently eased it upwards, being careful to ensure it didn't scrape along the rim, or crush her against the side. Up she and the object went until it was securely inside, and she fired several bursts from her thrusters to bring it to a complete stop.

'I'm in,' she said. 'The object and I are in the airlock. Close the outer door.'

'Roger.'

She could hear nothing through the suit in the vacuum, but looked down in time to see the iris hatch rotate shut.

'Repressurizing,' Floyd said. 'Wait for the lights to turn green.'

A minute later, the colour of the illumination changed, and Luana unclasped her helmet and breathed air from the ship once more. Above her came the clanking sound of clamps unlocking and the inner hatch slid open.

Floyd's head immediately poked into the airlock. 'Good work out there. You okay?'

'Fine,' she grinned up at him. 'Piece of cake. The readouts haven't changed. Still all showing green.'

Luana was surprised to see Max Landry also poke his head in, to the obvious irritation of Floyd.

'Well, well, well,' Landry said, staring at the object. 'Long time since I've seen one of those.'

'You know what it is?' Luana asked.

'Oh yes. That, my friends, is a high-yield contraterrene reaction device.'

'A what?' Floyd asked.

'Oh my God. A bomb,' Luana said. 'A matter/antimatter reaction bomb.'

'The lady's done her homework,' Landry continued. 'Designed to vaporize anything within a fifty-kilometre radius. They stopped making this model about fifteen years ago. I think it was something to do with gamma radiation levels making them dangerous.'

Luana retrieved her hand-held scanner and ran it over the device. 'Gamma radiation levels are slightly elevated, but well within safety tolerances. How do you know so much about this, Mr. Landry?'

'Oh, it's a hobby.'

'A hobby?' she said with a quizzical eyebrow raised.

'It's always good to have a hobby, ain't it, Mr. Floyd?'

'He's an arms dealer, amongst other activities,' Floyd explained. 'And not too concerned about what he sells or to who.'

'That's a bit harsh, Mr. Floyd. I prefer to think of myself as an entrepreneur.'

'You're a crook.'

Luana made a show of clearing her throat. 'We need to monitor the device and be prepared to eject it if anything changes.'

'We're not going to dump it right now?' Floyd asked.

'No. Paska wanted us to find it. Besides, the inquiry into the Aurora disaster will be needing any evidence it can get. Mr. Landry, would you get Conor to help you secure the device in here? We need to get back on course.'

'It'll be my pleasure, dear lady.'

— Nineteen —

Floyd had activated the lifepod's braking thrusters almost a day before, to bring their speed down to match that of the asteroid's. Now it approached the rock at a sedate thousand kilometres per minute and slowing.

From this distance, 349 Dembowska had a discernible disk, looking for all the world like a forlorn potato that had been left out in the sunshine too long, but no real details were visible to the naked eye. However, the lifepod was approaching rapidly and more and more features resolved themselves with every passing second.

'Okay,' said Floyd as an audible tone sounded in the cockpit. 'Passing the ten-thousand-kilometre mark.'

They were now within the exclusion zone that surrounded the asteroid.

'Well, pretty soon we'll know whether we're going to starve to death out here,' Luana said, and keyed the intercom. 'Cockpit to cabin: we're beginning our approach procedures. Powering down the gravity module so you'll lose gravity in a few seconds.'

'Seatbacks and tray tables in their upright positions,' Floyd deadpanned. 'Miss Lee will be round with gin and tonics in a jiffy.'

Luana switched off the intercom. 'You're an asshole, Floyd.'

'Till the day I die, he grinned mischievously, and reached for the gravity nacelle rotation control. 'Cutting power to the gravity section… now,' he said, flicking the switch.

Behind them, the nacelles began to slow. It took a little over a minute, but eventually they came to a halt and within, weightlessness was restored. The passengers had known this would be happening as Luana and Floyd had gone through this with them already, but even so, various tablets, pens, cups and eating utensils were suddenly liberated from the restraints that artificial gravity imposed.

Now they were in range, Floyd began running scans. 'Picking up low level energy readings from the asteroid. Organized patterns. Could be a fusion generator. There's definitely something artificial down there.'

'The question is: will we find any food? We've got six very hungry people back there.'

'And two very hungry people up here. Wait. What's this?'

The screen showed a blip on the surface of the asteroid, but now there were two more. And these two blips were moving extremely fast. An alarm began to sound in the cockpit, an alarm different to any other they had heard in the six weeks this had been their home.

'Missiles!' Floyd almost shouted.

'Oh, hell. Begin evasive manoeuvres.'

'Roger that.' Floyd increased power to the main engines, far more quickly than was healthy for the power units. As the thrust built, he flung the ship into a series of banks, dives and climbs.

Luana quickly flicked on the cockpit to cabin intercom. 'We're under missile attack. Brace for a rough ride.'

The two missiles moved with terrifying speed, at a much higher acceleration rate than the lifepod could ever hope to achieve.

'Dammit!' Floyd cursed. 'Missiles changing course. They're locked on and closing. Impact in twenty seconds. Get ready to take us straight down on full burn, on my mark.'

'I don't think that'll be enough,' Luana said, taking over control from Floyd as he unbuckled his harness and leapt from his seat. 'What're you doing?'

'I've got an idea.'

'Better make it quick,' she said, watching the two signatures from the missiles on her screen getting awfully close.

'I'm ejecting the distress beacon in three, two, one, mark.'

Floyd punched the button on the panel behind his seat. The was a sudden clank, followed by a whoosh as the distress beacon soared away from the lifepod.

'Now, take us down, Luana. Straight down.'

She did as she was told, praying that this worked. Luana would normally handle the ship with the deftest of touches. But now was not the right time for elegant finesse. She slammed the control column forward in a quick, brutal motion.

The lifepod lurched downward abruptly. Anything not bolted down was immediately slammed against the ceiling – including Ben Floyd. He hit the bulkhead with a grunt, and was paralyzed for a moment, pinned to the unyielding surface and unable to speak. After an interminable two-second delay, he managed to gasp out his commands.

'Right, cut power. All of it, including life support.'

Floyd pushed himself away from the ceiling and grabbed the back of his seat, dragging his body back into the co-pilot's chair.

Around them, they could hear the whine of the engines suddenly powering down. Luana frantically flicked switches to their off positions, and the cockpit was plunged into darkness, the only light coming from 349 Dembowska, which began to fill the screen.

Behind the lifepod, the missiles swirled in space, their on-board AIs trying to determine what was happening as a new target appeared, but the main one vanished. The first missile locked onto the beacon, which innocently transmitted its friendly message of distress. The missile didn't care what was being broadcast; it just knew it had a job to do. That little beacon, it reasoned, was now a justified target.

If it had any internal debate as to what qualified the noisy little object as a target, it didn't last long.

The missile slammed into the beacon and detonated in a disproportionately large explosion. The beacon was instantly vaporized, the detonation so violent it was reduced to mere atoms.

The blast wave, an expanding sphere of violent energy, hit the lifepod. In the cockpit, sparks flew from overhead electronic circuits, showering the two pilots.

With the entire area a confused mass of energy, it took the second missile valuable seconds to reacquire the lifepod. It twisted and rolled, like a fish evading a predator, but then it found something. It verified the weak signal. On its internal sensors, it could just make out the fleeing lifepod.

A microsecond later, it was back in pursuit.

Inside the cockpit, Luana stared out of the window. Ahead, filling the entire screen and getting closer all the time, was the asteroid. Craters became visible; then valleys; then individual rocks.

'Er... Floyd?'

'Power up on my mark,' he said, transfixed by the colossal lump of rock that they were seconds away from ploughing into.

'That asteroid's getting awfully big.'

'Not yet. There's still one missile out there.'

As if in response, the proximity alarm began to ping again. The missile was bearing down on them. But not quite. It was heading in their approximate direction, but not exact. However, the moment they reignited the engines, it would have them.

Floyd knew it would be tight. Fire up too early and the missile would hit them, reducing the lifepod to a superheated cloud of debris. Fire up too late and they would smash into the asteroid at a thousand kilometres per hour. And 349 Dembowska would have a fresh crater on its pockmarked surface.

The rock loomed, like a great, inescapable monster. Floyd waited until he was sure they couldn't escape, then forced himself to wait a couple of seconds longer. This was a trial of nerve, and he needed to keep his if they were to have any chance.

'Floyd?'

This was it.

'Now! Power up! Vertical thrusters, maximum drive!'

Luana had been waiting, her fingers poised and ready to flick the entire bank of switches on in one long, fluid motion.

Floyd did the same on his side of the cockpit, and was rewarded with the sound of the engines roaring back into life. He angled every motor, every manoeuvring thruster vectored downward and slammed them into maximum power. The ship began to rattle with the effort, then shook so violently their vision blurred and teeth rattled. The frame of the little ship creaked and groaned in protest as supporting struts fought against the colossal forces at work.

'Really hoping this works,' Floyd said.

With this much energy being deployed, the entire vessel shook with the immense power, and behind them they could hear the screech of metal as it was strained to the limit of breaking.

But was it enough?

A kilometre behind, the one remaining missile suddenly found what it had been looking for. In its targeting system, it now saw the bright, unmistakable silhouette of the lifepod. It made a minor adjustment in its trajectory and increased power to maximum.

In a few seconds, it would be able to fulfil its destiny.

'The missile has reacquired us and is closing,' Luana yelled over the roaring of the engines and scream of the tortured spaceframe. 'Impact in fifteen seconds.'

The nose of the lifepod began to rise. But slowly. Floyd dreaded to look, but glanced at the altimeter anyway.

The nose edged up a little more. Had he left it too late?

The ping from the proximity warning seemed to be getting louder, the chimes now so close together that they were almost forming a single, continuous note.

Floyd glanced across at Luana, who looked back at him and smiled. 'It's been a ride, Floyd,' she said.

He looked back at the horizon. They were levelling out. Was it enough? It couldn't be. Just a little more. Just a little more, he thought, involuntarily leaning his head back, away from the approaching rock.

The lifepod hit the surface of the asteroid at an angle of a little under ten degrees, smashing into the dusty ground.

The missile noted that the target was beginning to level out, and did its best to adjust its course, but realised three microseconds too late that it was committed to this trajectory.

It hit the asteroid not at a glancing ten-degree angle, but at a terminal sixty degrees. Fifty meters behind the lifepod, it smashed into the ground, the blast wave creating a new crater in the soil. White-hot rock was blasted clear, forming a broad ejector blanket that soared high above the asteroid before falling back and carpeting the ground.

The lifepod was deflected, lurching back up into the sky amid a cloud of dust and debris that it dragged along in its wake. It hung there for a few seconds before crashing back into the dust. It carved a furrow into the surface as it skidded along, churning up rocks that flew into the sky and came crashing back down to pummel the ship from above. It careered along and finally, with surface dust swirling around it, came to a juddering halt.

— Twenty —

A single red light winked on and off. But that was the only illumination in the cockpit. In fact, that was the only illumination in the entire ship. Outside was a swirling fog of dust that hung languidly aloft, slowly falling onto the battered remains of the ship like the first snowfall of winter.

And it was quiet. Eerily quiet. After six weeks, Floyd had always been aware of the noises within the ship. The constant rumble from the engines and hum of electrical systems were a ceaseless reminder that the little lifepod was a living thing, with a heartbeat. That heartbeat had been shut off abruptly, the safety systems sensing when there had been a catastrophic failure and cutting power.

Floyd started to stir, instantly regretting the action. He remembered reading somewhere that there are two hundred and six bones in the human body, or more, depending on your point of view. But he was fairly sure that, right now, whatever the true number, every single one ached. He opened his eyes and took in his surroundings. He was still in the cockpit, but viewing it from an odd angle. Somehow, during the crash he had been tossed out of his seat and deposited on the floor behind.

He waggled his fingers and toes. Yes, they all seemed to be there. They all ached, of course, competing with one another to see which one could ache the most, but miraculously none seemed to be broken. It was the same story with his arms and legs. He could barely believe it, but didn't question this remarkable good fortune.

'Luana?' he croaked, hearing the rasp of his own voice. He cleared his throat and tried again. 'Luana?'

'Yeah, I'm alive,' came the uncertain response. 'I think. You okay?'

'Yeah,' he grunted, heaving himself to his feet. It was a strange sensation, feeling gravity in the cockpit again. The last time he had experienced it in the cockpit area had been a few seconds prior to their desperate escape from the Aurora. He was getting a little tired of having to fight just to stay alive. It was about time the universe started taking pity on them and made their lives a little easier. Just a little.

Luana went feeling around for the emergency lighting and switched it on. It should have activated automatically; an indication that the lifepod was in an extremely poor state of repair. Next, she reached for the intercom. 'Cockpit to cabin: is everyone okay back there?'

There was a disturbing pause before anyone answered.

'Still in one piece back here,' Max Landry replied.

In the starboard nacelle – now that port and starboard had some justifiable meaning – Landry looked around him. In the next seat, Celeste gave him a half-hearted thumbs up. At the far end of the nacelle, Suzy's seatbelt must have come loose, as she was now upside down on top of Dane Jefferson. Not that the man looked like he was about to start complaining too vociferously.

Landry unclipped his seatbelt and staggered over to the access tube that connected the port and starboard nacelles.

'Conor?' he shouted.

Conor and Tamara appeared at the far end and gave another hand signal, gesturing that they were both okay.

'No broken bones?' Landry asked no one in particular. When there were no affirmative responses, he spoke to Luana again. 'No, we're all okay back here.'

'Glad to hear it,' Floyd said, taking the mike from Luana. 'Thank you for flying Lifepod 11 Airways. On behalf of the crew, we hope you enjoyed your flight. Dane, I've got something here I need you to look after. Can I trust you to do that?'

'You got it, boss. Need me to take that little lady of yours in hand?'

Luana rolled her eyes. 'Funny Dane, funny.'

'Regular goddamn comedian,' Floyd grumbled. 'Cockpit out.'

He shook his head and smiled. Dane really was one of a kind. He turned to look at Luana, and the smile froze on his face when he saw the expression on hers.

'So I take it you told Dane about me and you?'

'Ah. Yeah, about that—'

'You just couldn't keep it to yourself, could you?' There was a smile there, tugging at the edges of her lips. A small one, but it was there.

'It wasn't like that. He happened to look in the cockpit window one night while we were... You know. On aerial manoeuvres.'

She let out a bark of a laugh. 'Is that what we're calling it now? So how much of our aerial manoeuvres did he see?'

'Enough. He wanted to know how you got a bruise on your butt the size of Texas.'

'My butt is the size of Texas?' she said with a frown.

Uh-oh. 'No, of course not!' he laughed nervously, and the moment he did, knew he wasn't going to get out of this without something to avert his imminent execution. 'No, the bruise is that size; your butt is *barely* the size of Dakota.'

'Hmm. North or South?'

'Both. One for each cheek.'

'Okay, whatever. I'll let you off, considering we are still staring death in the face and I may need you without both legs broken in multiple places.'

'The lady is too kind. I'm guessing the ship is not in great condition, from all those red flashing lights?'

Eden's Gate

She shook her head, seeming to find the motion curious in a gravitational field. 'You won't be surprised to hear she'll never fly again. Main engines: offline. Take off thrusters: offline. Navigation: offline. Communications: offline. Life support offline, but I've rerouted power from the manoeuvring thrusters. I doubt we'll be needing them again. It'll at least be enough to keep the system circulating for a while. Structural integrity is holding. No sign of any hull breaches that the system has detected.' There were a lot more items on the list of damages, but she thought she'd stick to the most serious now.

'What about the bomb,' he asked, and from how wide her eyes went, it seemed that she had forgotten their little antimatter friend in airlock two.

Luana brought up the readings from the airlock. 'Seems to be okay. I think. Gamma radiation is holding. No discernible power increase. No ticking.'

Floyd found the notion of their high-yield contraterrene reaction device actually having an audible tick quite amusing. 'I'll get Landry to take a look at it, just to make sure. I think it's a fair bet he knows a lot more about these things than we do.'

'Fair point. You go organize that, and make sure they're all okay in the cabin.'

Getting from the cockpit to the nacelles was a lot more arduous now than it had been in zero gravity. It was at that point, while he was trying to get his aching, recalcitrant body from the central cylinder into the access tunnel to the starboard nacelle, that a troubling thought occurred to Ben Floyd. This asteroid was around a hundred and forty kilometres at its widest point. It should be producing such a tiny gravitational field that a good sneeze should be enough to achieve escape velocity. And here he was, feeling every bit as heavy as he did on Earth. He remembered feeling surprised that the lifepod took so long to level out during its dive. An unanticipated one gee might have a lot to do with that.

This asteroid was just throwing up more and more puzzles.

He clambered along the access tunnel and eventually came out inside the starboard nacelle, where he found four of his comrades. That's what they were now. Comrades. He had even mellowed towards Landry. A little. The man was still a crook and a gangster, and he was still going to enjoy clapping him in irons and delivering him into the waiting arms of EarthPol Security. But for now, the man might prove useful.

'Oh, Mr. Floyd,' Landry greeted him with a smile. 'I have to compliment you on an outstanding landing.'

'Thanks, Max. I can just feel the sincerity oozing out of you.'

'Something's oozing out,' Dane mumbled, 'and it sure ain't sincerity.'

'Ever the action hero, eh Dane?' Floyd said, wandering over to the Jamaican. He held out his hand and dropped a small object into Dane's palm. 'Look after that for me,' he whispered. 'Guard it with your life.'

'You got it boss,' Dane replied with a wink.

'Max,' Floyd said, turning back to the gangster, 'I need you to come and have a look at that bomb with me.'

'Always happy to help, Mr. Floyd; you know that.'

That did not inspire him with confidence. Floyd wondered at what point Landry would make his move. He had no illusions that this constant show of bonhomie was as false as a real estate agent's smile, and that at some point, Landry would turn on him. The question was, when? He doubted it would be before they were out of danger, but it would not be long before any kind of trial could take place. No, it would happen at some moment in between, at the exact instant between danger and safety. That was when Landry would make his move, which meant that Floyd was probably safe for now. However, if the people on this asteroid proved to be friendlier than they at first appeared, it wouldn't be long.

Ten minutes later, the two men dropped into airlock two. Floyd was amazed that it had survived. Being just a hollow tube on the underside of the ship, he would have bet a month's salary on it shearing off as the lifepod had skidded along the rugged terrain of the asteroid. But, survive it did, and now they needed to check that their extremely delicate and volatile cargo was undamaged.

The Arcadia Series

Sensibly, Floyd left most of this to Landry, and the cockney carefully went through all the bomb's systems, checking radiation levels, detonators, timing systems, magnetic containment fields, chamber integrity and a couple of dozen more vital systems.

'So, what's the next move, Mr. Floyd?'

While Landry went through the device's systems, Floyd just checked that's its restraints were still secure. 'I think that's pretty obvious, don't you think Max?'

'Yeah, someone's going to have to go out and meet our new neighbours,'

'Exactly.'

'And hope they don't kill you the moment they clap eyes on you.'

'That is an annoying little detail,' Floyd conceded. 'But if they did, it would save you the trouble of being arrested and being taken to court.'

'Not at all. If you die, then so do I, just a little while later. It's in my best interests for you to stay alive, Mr. Floyd. So, did you want me to come with you?'

'Sure, although it might be easier if I just shoot *myself* in the back.'

'Oh Mr. Floyd, that's unworthy. Would I ever do that to you?'

'You sent three guys to do that to me.'

'Apart from that.'

Floyd had to laugh. 'No, I need you to keep things together here. You're the strongest one in the group. They'll need that strength and leadership once we're gone.'

Landry stopped what he was doing and looked at Floyd, his expression unfathomable. 'Thanks. I won't let you down.'

Floyd just nodded, and with no more words exchanged between them, they headed back, Landry to the nacelle and Floyd to the cockpit.

When Luana heard Floyd scrambling in through the cockpit hatch, she looked up and smiled.

'Everything okay down there?' she asked as she ran a diagnostic scanner over the environment console. The panel was off and the delicate electronic boards behind were a jumbled mess of optical cabling and mostly red flashing lights, with a few amber to add some variety. She had diverted power to the system, but that only solved part of the problem. She had had to engineer physical bypasses that circumvented various systems, just to keep the environmental network operating at a minimal level. She couldn't be sure even this would work for long, one bank of relays having burnt out twice already.

'Could've been worse,' Floyd said. 'Actually, it could've been a lot worse. No injuries, except a couple of small cuts and bruises. There's air, water and heat, and the bomb's secure and functioning well. I got Max to go with me to check it.'

'Good. I wish I had equally positive news.'

'The ship's dead?'

'Dying. We're running on battery power, but those batteries have enough juice to last twelve hours. Fifteen at the most. After that we lose heat and air purification. I've jury-rigged various get-arounds but it's only temporary. If the system doesn't burn itself out beforehand, the ship will be dead in a few hours.'

'It's pretty much as I thought,' Floyd said, stroking the stubble on his chin.

'So, we're here. Now what?'

'The natives don't seem all that friendly, but unless you want to suffocate or freeze to death, we'd better go introduce ourselves.'

It was clear she had been thinking along similar lines. 'How?'

'That power source we tracked just before the attack? By my reckoning it's around fifteen klicks in that direction.' He gestured towards the front of the cockpit, and a little to the left. He scared himself with how vague that was.

'And if they decide to kill us as soon as they see us?'

'Whether we get shot over there or suffocate here, we're dead anyway, so we're really not risking much.'

'Nothing like looking on the bright side,' she said, opening the environment suit storage locker and tossing one of them to him. 'And that's nothing like looking on the bright side.'

— Twenty-One —

The two forlorn figures set off, trudging through eons-old dust that probably hadn't been disturbed in the last four billion years. Fifty meters from the ship, Floyd tapped Luana on the arm, and gestured back to where they had just come from.

'Do you see that?' he said, his voice little more than a whisper.

'I sure do. Incredible that we just survived that. And if we don't find some food and shelter in a little over half a day, everyone in there will be dead.'

Lifepod 11 seemed a terribly impersonal name for such a valiant little ship. She had whisked them away from the dying wreck of the Aurora, had sustained them through all those long weeks, and finally had sacrificed herself to get them to safety. Now, she looked such a sorry sight, half buried in earth and rocks, battered to the point of being unrecognizable. Dust still hung suspended above her, like a shroud of death slowly descending around her.

'You're right,' Floyd said. 'Not exactly time to go sightseeing. Come on.'

He and Luana turned away, and began their journey in earnest, traipsing through soft dust that had been pulverized over billions of years. It was so fine, it was almost like a liquid, rippling as they passed, hanging in hollows and crevices while naked bedrock protruded, as if reaching through the dust to touch the raw sunlight.

Floyd had estimated that they were around fifteen kilometres from the energy source, but he had not let on just how much of a guess that was. Fifteen kilometres was a conservative estimate. Twenty-five or thirty might have been nearer the mark. Unfortunately, the ship's sensors were now just useless scrap, and those that were not destroyed by the crash had been fried by the static build up from the dust that now cocooned the ship.

'You realise,' Luana said, slightly breathlessly, 'we're probably going to be dead in the next hour or two?'

'No, we'll be fine,' Floyd replied with far more positivity than he felt.

'I take it you've noticed the gravity?'

He nodded, before realising how stupid this was when his helmet just stayed pointing straight ahead. 'Yeah, noticed it on the ship. Any thoughts as to what's causing it?'

'I was hoping you might have some ideas. I don't see how it could be occurring naturally. With every step we take, we should be flying fifty meters into the sky, but we're not. As far as I can tell, this is more or less Earth gravity.'

'Could it be some kind of magnetic field?' Floyd asked, postulating wildly.

'I don't see how. We'd need to be made of metal for one thing. I just can't even begin to imagine what forces are at work here to create a gravity field this strong in such a small object.'

'A black hole could.'

'A black hole would need to be inside the asteroid and in perfect equilibrium, exerting just enough force to create comparable gravity to Earth, without sucking the asteroid in. Same goes for a super tiny neutron star.'

'That does sound a little far-fetched,' Floyd admitted.

'Call it something like a thousand trillion to one against.'

Floyd stopped and took a few drops of water from the suit's built in feeder straw.

'It's getting rockier,' he said, gesturing toward the surrounding terrain. The largely flat plain was coming to an end, jagged rocks jutting out of the ground. 'We'll soon have some climbing to do.'

Luana mumbled an affirmative, not sounding too thrilled at the prospect.

Soon, they were stumbling through rocky foothills, sliding every so often on loose stones. Above, crags overhung them, looking menacing, like cloaked figures about to swoop down and scoop them up.

'What if it was artificial?' Floyd asked.

'What if what was artificial?'

'The black hole. What if somebody made it?'

'Made it? Have you any idea of the quantum engineering that would be involved in something like that? Hell, I don't recall anyone even theorizing about trying something like that, to produce a stable gravitational field.'

'But it's not impossible, is it? Theoretically, it could be done, right?'

'I guess so, but it's way beyond anything we're currently capable of. Which brings us back to this.' She stopped momentarily to stamp one foot on the ground, dust flying up around it and dropping straight back down. 'This being some kind of naturally occurring phenomenon.'

So, on and on they went, mildly bickering as they walked, stumbled, climbed and slid.

'What do you think we're going to find?' Luana asked, hoping the answer wouldn't have anything to do with artificial black holes.

'I don't know, some kind of covert defence operation? Maybe an unmanned station with an automated defence system.'

'Which would mean no food.'

'So much for looking on the bright side,' he grinned, and gave her a friendly jab in the arm.

'At this point I couldn't even tell you which direction to look for the bright side.'

'Or...' Floyd said, leaving the word hanging there like a smelly, unwanted sock.

'Or?' Luana asked, knowing she would regret the answer.

'Or it could be a manned, secret black hole research station.'

She wasn't sure that extreme eye rolling would come across in their current situation, so she repeatedly banged her helmet with both fists.

'Okay, I'm not feeling we're both on board with the whole artificial black hole scenario.'

'Oh, you think?' shouted Luana.

As they scrambled down an embankment, Floyd thought it best not to pursue his new pet theory, and decided to leave it for now. Maybe they could revisit it later, when he didn't feel his life was in such imminent peril.

Another hour went by and they trudged on. Floyd's best calculation estimated they had passed the fifteen kilometre mark some time earlier. A niggling little voice in the back of his mind was beginning to wonder whether he had made a dreadful mistake, and that they were heading off into an inhospitable desert more deadly than any that had ever existed on Earth.

They were stumbling through a small valley, with rocks high on either side. There were cracks in the ground and surrounding rocks. Some of these weren't just cracks, but great fissures, which could swallow one of them easily. Floyd didn't know how far down these cracks went, and really didn't want to find out. He had a feeling it would be a long way down to the centre of the asteroid (and the black hole that might be there, although he kept that little thought to himself).

'Cheeseburger or hot dog,' Luana said suddenly. He realised that they had not exchanged a word for over half an hour. She sounded tired and perhaps a little dejected.

'Hmm? Oh, er... Cheeseburger. You?'

'Hot dog.'

On and on and on it went, every footstep taking them further away from the crashed lifepod, but hopefully closer to the elusive power source.

'You can't eat a carbonara without parmesan,' Luana said, truly dismayed. 'That's just wrong. But you have olive oil, right?'

'Nope. Just as nature intended it.'

'I can't believe I let you touch me with those fingers.'

'I didn't hear you moaning at the time. Oh, wait a minute; I think I did...'

'Can it, flyboy. For the carbonara comment alone, you deserve to be...'

As they rounded the next rock, they were confronted by six figures, each holding a high-powered assault laser rifle.

'...shot,' Luana finished as she stared at the six spacesuited figures.

As if the large and extremely destructive weapons weren't intimidating enough, their visors were darkened and their suits gunmetal grey. Covering this were panels of black armour, strong enough to deflect glancing laser blasts, or small projectile weapons.

Floyd and Luana slowly raised their hands in time honoured fashion. One of the figures gestured with the stubby barrel of his laser toward a small gully off to one side. The man gestured again, and from the body language, he was becoming quite insistent.

'It's a wild guess,' Floyd said in a jovial tone, totally inappropriate to the occasion, 'but I think he wants us to go that way.'

A shove from one of the other figures confirmed this, not that Floyd was in any doubt.

'Where do you think they're taking us?' Luana asked as she stumbled through uneven rocks covering what passed for a path.

'I don't know, but we're still alive, which I take as being a good sign.'

'I don't recognize the suits. They could be private contractors. Or maybe—'

The shove from the gun caught her at the wrong moment, and Luana stumbled, falling forward. Floyd reached for her but was too late as she went crashing to the ground. The butt of one of the rifles found his midriff and Floyd doubled over, the wind knocked from him.

'No!' Luana shouted.

Floyd looked up to see the barrel of a rifle pressed hard against his visor, the hard metal scratching its surface.

A second later, a breathless Luana was up and standing between Floyd and the man holding the gun. A moment elapsed, where he was fairly sure that the man was pondering whether or not to kill him where he stood. But then the rifle was lowered and the two of them were pushed forward again to stumble through the uneven track.

Right around the next corner, the path widened out into an open area, where the slopes were shallower. They were entering a crater, Floyd realised. Something had impacted here countless eons ago, blasting out a bowl fifty meters wide. However, it was not the crater that garnered his attention, but the enormous dust-crawler that sat at its centre. It was more like an open backed truck with half a dozen huge wheels on a side, each one taller than he was. The drivers' cabin was a pressurized unit, the rear dominated by a formidable crane and open to space.

Floyd and Luana felt rifle barrels in their backs again and they were pushed forward toward the vehicle. Two of the figures made for the drivers' cabin, while the other four were to ride in the back with their two captives.

'Not exactly a small-scale operation, is it?' Floyd mumbled out of one corner of his mouth. For a moment he caught sight of Luana's face, and she gave him a look that somehow managed to convey that the men could probably hear them and to keep quiet. In return, he winked at her.

They were quickly loaded onto an elevator. There was a ladder, but the vehicle was so large, it was clearly deemed a necessity. Once loaded and the captives secured, the crawler silently moved off.

The mysterious figures had still not spoken a single word to them, either unable or – to Floyd, most likely – unwilling to talk. These were clearly the foot soldiers, the grunts required to do the dirty work. That dirty work did not seem to include execution on sight. They could only guess where they were being taken, but Floyd was pretty damned sure it was the power source they had been seeking.

Something told Floyd that this would not end well.

The Arcadia Series

— Twenty-Two —

The journey was slow and plodding, the dust-crawler unable to achieve a much better speed than Floyd and Luana had managed on foot. However, not having to concentrate on walking, for fear of stumbling into hidden crevasses or just slipping and breaking an ankle, the ride gave them a chance to appreciate the scenery. Unfortunately, this seemed to be the blandest and most monotonous scenery he had ever seen. And he had taken an air car from Albuquerque to Farmington, so he knew what bland looked like.

They didn't have to wait long though, which was the only saving grace on the small asteroid. No journey would ever take *that* long. After twenty minutes, the crawler came to a halt, dust swirling around it and quickly falling to the ground again like rain. The gravity may have been equivalent to Earth's, but there was barely a whisper of an atmosphere to suspend the tiny particles.

Floyd tried to look around to see where they were, earning himself a clanging whack on his helmet. He cursed whoever was responsible silently. When the time came, he was looking forward to dishing out some payback.

They didn't have long to wait as, with his head still ringing, Floyd finally got to see where they were.

The dust-crawler sat at the foot of a mountain. At least, it was the nearest thing that might qualify as such on 349 Dembowska. It was a rocky mound, possibly a hundred meters high and three times as much wide. The mountain may have been unimpressive by the standards of Earth or Mars, but what did command their attention was a huge double door set into its base. It must have been twenty meters wide and fifteen high.

'So much for a small prospecting operation,' Floyd said.

'This is no mining operation,' Luana replied.

They felt a rumble of heavy machinery beneath their feet and as they watched, the double doors cracked apart and began to slide open, a shaft of glaring white light illuminating the track ahead. The glare from within was initially dazzling, but once it had subsided, they could make out the details of a large hangar.

At some silent signal, the huge crawler lumbered toward the hangar. Floyd and Luana looked around them as they were taken inside. It felt like the cavern was swallowing them, taking them into its giant, dazzling maw. There was too much to take in with a single glance. Floyd had an impression of piled up storage containers, machinery, forklifts and small tractors, pipes, gantries and that piercing, pain-inducing light.

The crawler came to a halt and began to turn, and Floyd realised they were on a turntable, rotating the crawler so it could drive straight out of the hangar the next time it was deployed. The double doors slowly trundled back into place and locked together with a slight bump transmitted through the floor and the bulk of the crawler.

Once the vehicle had stopped rotating, they were finally released and lowered to the ground on the elevator, along with their four guards. Floyd could hear a whooshing sound. The fact that he could hear anything at all other than his own breathing felt like a novelty.

Through his helmet, he heard the muffled words of a public address system, echoing in the hollow chamber.

'Repressurization complete. Hangar internal Absolute Air Pressure ten-point-nine. Ambient temperature: five degrees Celsius. Conditions safe for unprotected human operations.'

A pulsing red light on the wall changed to green, the harsh rattle of a klaxon cutting through the freshly pumped air, echoing around the chamber. The six mysterious figures became less mysterious as they each unclipped their helmets and stowed them on a rack. Four men and two women eyed them mistrustfully, waiting and perhaps hoping they would try something. At least two ensured they kept their weapons trained on the two captives at all times.

Eden's Gate

Luana and Floyd followed their lead and removed their own helmets, but held onto them for now. There was no telling when they might be needing them again.

Floyd inhaled a deep breath of cold, metallic-tasting air. Just a couple of minutes earlier, the hangar had been open to the frigid vacuum of space, and it would clearly take time to heat up.

'Smells of engine oil,' Luana said, taking her own initial breaths. 'Quite an operation you have here.'

One of the people, a grizzled man with military haircut and eyes like chipped granite, opened the nearest doorway and gestured for them to go forwards.

'This way. Move.'

This didn't seem the time to argue, and Floyd was quite sure that this man was just a grunt, a foot soldier with little authority. His swagger may have impressed the other five, but he was clearly just a loud noise in a small room. There would be little point wasting time negotiating with him when, hopefully, they were being taken to see his superior.

'Not very friendly, are they?' Floyd muttered to Luana.

'I'll definitely be taking this up with the management.'

'Keep moving and cut the chatter,' the soldier barked, clearly not amused by the banter.

A few minutes later, they emerged into a room ten meters square. The walls were native rock, smooth-hewn by laser cutters. The ceiling was low at the edges, but curved to form a shallow dome, strengthening it against the weight of millions of tonnes of rock above them.

There was a welcoming party, of course. Eight marines, as well as the six that had accompanied them from the hangar. There were also two other men, who appeared to be senior officers. One was tall, his grey hair speckled with white and probably staring sixty in the face. The other was younger, still clearly a soldier and with boyish good looks that seemed to set him apart from most of the others. Luana would wager he had broken more than a few hearts during his short career.

But it was not the younger, more amiable looking man who spoke first. The white-haired man stepped forward.

'You are in a restricted area,' he said in a broad, Texan drawl. 'Who are you, who do you work for and what are you doing here?'

Luana glanced nervously at Floyd before answering. 'I am Third Lieutenant Luana Lee, the only surviving officer of the Aurora disaster. And this is—'

'Ben Floyd, special investigator with Sub Rosa Security, on special assignment on behalf of EarthPol. And you are?'

'Colonel Rye Calvert, Earth Defence Force. This is Lieutenant Calvin Casey.' He nodded to the younger man. 'You say you were on the Aurora?'

'We were,' Luana said quickly, hoping this dialogue was improving their chances of surviving the rest of the day. 'There was a terrorist attack. Ours was the only lifepod to make it off before the ship was destroyed.'

'And you entered a restricted zone because…?'

And with that, Floyd was convinced he had heard the stupidest question of the day, but Luana answered without so much as a heartbeat.

'There was a collision when we were escaping from the Aurora. We lost most of our food reserves. The ship's sensors found a power source on 349 Dembowska, so this was our only possibility of survival.'

Calvert nodded slowly as he digested this. He was clearly a man who liked to have all the information available before acting. With a final nod, he turned to speak with Casey.

The conversation was little more than a whisper, and Floyd couldn't quite catch what was being said, but things seemed to be going well; better than he had expected, considering this colonel had tried to blow them out of existence not so long ago.

Calvert turned back to face them, his expression unfathomable.

'I'm sorry, Lieutenant Lee, Mr. Floyd. My orders are specific and with no exceptions. Any unauthorized ships entering the ten-thousand-kilometre exclusion zone are to be shot down. Survivors are to be executed.'

'What?' Floyd spluttered. 'We're civilians. Non-combatants.' He wasn't sure who this man might be combatting but it was the best he could come up with.

'That's coldblooded murder,' Luana fumed. She didn't look the least bit afraid. No, she was way beyond fear, Floyd could see. She was in a barely suppressed fury.

'Lieutenant Casey, prepare an air strike to ensure no others make it off the enemy ship.'

'It's not an enemy ship,' Luana spat. 'It's a lifepod.'

'You're murdering innocent men, women and children,' Floyd said, earning himself a brief look from Luana.

Calvert also looked at him for a moment, his steel-eyed squint revealing nothing, but the glance itself told Floyd enough.

'Prepare your weapons,' Calvert said, addressing the eight heavily armed marines, and the other six pushed him and Luana back against the wall. 'Chest shots only, on my order and not before.'

'You're carrying out illegal orders, Calvert,' Floyd said. 'You let that air strike go ahead and you'll be known on every inhabited planet in the Solar System as the butcher of innocent children.'

'I know you don't want to do this,' Luana said.

Calvert's face twitched. It wasn't much, but it was there. 'Assume firing positions.'

The eight marines, five men and three women, formed a semicircle around them, raising high-powered laser rifles, barrels pointed directly at their hearts.

'Illegal massacres like this are never kept quiet,' Floyd said. 'News of this will get out. You will be remembered as the one responsible.'

Eden's Gate

'Take aim.' They already had, but Calvert's mind was racing through a thousand different scenarios at once and he hadn't noticed.

'Do you have children, Colonel?' Luana pressed. 'Grandchildren? Do you want them to remember you this way? As a butcher? As a murderer?'

'Be quiet!'

'Do you? They will if you do this.'

Calvert raised his hand, ready to bring it down again with the order to fire. It stayed there, quivering in the air as conflicting thoughts and emotions churned in the man's head. He was an officer, a lifelong adherent to order and the strict chain of command. Orders were to be followed without question. That was why the chain of command existed, as it always had. Follow orders because those in more senior positions knew better and took the responsibility.

But.

But there was more than one type of courage in the military. Physical courage was easy, especially when all those around you were in the same position. But moral courage was far more difficult. It meant possibly defying orders to "do the right thing". The right thing. It's easy to issue a blanket command to execute any who stray into the exclusion zone. Far more difficult to carry them out and murder innocents.

The hand was slowly lowered. 'Stand down,' Calvert muttered, almost in a whisper.

'Say again, sir?' Casey said, not sure he had heard his superior officer correctly.

'You heard me. I said stand down. Belay the order for an air strike.'

Floyd and Luana both sagged as the tension swept from them.

Calvert strode toward the door and shouted over his shoulder: 'Find some clothes for our guests and have them brought to my office.'

Floyd turned to Luana and grinned. 'You see? I told you it'd all be fine.'

— Twenty-Three —

A pair of extremely confused but relieved guards escorted Floyd and Luana from the would-be execution chamber to guest quarters. Considering what had just happened – or nearly happened – Floyd guessed they didn't have too many guests at the facility.

One of the guards used his key card to open the door to the quarters and gestured for them to enter. It made a refreshing change for this to be accomplished without having a gun shoved into their backs.

'Wait here,' he said gruffly as he went to lock the door again.

'Oh, I thought we'd go for a nice walk,' Floyd shouted as the door slid closed. 'You know, stretch our legs for a bit!'

'That's it, Floyd, you go and really ingratiate yourself. Our host could change his mind, you know.'

He snorted. 'Well, I'm kind of getting tired of being led around like a prize bull.'

'Prize bulls are led around just before they're slaughtered, aren't they?'

'There you go,' Floyd grumbled, 'bringing logic into the argument again. It takes all the fun out of it.'

The quarters were spartan at best, with one bunkbed for them. Presumably sexual relations were discouraged on the base.

There was a chime and Luana sighed, happy that Floyd had been cut off. He was just starting to get into full flow. She pressed the intercom button on the wall.

'Yes?'

The door slid open and a guard handed her two sets of clothing. 'These should be close to your sizes, Mr. and Mrs....'

'Oh, we're not married,' Floyd said.

'And not likely to be at this rate,' she finished for him.

The guard looked a little confused, but continued regardless.

'If you could be ready in ten minutes, I'll return to take you to Colonel Calvert's office.'

'No problem, and thanks,' she said with a smile. The poor guard seemed quite nonplussed by their strange new guests.

The clothes, it turned out, were standard charcoal grey sweats and pants, and hefty boots. Not the height of

Eden's Gate

Paris fashions, but after a day cocooned in their spacesuits, they weren't about to complain.

They were escorted to Calvert's office, bedecked in their new uniforms which almost, but not quite, fitted. The guard pressed the intercom button and a second later, they heard the soft, resonant voice of Calvert.

'Enter.'

The door swished aside and they walked in, hoping to finally get some answers. Calvert sat behind a simple office desk, focused on a picture he held in his hard, weathered hands.

'Please sit down, Ms. Lee, Mr. Floyd.' He gestured to the pair of guards. 'Wait outside.'

They immediately did as instructed and disappeared, the door sliding shut behind them.

Luana took one of the two seats, but Floyd wasn't ready to sit down just yet.

'What the hell is going on here, Colonel?' he fumed. 'Threatening civilians?'

Calvert placed the picture back on the desk in a very careful, almost tender way. Luana could see a woman, perhaps around thirty years old, and three young children that looked as if they'd be an unruly handful at the best of times.

'Please, sit down,' Calvert gestured for Floyd to take the vacant seat.

Still, he remained standing. As Luana's fury had subsided since the stand-off, Floyd's had merely increased. At this point he felt ready to explode and hit someone. Although even he would concede that this would probably be a bad idea. So, he stood. That would be his act of defiance.

'Look,' Calvert said with a weary sigh, 'I could get the guards back in here and they could make you sit down, if that's what you wish?'

On balance, Floyd reasoned that this course was best avoided, so petulantly plonked himself down, like a teenager about to get a parental lecture.

Once his guests were seated, Calvert could continue.

'I've sent a pair of dust-hoppers out to retrieve the rest of your party. How many are there?'

Floyd suddenly felt uncomfortable, some of his bravado evaporating. 'Six. Three men and three women.'

'You mentioned children,' Calvert queried, the piercing squint returning.

'Ah, yeah,' said Floyd. 'That was a lie. You were going to shoot us; I needed a bargaining chip. My bad. But it worked.'

Calvert stared at him for a full, uncomfortable ten seconds, before harrumphing and shaking his head. 'Nicely played. The news is not good, I'm afraid. You see, we are monitored here constantly, just to ensure that such an incident as occurred earlier does not happen. Or at least, if it does, it is quickly dealt with. I attempted to contact our command headquarters on Ceres a few minutes ago. There was no response.'

'Meaning?' asked Floyd.

'Meaning that the assumption will be that the base and its staff have been compromised. A Black Star assault force will be leaving Ceres as we speak, to neutralize the problem.'

'They're coming to kill the Aurora survivors anyway?' Luana said, appalled.

'Talk about out of the frying pan,' Floyd murmured.

'Not quite. At least, not just you. Myself, my officers and the forty or so men and women under my command will be categorized as a renegade force as well.'

'What?' Luana almost shouted. 'They're going to come here and kill all of you as well? But why? Because you showed some compassion? Because you showed you are a human being?'

Calvert shrugged. 'They will be here within three days. Black Star cruisers are fast. Unlike the Aurora or your lifepod, they use a PLT Drive.'

'A what drive?' Floyd asked.

'A Photonic Laser Thrust system,' Luana explained with a wave of the hand. 'Very fast, very efficient. Very expensive.'

'Money isn't exactly an obstacle to these people,' Calvert said.

'Wait a minute,' Floyd said, his anger now turned to confusion. 'I still don't get it. What's so special about this asteroid that they'd kill absolutely everyone?'

'Some secrets are meant to remain secret.'

'What secret? What's so important here?'

Calvert said nothing for several seconds as he considered things. He'd broken the rules already, and was now facing a death sentence. A penalty not just for himself, but for everyone under his command. He'd betrayed them. They would die because of his weakness; because of his humanity. Floyd had spoken of illegal orders, and he was probably right. Killing civilians who had landed here in desperation had to be illegal. Calvert was beginning to wonder whether the Earth Defence Force was the same organization he had joined forty years before. Its goals certainly seemed to have diverged from his own in the interim. There was no way he would have been asked to murder civilians when he joined, just to protect…

Calvert stood abruptly. 'Lieutenant Lee, Mr. Floyd, I think it's time I showed you something. This is the reason we're all going to be executed in three days. Would you follow me, please?'

He walked to the door, which swished open. Floyd and Luana stared at each other, both giving a slight "search me" shrug.

'Only I have to warn you,' Calvert said, 'it's probably not what you're expecting.'

— Twenty-Four —

Blade was not the most feminine of names, but Katherine Blaize was not the most feminine of lieutenant commanders. The nickname had originally just been a bastardization of her surname, but she had soon proven that it far more accurately described her as a person, and her preferred weapon of choice.

At one point eight meters, she was tall for a human female, but not for a woman born within the low gravity of Mars. In her jet-black uniform she looked slim, but the uniform hid the rangy muscles beneath. She wore her dark hair shoulder length. It was, to many, the only feminine thing about her.

She had very quickly risen through the ranks. Or, more accurately, carved her way through the ranks to establish herself as a brutal soldier who would do whatever was needed to complete her mission. Personal relationships, family and friends were of secondary importance. All that mattered was the mission. All that mattered was to serve Earth, at absolutely any cost.

For her to be recruited by the Black Star Corps was as inevitable as the setting Sun, but her utter devotion to the corps had gone far beyond what had been expected, or even hoped for.

Lieutenant Commander Katherine Blaize was a born killer, and a born leader. What her superiors did not realise was the level of hatred she had harboured toward Colonel Rye Calvert, ever since he had been assigned control of 349 Dembowska. That should have been her posting. From that small, innocuous little asteroid, she could have built her own special force, established her own power base and demonstrated that she had the skills, the drive and tenacity to run the entire Black Star operation.

It should have been hers.

The drone was elusive, as wily as they came. The Nemesis had pursued it though asteroid fields and mountain ranges, and finally its quarry was in sight, ducking and weaving through the uneven terrain of Zadeni crater.

'Strafe the crater rim,' Blade ordered. 'Now we have him, I don't want the little bastard getting away.'

Eden's Gate

As it crested the rim, the Nemesis's forward batteries opened fire, the line of low mountains erupting in dust.

'Keep firing!' Blade shouted as she scanned the crater. The drone was here; she knew it. 'Bring us around, and give Thrud some attention.'

A bank of lasers broke off from their pounding of the hills at the massive crater's rim, and instead began to pummel Thrud, a smaller crater within the great bowl of Zadeni.

'There it is!' she shouted, and leapt from her seat to point at the tiny silver drone as it broke cover. 'Concentrate all fire—'

'Commander,' a voice from behind cut in. 'Incoming communication from Black Star Command.'

'Not now, damn you,' Blade spat, tearing her eyes from her prey to glare at her communications officer.

'But Commander, this is priority one.'

Blade looked back at the screen in time to see the little drone scurry between twin laser beams and zip over Zadeni's crest and hurtle toward the next crater on the heavily pitted surface of Ceres.

'Stay with him,' she ordered as she quickly scanned the message from Black Star Command: "Training mission aborted. Return to Occator Base immediately".

'Well ain't that just peachy,' Blade cursed as she watched the drone disappear into Thrud crater. 'We're aborting the exercise,' she sighed. All around her, she saw the shoulders of the bridge crew sag. Chasing drones around the largest asteroid in the Solar System was not exactly hunting renegades on Mars or insurgents on Ganymede, but it was a hell of a lot more interesting than languishing is Occator Base's rec room or mess hall.

'Say again?' her X-O said, clearly hoping that this was some kind of mistake.

'I said cease firing and prepare to bring us about. And start preparing the ship for offensive operations.'

'What's happening then, Commander?'

'Beats me, but if they're pulling us off this exercise just because the admiral's cat is stuck up a tree, then I'm going to tear the base apart until I find the bastard. Then I'll rip his head off, scoop out his brain and use his skull as a soup dish.'

This at least earned her a few smirks from the bridge crew.

The Black Star cruiser, Nemesis, swung her bow around with considerable agility, considering the size of the vessel. She was a magnificent craft, packed with laser emplacements, assault craft, fighters, landing craft, missiles and mines. There were only three of her kind in existence, and all three served the Black Star Force. Their purpose was to do the dirty work that other branches of the Earth military shied away from because they were too difficult, too dangerous or too politically sensitive. The Black Star Force had no such qualms, and the Avenger class heavy cruisers were the force's iron fist, ready to obliterate whoever or whatever threatened Earth's security.

Blade did not need to give specific orders to the bridge crew. She had trained them well enough to know what to do. The helmsman brought the main engines up to full power and the ship surged forward, the energy of five photonic laser thrust engines quickly bringing the ship up to a full half a gravity of acceleration.

It would not take long to cover the twelve hundred kilometres to Occator Base.

'What the hell are you doing, Viktor?' Blade shouted the instant the door to Viktor Barkov's office slid aside. She strode in, full of magnificent fury and a force of personality that few could withstand.

Fortunately, Barkov was among those few. He held up a hand, but did not look up from his desk.

Blade stood there, her heart pounding within her chest. She counted one, two, three, four.

'We were in the middle of—'

He held up his hand again, and if it were possible, made the gesture slightly more forceful. So Blade waited, and counted again. One, two, three, four, five.

'God damn it, Viktor!'

'You never could keep your big, fat mouth shut for more than five seconds, could you Katherine?'

She did not reply, merely fumed silently.

'You are wondering why I aborted your training mission early? And dragged you all the way back here? Well, there has been a worrying development at Shadow Base, Dembowska.'

She finally stopped fuming, her anger dissipating as reason pushed its way through. 'What kind of development?

That was better. He could reason with her now. 'Shadow Base has been compromised. A ship landed there nine hours ago, under the auspices of it being a humanitarian emergency. Colonel Calvert sent a peculiar message an hour ago, stating that he had not eliminated the intruders immediately. In fact, it seems he has given them refuge.'

Blade was stunned. This was just inconceivable. Calvert was a trained soldier, just as she was. He knew better than anyone, the standing orders that existed – and the inevitable response that would come from Black Star Command.

'I see you appreciate the significance of this development, Lieutenant Commander.'

'I do, sir,' she replied, although her mind was clearly going through every possible scenario. It did not matter whether this was a genuine humanitarian emergency. That was not for her or Calvert or anyone else in the Black Star Force to worry about. What *was* their concern was the response, and any deviation could have only one outcome.

She had wanted the Shadow Base command for herself, and she would probably now get it. She had wanted it, but not like this.

'I've got my crew preparing the ship already,' Blade said.

'You knew about this?'

'You don't abort one of my exercises without a damned good reason. I knew *something* was happening.'

Barkov laughed, but it faded quickly, his face once again becoming serious. 'You are going to have to kill Colonel Calvert.'

'I know,' she shot back. 'Calvert is probably dead already, and if not, then he's compromised. Either way, he and his platoon will be dead in three days. He knew that would happen.'

'Yes, yes, but he is your friend, is he not?'

'That doesn't make any goddamned difference.'

'You're sure? The Vengeance is on a covert exercise on Deimos, and the Retribution is undergoing maintenance, but I could reassign the Retribution's captain to take command of the Nemesis.'

'No. I'll be commanding the Nemesis, and I'll be the one to kill Rye Calvert. Is there anything else?'

Barkov stared into her eyes, looking for something, some sign of regret, some sign of humanity, but there was nothing. Katherine Blaize was just a cold, merciless killing machine. That was how she had been designed, and nothing would ever change that. All he knew was that when it came to it, when she killed Calvert, it would be a swift death. She was many things, but had never been a cruel woman.

'Then I won't keep you any longer. Good hunting, Lieutenant Commander.'

She nodded curtly and walked out of the office. Barkov could be sure of one thing: in just three days, this incident will have been taken care of and an exceptionally good officer would be dead.

Forty minutes later, the Nemesis powered up its five immense photonic light thrust engines and set a course for 349 Dembowska.

— Twenty-Five —

Calvert led them through corridor after corridor, the two guards trailing behind, seeming reluctant to be in this part of the base and only there because they absolutely had to be. Even Calvert himself seemed abnormally tense coming down here into the depths of the complex.

The base was huge, far larger than Floyd had expected, judging by its outside appearance. Down they went, further and further, deeper and deeper. Were they close to the asteroid's centre, he wondered? No, the asteroid was around a hundred kilometres thick at this point, and they had probably penetrated no more than a couple of hundred meters.

'I'm telling you,' Floyd muttered to Luana. 'They've got a black hole down here.'

She rolled her eyes, and now with her space helmet gone, he was treated to the full, unrestrained spectacle. 'Floyd, let's get one thing straight, can we? It-is-not-a-black-hole. I don't know what *is* creating this gravitational field, but it is definitely not – repeat – *not* a black hole. Understand?'

'Completely.'

'Good. Finally.'

'But I still think it could be.'

He heard a noise from her that sounded distinctly like the threatening growl of a jaguar.

After a final flight of steps, they found themselves in another corridor. It was indistinguishable from a dozen or more similar passages, but Calvert slowed, and spoke to them for the first time since they had left his office, several minutes before.

'This is the final tunnel,' he said, his voice reverential, as if this unremarkable corridor were particularly special.

At the far end was a doorway, again, just like dozens of others. When they reached it, Calvert turned.

'Are you ready?' he asked.

Floyd and Luana shrugged, both beginning to think that the colonel's entire performance was a little melodramatic.

'I think,' said Floyd, 'that after all we've been through, what with spaceship collisions, missile attacks, crashes and execution squads, we're pretty much ready for anything.'

Calvert smirked with a mirthless grunt. 'We'll see.'

He raised his hand and keyed in the code that would unlock the doors. An instant later, they slid aside.

Eden's Gate

What they saw on the other side was... not what they had been expecting. Floyd stared in open-mouthed wonderment. It was a cavern. A vast, irregular cavern. Its scale was extraordinary, even by the standards of most caverns on Earth. All around them, rocks lay strewn, lining a pathway. Colours rippled over the rough terrain in aquamarine blue, vivid purple, soft mauve, vibrant pink and every shade in-between. It flickered and flowed over the rocks, over the vast cavern walls.

But far off, on the other side of the great edifice, was the source of this incredible swirl of coloured patterns. Like the most glorious sunset that ever graced the Earth, viewed through the most magnificent kaleidoscope ever made, it shone with an epic incandescence that mesmerized the five onlookers. Colours flickered on its surface, swirling in a maelstrom of light, enclosed in a cocoon of eons old stone. Fingers of granite seemed to hold the sphere of light aloft, as if proffering it to a disinterested god.

Floyd stumbled forward and stopped. It was all he could do not to drop to his knees before this magnificent thing. And then an even more astonishing and terrifying realisation hit him.

The stones that held this miracle aloft were not naturally occurring, but had been hewn by hand.

'What is it?' he heard Luana whisper next to him, her voice full of wonder and joy.

'We don't know,' Calvert said. 'I don't think anyone knows, really.'

'It's so beautiful,' she said, completely transfixed by the swarm of colours that danced over its surface.

Floyd tried to tear his eyes from the object, but could do so only for a second, as if they were physically linked to it, tethered in some invisible, impossible way.

He made an effort to turn his body, and his head reluctantly followed, eyes breaking contact with whatever it was. A sun? No, it was bright, but not that bright. He blinked repeatedly, the after image burned onto his retina, but not indelibly. All manner of words flashed through his mind: nova, anomaly, object, phenomenon, thing, whatchamacallit, doohickey, thingamajig. Nothing, not even whatchamacallit, seemed to do it justice, or managed to encapsulate all it meant or how it made him feel.

Now his eye contact had been broken, even if only briefly, he could get some idea of his surroundings. The cavern was huge, like being inside one of the great cathedrals on Earth. It seemed to be separated into two halves, with an uneven, rocky causeway leading up to the thingy. He had to come up with a placeholder noun better than "thingy". He held a hand up to protect his eyes from the glare, shielding them so he could study the surrounding stonework more easily. He felt his stomach churn and a wave of dizziness overwhelm him for an instant as the incredible ramifications of this discovery embedded themselves in his brain.

As his eyes roamed over the stonework, he realised he had seen something like this before. It was a long time ago, when he was still a child. He had stood and stared in wonder then as well. His parents had taken him on a little trip, and for some reason they had ended up at Saint Paul's Cathedral in Minnesota, of all places. But it was within this great building that he had stared in mute awe at the Rose Window, a perfectly round image of exquisite beauty. Yes, this place reminded him of that, like being inside a cathedral. This giant edifice was tens of millions of kilometres away from that place, yet the feeling of familiarity was still there.

That was the realisation that swirled in his mind and almost caused him to topple over.

This place had been constructed. Someone in the distant past had come to this lonely asteroid, dug deep beneath its surface, and built this.

'Calvert,' he said quietly, 'what do you call this thing?'

'Officially, we don't call it anything because officially it doesn't exist. Unofficially, it's designated the 349 Dembowska Anomaly One. Unofficially, we unofficially call it the anomaly, and leave it at that.'

Luana slowly edged toward it.

'Careful, Ms. Lee,' Calvert warned.

'Oh, don't worry, I will be. And it's Luana.'

She moved a little closer, and Floyd followed close behind, ready to grab her in case some unseen alien force tried to snatch her away.

'It was discovered seven years ago by mining prospectors,' Calvert explained, not for an instant tearing his eyes away from the anomaly. 'The military immediately took control and that's the way the situation has remained ever since.'

Luana managed to drag her eyes away. 'Are you telling us there's been no scientific study? Nothing at all? In seven years?'

'That is correct.'

'What a wasted opportunity,' she said, shaking her head. 'What does the military think it is?'

'The military has no official opinion on 349 Dembowska Anomaly One.'

She snarled in frustration. Only the military could be this obtuse and narrow minded. Well, apart from most governments on Earth and in the rest of the Solar System.

'However,' Calvert said, holding up his hands to placate her. 'I do have my own opinions. I believe it could be a power source, an unlimited new form of energy.'

'What do you think it is, Luana?' Floyd asked.

She barely hesitated before replying. 'I think it's doorway – a doorway to somewhere else. Wait a minute.'

'What is it?' Floyd asked.

'I just thought of something. Colonel, you say this is a closely guarded secret?'

'That's right.'

'How closely?'

The question seemed to catch him off guard. 'Well, er… Absolutely top secret. I mean level-one, maximum security. No one else outside the Earth Defence Force Elite Command and senior levels of Earth government know anything.'

Eden's Gate

'But you haven't maintained the same staff here for seven years, have you? Crews rotate. People go back to Earth, right?'

'Listen,' Calvert said with a hint of indignant menace, 'my people are professionals. They're not—'

'They're professionals, but even professionals talk sometimes,' she said, ignoring his tone. 'Someone has a few drinks, tells their partner, a brother, a close friend. Stories start to circulate. Or maybe it's nothing to do with your troops. Maybe it was someone in government. Somehow, an agent from the Martian Independence Movement heard about this place.'

'That's a lot of supposition,' Calvert said, but the harshness had disappeared from his voice.

'That's what Kyle Paska was doing. He knew about this anomaly. That was the reason the Aurora was destroyed. That was why it happened precisely where it did.'

'To what end?' Calvert asked.

'I don't think we've thought this through completely, yet,' Floyd interjected.

'But—'

'We'll deal with that later,' he cut her off. 'Right now we need to focus on understanding whatever this is.'

Luana glanced back at the anomaly for a few seconds, its kaleidoscope colours dancing over her face. She looked back at Floyd and Calvert. 'Someone has to go through.'

The Arcadia Series

'Now hold on there,' Calvert said in a no-nonsense tone. 'We have no idea what this thing is. Anyone going through that would most likely die instantly.'

'Most likely?' she repeated. 'You mean no one's ever tried?'

'No, but you only have to look at the thing to see how much energy it's producing. You would be atomized the instant you touched it.'

'Not necessarily,' she persisted. 'Anyway, that's a risk I'm willing to take.'

'You?' said Floyd.

'Floyd, someone has to go. Just imagine the possibilities. Just imagine where I might end up. Who in their right mind would pass up a chance like that?'

'In case you hadn't noticed,' Calvert said irritably, 'I am still in command here. I will decide if someone is to go, and who that might be.'

'Fine, as long as you see sense and send me, I don't care. One thing is for sure: this anomaly isn't a weapon. It's an opportunity. And besides, if what you said earlier is correct, we're going to be executed in three days anyway. Better to die doing something worthwhile than at the hands of a firing squad.'

Calvert started to pace up and down, although there was minimal space to do this on the causeway. 'We should at least send a probe through first.'

'Colonel,' Luana pleaded, 'this is no time to send a robot. It has to be a human being.'

'Two,' Floyd said.

'What?' Calvert and Luana said in unison.

'It needs to be two human beings. Let's face it Luana, I'm hardly likely to let you go through there alone, am I? We both go. End of argument.'

Calvert turned on him. 'It's most certainly not the end—'

'Listen to reason, Colonel. If Luana is right, this thing is too important to leave to the military. It's our decision, our lives we're risking. And Luana's right: if we die today, or in three days' time, we're not exactly losing much.'

Calvert sighed. 'Go.'

'Sorry?' Luana said, not certain she had heard him properly.

'I said go. See what you can learn. God knows, the human race needs all the help it can get right now. Take whatever you need. Just remember: we have less than three days until a Black Star heavy cruiser arrives and wipes out everyone on this rock.'

Luana looked to Floyd with the biggest grin he'd ever seen on her face.

'We'd better go get ready,' he said, and reluctantly they dragged themselves away from the thingamajig.

— Twenty-Six —

Back at their rudimentary quarters, Floyd and Luana showered and ate something that almost tasted like food, but they were both so hungry, they didn't care about nuances of flavour and texture.

'Floyd, why did you cut me off back there in the cavern?' Luana asked as she finished her meal.

'Oh that. Well, I could see where your line of reasoning was going and I didn't want our new friend, the colonel, knowing absolutely everything. I wanted to…' He leant closer and whispered into her ear. 'I wanted to keep our asset in the lifepod a secret for now. I don't trust him that much.'

'I'm right though, aren't I? About what Paska was up to?'

'I'm not sure. What's your full theory?'

She grinned. 'I think I know what he was going to do. His plan was to destroy the Aurora, which succeeded, and take the only surviving lifepod to rendezvous with the—'

'Asset,' Floyd interrupted.

'Right, the "asset".' She made quote bunnies with her fingers.

'That much we'd pretty much already figured,' Floyd said. 'You have something more?'

'Yep. I think the MIM terrorists knew about this anomaly. Paska's job was to float the asset in quietly until it was in range, and then hold 349 Dembowska to ransom. This anomaly is, to the best of our knowledge, a priceless, one-of-a-kind artefact. Calvert could be right. Maybe it *is* a new limitless power source. Whatever it is, the MIM thought it was worth Martian independence to the Earth.'

'Give Mars its independence or we blow up your shiny anomaly?'

'Exactly. It would depend on which the Earth government thought was more valuable: holding onto Mars or this new anomaly.'

'I'll be damned,' he said quietly as he thought the matter through.'

Luana slouched back in her chair. This puzzle had been consuming her for weeks, and she was certain she had finally cracked it. Everything fitted. It was actually a very good plan, except, as Max Landry of all people had pointed out, there were too many links in the chain – too many points where something could go wrong.

'Are you sure you don't want to change your mind?' Floyd asked.

'A little late now, I've already eaten.'

'I didn't mean menu options! I mean—'

'I know what you meant. And no, I haven't changed my mind about that either. This is an opportunity to do something no one has ever done before. Something that no one has had the chance to do. It's why I went out into space to begin with. I wanted to be an explorer.'

'Strange new worlds and civilizations? Or however it was supposed to go.'

'Close enough,' Luana grinned. 'Okay, time to suit up again,'

Despite the fact that they had already decided to walk into an immeasurably powerful energy field, even Luana baulked at the idea of going completely unprotected. They would be borrowing a pair of spacesuits from the base. These were broadly similar to the ones carried on the lifepod, but came with a few added extras like supplemental sensors, food and water tubes, lightweight ablative and reactive armour, cherry bombs and sidearms.

They elected not to bother with the cherry bombs. But they would keep the hand lasers – just in case.

They checked the seals on each other's suits. There had never been a better substitute for a last-minute visual inspection. Despite the armour, Floyd reckoned Luana's suit went in and out in all the right places. He wasn't quite so thrilled to have his own anatomy open to such scrutiny.

Aside from the helmets, they were ready.

'Any idea what's going to happen?' Floyd asked.

'Ideas? Plenty. But – and it's an enormous big but – what I think is that the anomaly is a doorway to another place. Or possibly to another time. Maybe our Solar System isn't quite as isolated as we thought.'

'So we could be about to meet—'

The door pinged, and Luana opened it immediately.

'Ah, Lieutenant Casey,' Luana said. 'Come to escort us?'

Casey smiled, not entirely sure what the protocol was for this situation. 'Aye, Ma'am. Colonel Calvert is already down there. He wanted to make sure you didn't get lost.'

She looked left and right at the guards that flanked the door. 'I doubt we'd get too far, Lieutenant, do you?'

'I er… I guess not Ma'am. Shall we?'

They began to follow the lieutenant down the hall but were brought up short by the sound of a familiar voice.

'Hey you guys!' Dane Jefferson yelled from five meters behind them, just emerging from a side door. 'Wait up.'

Luana turned and ran back to him. 'Dane, when did you get here?'

Floyd took a peek into Dane's quarters – just in time to see Suzy emerge from the shower cubicle, wearing a towel that almost covered the very tops of her thighs. It was immediately clear that the showgirl and the geek had become a lot closer than just lifepod buddies.

'Hey Suzy,' he said with a wave, feeling a little self-conscious as he tried desperately not to ogle the half-naked woman.

'Hiya Floyd,' she said with a big grin, seeming not to care in the least that all she wore was a towel that was held aloft by a tucked in corner and some will power, and not much else.

'We got here a few minutes ago, so me and Suze jumped straight in the shower.'

Luana raised an eyebrow, only just now catching on. 'You mean you two are... er... friendly?'

'Yeah,' Dane said with a grin you could fly a shuttle through, 'like rabbits are friendly.'

Suzy stood there, mouth agape and looking scandalized, but one wink from Dane had her giggling like a starstruck schoolgirl. It was just so unlike the sad and withdrawn figure they had known on the lifepod.

'So much for a mining operation,' Dane said. 'This place is huge!'

'And battening down the hatches for a major assault,' Floyd said. 'We've got less than three days until hell flies in.'

'Yeah, you could cut the tension in this place with a baseball bat. I thought these guys seemed like an unfriendly bunch. Used some of my best gags. Nothing. Nada. Zilch. Not one so much as cracked a smile. Not even the hot one with the dimples. Are you two going back out there?'

Eden's Gate

'No, not exactly,' Luana said. 'They found something here. Something…'

'Something that'd take too long to explain,' Floyd finished for her when he saw the anxious look on Lieutenant Casey's face.

'Talk to Colonel Calvert,' Luana said, feeling the pressure of Floyd's hand on her shoulder. 'He's a little stiff but basically a good guy. Everyone else okay?'

'Sure. Conor and Tamara seem relieved to have some actual privacy for once. I get the feeling they're putting Suze and me to shame. Max has been telling all the soldiers he can get them state-of-the-art assault weapons for a good price, and Celeste has been explaining to him all the legal reasons why he shouldn't. So, all-in-all, nothing's changed really.'

'Excuse me,' Casey interjected, 'but I think we really should be going.

'He's right,' said Floyd. 'Time to boldly go. We'll see you when we get back.'

They finally managed to get away, much to the relief of Casey. He knew just how bad-tempered Colonel Rye Calvert could get if he was kept waiting.

'Good luck you guys,' Dane shouted after them.

'Thanks,' Luana shouted back. 'And give Suzy a kiss from us.'

'Will do.'

He did. It was a huge, slobbery kiss.

The Arcadia Series

The doors to the chamber slid aside and the trio stepped through. They knew this time what to expect, yet still the sight of the anomaly took their breath away as it hung there shimmering in magical brilliance as presumably it had for countless eons.

Calvert was already there, standing stiffly in an 'at ease' pose, staring at the incandescent disk.

'It doesn't get any less beautiful, does it Colonel?' Luana said reverentially.

'Sure doesn't. I thought you two might've changed your minds.'

'Not a chance,' Luana said breathlessly; not from exertion, but from excitement.

'I'm almost disappointed,' Calvert said. 'I've thought about this for a long time. It's been here all along, and I've done nothing about it. Because, orders are orders, and I am a man of orders. Giving them, obeying them. Always orders. I never stopped to think that perhaps the orders I received might, just might, be wrong.'

Luana stood on tiptoe – not an easy feat to accomplish in spacesuit boots – and gave Calvert a kiss on the cheek. If he was moved by this, he gave nothing away.

He turned to her with a rueful smile. 'I should have done this a long time ago.'

'We all have missed opportunities that we regret.'

Eden's Gate

Calvert harrumphed and straightened up, as if awakening from a dream. 'We've picked up a contact approaching at high speed. That will be the Black Star assault cruiser Nemesis. They won't negotiate; won't accept a surrender, no matter how unconditional. We estimate it'll be here in sixty-five hours. Maybe sooner.'

'Then we'd better get going,' Floyd said, lifting his space helmet and securing it in place. Luana did the same and they checked each other's seals. They were now totally enclosed and separate from themselves and the world around them.

'Radio systems check,' Calvert's electronically modified voice came through.

'Radio check A-OK,' Floyd responded.

'Radio check positive,' Luana confirmed.

'Then let's go.'

Floyd reached for Luana's hand and felt her fingers, delicate even covered in the spacesuit's mesh, intertwine with his. They shared a quick, nervous glance, and stepped forward until they were within touching distance of the anomaly.

Floyd could feel no heat, no vibrations and no sound. But he could feel something. He couldn't pinpoint what it was, but there was definitely something there.

'Good luck,' they heard Calvert say.

As one, the pair stepped forward into the shimmering veil of kaleidoscope colours, and disappeared.

The Arcadia Series

— Twenty-Seven —

Ben Floyd felt his body immediately enveloped in warm light, colours dancing around him like flames flicking around his limbs. But there was no pain; no discomfort at all. That feeling he had experienced just before they had stepped through into the anomaly was amplified, and now he had the impression that a trillion others were in his suit with him: observing, touching, smelling, listening and a hundred other sensations that he could never describe.

His body whirled through this realm, gravity a memory. He felt he could fall for all eternity and never touch the ground. Luana's hand clutched his as her body was also twisted and coiled and stretched.

There were so many voices, so many minds. And they were all in there with him, calling to him. They knew his name. They knew everything about him. He was naked before them as they stared, a million questions on their lips.

Eden's Gate

And the colours. The colours were so bright. So incredibly bright. And yet, it didn't hurt. The colours were like warmth, cascading around him, enveloping him in their magnificent brilliance.

He wondered if this was how they communicated – speaking in colours instead of words, communicating emotions with vibrant tints, lights of such broad intensity.

Floyd and Luana stepped from the maelstrom as easily as stepping through a doorway. They both stumbled, the whirl of colours and sounds disorientating them, but they were standing on something solid.

Floyd realised that his eyes were screwed shut and his free arm was covering the visor. He slowly, tentatively lowered it and took in the scene around him. He hadn't known what to expect. Indeed, he had not expected to survive the ordeal.

He stood on a path of smooth, well-worn stones. Either side was lush, verdant grass and trees as dense as he had ever seen.

'Luana,' he said weakly, and turned to look at her.

She was stood up straight, her helmet cocked backwards as she stared at the sky. Floyd followed her gaze and nearly collapsed when he saw it. Beyond the trees were immense, truly, staggeringly massive structures. The organic shapes towered above them, as Everest would tower above an ant. They reached out, through the crimson sky and far into space.

And in that space were planets, ludicrously close. So close that for a moment, Floyd thought they were about to impact with each other. Each planet was covered in similar organic structures, great strings of spheres reaching into space and... touching. It was a spiders' web of interlocking structures, holding all these great planets together.

Floyd had never imagined such a spectacle, had never dreamed that such a thing could be possible. Yet here it was, the most magnificent feat of construction in the universe. He was sure that nothing else, anywhere, could ever rival this incredible tableau.

Luana dropped to her knees and lifted the visor on her helmet. She was crying, sobbing like an infant, overwhelmed by the majesty of this impossible place.

Floyd quickly checked the environment gauge on his wrist.

Apparently, wherever they had ended up, the atmosphere possessed the same elements, in the same proportions, as Earth. Not to mention a comfortable eighteen degrees Celsius ambient temperature. He did not believe for one moment that this was a coincidence. Of course, coincidences did occur in the universe, but not like this. Also, although he hadn't checked lately, he was fairly sure that eighteen degrees Celsius would be the perfect average temperature for a human being.

There was only one conclusion that could be deduced from this: their arrival was expected, and had been prepared for.

Floyd lifted his own visor and smelled the air. It was perfectly fresh with a hint of citrus.

Luana looked up at him, her cheeks running with twin rivulets of tears. She smiled weakly. 'Oh my God, Ben, what are we doing here?'

In all the weeks he had known her, through all the crazy brushes with death that they had shared, he had never seen her broken like this. She was now a lost child, wanting, needing someone to take her and tell her that it was all right. He helped her to her feet and held her tightly.

'It's okay, Luana. Whoever built this, they're a lot more advanced than we are. But they brought us here for a reason.'

'What kind of reason? What could they possibly want us for? Do they want us as exhibits in some kind of galactic zoo?'

He laughed, but knew that this was probably inappropriate. 'I doubt they went to all the trouble to bring us here just to ogle us behind their funky space bars.'

She chuckled and sniffed the tears away, and he could feel the tension ebb from her body, just a little. Luana pulled away, not too far, but enough to kiss him.

'Thanks,' she said. 'I think I'm okay now. I just had a wobble there.' She braved another look up at that incredible sky and shook her head. 'But just look at it, Ben. Have you ever imagined that something like this could exist?'

'No.' he admitted. 'I'm still trying to work out whether this is real, or just a dream.'

She waited a couple of seconds, then punched him in the arm.

'Ow, what did you do that for?' he asked.
'Did that feel real?'
'Real enough.'
'Then this isn't a dream.'

Rubbing his arm, there was no faulting her logic. He looked back at where they had come from. The path on which they were standing ended with a shimmering disk of colour, identical, as far as he could tell, to the one back in the cavern, deep within 349 Dembowska. In the opposite direction, the path led around a corner where it disappeared.

'I'm guessing our hosts aren't expecting us to go straight back,' Floyd said, even though he was nervous at the prospect of losing sight of the anomaly.

'I guess we follow the yellow brick road,' Luana shrugged, and the pair of them set off.

They did not have to walk far. Just around the bend in the path, they came to what they assumed to be their destination. It was as unexpected as the sight of the connected worlds had been.

Immediately in front of them was a small wooden cottage, set against the crimson sky and those vertiginous towers. It was so ordinary, so inexplicably mundane, that it would not have garnered a second glance in Middle America. It was a single story, its timber walls painted a pale eggshell blue. Of course, Floyd doubted they had come from anything remotely resembling a tree. This whole set up, he was sure, had been constructed purely for their benefit. A brick chimney sprouted from the roof, a slim funnel of white smoke issuing from it and swirling into the vermillion sky.

Everything was perfectly normal, as long as you discounted the planets above and the unfeasible structures that seemed to hold them together.

As they rounded the corner, they stopped and shared a glance.

Ten meters ahead, a figure stood in the middle of the path.

It stood there, immobile, an image of placid countenance. It was an old man, lines of great age embossed onto a pleasant, if inscrutable face. His hair was pure white, its wispy strands cocooning pale flesh that looked like it had seen eons come and go. He wore a simple gunmetal grey cloak with a rope tie, wrapped around a stooped frame.

'Well I don't know about you,' Floyd whispered, 'but I have to admit I wasn't expecting this.'

Luana didn't respond, but reached up to unclasp her helmet and held it loosely at her side. Floyd did the same. He figured that if their hosts did decide to kill them, a pair of tin helmets would not present much of an obstacle.

'Hello, hello,' the old man said in a surprisingly strong voice. 'Wondered when you'd get here.'

The language was standard English, but the accent was difficult to place. It could have been American, or English, or Australian or any number of a dozen different dialects. Floyd settled on 'mid-Atlantic' and left it at that.

'Hello,' Luana said weakly, as if speaking too loudly would incur the man's wrath.

'Why not come join me for tea. Or I think I may have some coffee somewhere. Never drink the stuff myself. Keeps me up at night.'

He turned and limped off toward the cottage at a painfully slow pace.

'Excuse me, but who are you?' Luana asked, perplexed and enchanted in equal measure.

'Oh, I'm most dreadfully sorry,' the old man said. 'You can call me... Kevin. Yes, Kevin would probably be best. Kevin. Nice and uncomplicated. Now, refreshments beckon.'

He turned once again and hobbled off in the direction of the house, taking over a minute to do so when it would have taken his new human friends under ten seconds without breaking a sweat.

Floyd looked at Luana with a quizzical expression on his face, while she just looked like she was making a monumental effort not to burst out laughing.

'Luana, we have to go back and tell Calvert that we travelled through space and possibly time and met an alien called Kevin who has a limp and doesn't drink coffee because it keeps him up at night.'

'But on the plus side he does appear to be a fantastic gardener. That's assuming we *can* go back.'

'This should prove interesting. I just hope we can return with something a little more tangible than expert horticultural advice.'

Eden's Gate

They waited a couple of minutes for Kevin to reappear, and when he did, he was carrying a tray of hot drinks. Floyd was ready to rush to the old man's aid but Kevin lifted both hands to keep him at bay.

'Not to worry, young man,' he said, and the other two stared with wide eyes as the tray stayed floating in mid-air. 'I can manage, I can manage.' He set the tray down on a garden table, that Floyd could have sworn was not there a moment before.

'Sit, sit,' he said, gesturing for them to join him.

Judging that a refusal might be interpreted as rude (and possibly fatal) they joined him at the small table, stowing their helmets and gloves under their chairs.

Lightning scythed across the crimson sky, catching one of the giant structures and rippling along its surface.

'Now,' Kevin cooed, pouring tea for the three of them into what appeared to be ceramic cups, his long, bony fingers quivering slightly with the effort. 'I suppose you're wondering how you got here, where you are and with whom you are having tea?'

'The thought had occurred,' Floyd said, trying to stay focused on the old man, but his gaze constantly flicking up to the planets hanging precariously above them, that seemed ready to crash together at any moment. As if to offer a soundtrack to this amazing spectacle, a rumble of thunder drifted across the sky.

Luana leant forward, taking her cup in the palms of both hands. 'I'm guessing that what we have called the anomaly, was actually the entrance to a wormhole of some kind. This isn't Earth, or any other planet in the Solar System, so – assuming all this isn't an illusion – we must have travelled to another star system.'

'Very good, very good. And logically deduced,' Kevin said with a smile, pointing a gnarled finger at her. 'You are quite correct. It is not an illusion. You have travelled beyond your star. A wormhole is not a terribly accurate description, but reasonable enough for our purposes. To be honest, how you got here isn't important. Where you are, is.'

They waited for him to elaborate. And they waited. When it became clear that Kevin was not going to continue, Luana prompted him. 'So, where are we?'

Kevin smiled in a strangely enigmatic way, a smile that the two humans were beginning to recognize. He blinked once, and suddenly they found themselves swirling through space.

In a moment of near panic, Floyd choked and looked at his hands, expecting to see his fingers turning blue from the ravages of frostbite. But they were perfectly healthy, as were his lungs which should have erupted as air was wrenched from them. Physically, he was as healthy as ever. Mentally, however, he was not sure he would quickly recover from being flung into the orbit of an alien world.

Looking round, he could see a similar look of horror on Luana's face, before it turned to utter joy.

# Eden's Gate

Kevin was also with them, seeming much more alive than he had on the planet's surface. His hair rippled and swirled, his cloak billowing around him.

Then a thought occurred to Floyd: they were looking down on a single world – a world of crimson oceans and golden continents, a world alive with the bustle of people, technology covering every meter of the land. But, it was a single planet. Where they had just been was a world among many, interlinked and interdependent. Before he could say anything, Kevin continued.

'You are on Arcadia. The first world. My world.'

They stared in mute awe at this magnificent scene, at the wonders of being in another solar system.

'We are the progenitors,' Kevin said with more than a hint of pride. 'Does that explain things?'

Floyd looked at Luana in confusion, then at Kevin. 'No, not in the slightest.'

'Yes, I think it does,' Luana said, clearly working things out as she spoke. 'Life evolved here first… Oh my God. You mean you are the progenitors of humanity?'

'What?' Floyd said.

'That's it exactly!' exclaimed a beaming Kevin with a clap of his bony hands. 'And not just humanity. All life. Everywhere.'

He pointed back to the planet. Huge starships were leaving the surface, breaking through the clouds. They were unlike anything Floyd had ever seen, had ever envisioned. They rippled like oil on water, creating fantastic, organic shapes, and moulding themselves as they went.

'You see, when we first spread out among the stars, we were but children, with a naïve sense of wonder and expectation. We hoped to meet others, to learn about their cultures and share knowledge.'

One of the ships passed fairly close to them and Floyd caught a glimpse of the creatures staring out at him. Their bodies seemed to be as liquid and malleable as their ships, growing, shrinking, swirling into ecstatic coils. One thing of which Floyd was sure: these creatures were nothing like humans – nothing like the image that Kevin was projecting. Like the garden and cottage, he was merely an image. A mask that concealed its true appearance for their benefit.

The scene changed, and Floyd could see several of the creatures on an ice field. In the distance was an ice-bound volcano, a great column of frigid magma frozen at the instant of eruption hung in the sky, as it probably had for countless generations.

'We travelled to many, many worlds. We saw some truly stunning sights, wonders that we could not have imagined.'

The scene changed again to show a barren mountain, its lower slopes as devoid of life as its frozen summit. A hand reached into the dirt, a hand unlike anything Floyd and Luana had ever seen. Long, tentacle-like fingers delved into the earth, but as they shrunk back to tiny stubs, found only dust.

Eden's Gate

'Yet it was barren,' Kevin said sadly. 'A universe of exquisite beauty, but utterly devoid of life. We searched for eons, but alas, never found so much as a microbe. This wondrous galaxy was an empty shell, and we eventually had to accept that we were alone.'

Floyd looked around him, and found that he was back in the garden, sipping tea as though he had never left. It was then that he realised that they never had. It had all been an illusion. He felt foolish, having thought that he really had left the garden and floated above the world. He was beginning to come to the conclusion that this was a race of beings that only presented what they wanted them to see, a race of smoke and mirrors, a race of masks and false identities.

'That is the story of Arcadia, my friends,' Kevin said. 'My beloved Arcadia. Alone, among the great expanse of the early universe.'

'It must have felt like a lonely place,' Luana said.

'Oh, indeed it was. Desperately lonely. It is a terrible thing to realise that one is totally, utterly alone. Beauty is meaningless, if there is no one there to appreciate it, don't you think?'

'So... you populated this universe, using your own genetic code as a blueprint?'

Kevin looked at her like the proudest parent who ever lived. 'Such glorious clarity of thought. I'm awfully glad you were the first to make it to Arcadia, Luana. Oh, and you too, of course, Mr. Floyd. Yes, this was our great experiment. Thousands of worlds were seeded. Including your own Earth. But now it is time for the next step in your great adventure.'

'What next step?' asked Floyd. He wasn't sure he liked where this was going.

'It's time for you to leave the cradle, to meet new challenges, to make fresh discoveries. You are free to return home to your lives and never pass through the gateway again. Some species do. Some are content to find their own way. Some are content to remain on their own worlds and lack the genetic imperative to explore the great cosmos. You could be like them. There is no crime in embracing the familiar. Or… you could embark on this adventure, could face these challenges. If you do choose this path, the next time you use the gateway on the asteroid, it will not bring you here, but to a new place. A wonderful new place to call home. A new world to mould in your own image.'

'As part of your great experiment? It makes you sound like gods.'

'Oh, I'm certainly no god,' Kevin chuckled. 'Goodness knows whether one truly exists, but the concept is present in every culture we have nurtured. Almost every culture. All but one…'

Silence descended on them, the only sound the distant rumble of thunder as jagged spears of lightning skewered the sky. Kevin stared at a drooping patch of plants that skirted the little cottage.

Eden's Gate

'The ooga tubers aren't faring well, I'm afraid. I might have planted them a little early this season. You'd think I would have the hang of it by now.' He tutted sadly.

'Kevin,' Luana asked, 'is this place real? Or just an illusion.'

'Oh, it's real enough. I have waited a long time for you to arrive. Four point one billion years or so, give or take an eon or two either way.'

Luana was stunned. She knew life had begun on Earth early. So early, it hardly seemed possible. The Earth had barely solidified when the spark of life had first ignited. This was incredible enough, but the old man's statement was almost beyond imagining.

'You? You mean your people?'

'No, I mean me. Myself. We're quite long lived these days, you see. I was lucky enough to be the one overseeing the seeding of your world.'

'My God,' Floyd uttered, the enormity of the statement confounding him. 'You have literally been waiting here for us to arrive? For four billion years? I'd be a little disappointed if I were you.'

'Oh no, not in the slightest. This is my life's work. Forgive me. It is not my wish to patronize you, but it is like meeting my children for the first time. I'm pleased to see how you have evolved. A little different in some ways; the results of environmental variations, no doubt. But overall, I couldn't be happier.'

A fresh lightning flash scudded across the crimson sky, followed an instant later by a wrenching explosion of thunder. It latched onto one of the nearer giant structures, and Floyd watched as it clawed its way up into the heavens.

'Now, it is time for you to return home,' Kevin said, setting his cup down. 'You will not see me again, so I will wish you the best of luck in your new adventure.'

'But… that's it?' Luana said. 'That's all you waited four billion years for?'

'Isn't it enough? If it makes you feel any better, yours is not the only race I have nurtured. I have overseen the rise of over a thousand species. Some long ago; others still have not come to fruition.'

'I just wish…' Luana said trying to enunciate the feelings that swirled in her head. 'I just wish we could spend more time with you. You could teach us so much. We could learn—'

'The meaning of life?' Kevin said with a chuckle. 'No, these things you must learn for yourselves. And you will learn some of it if you choose to go to the new world. Now, twilight approaches,' he said, dragging his weary old frame upright.

Floyd wondered how much of that was for their benefit. Yet again, he had the impression that they were only shown what the aliens wanted them to see.

They too stood and collected their helmets and gloves, recognizing that they were about to outstay their welcome, and Floyd thought it would be prudent not to antagonize their hosts.

'It has been a pleasure to meet you,' Kevin said, shaking first Floyd's hand, and then Luana's. Floyd half expected to feel tentacle fingers squelching between his own flesh and blood digits, but the handshake felt human enough. 'I am so proud of what you have become, and I do hope you choose to travel through the gateway again.'

'We will have to discuss it with our people,' Luana said. 'But I hope so too.'

'Come, I will see you safely on your way.'

They made the short walk to the gateway, Kevin still ambling along in an awkward, laboured fashion. When they finally reached the gateway, Luana turned to Kevin. 'What will you do now?'

'Me? Oh, I have a few more species to welcome and nurture. Then, retirement will beckon. I shall go to the sea to live out the rest of my days.'

Luana smiled, but Floyd could tell there was a sadness behind it, a despondency at the thought of never seeing the sweet and kindly Arcadian again. Despite what Kevin said, a few minutes with them seemed extremely poor reward for four billion years of patient waiting. Still, the old man seemed genuine enough when he said he did not mind, and it wasn't their place to question that commitment. If he was being honest with them.

'Goodbye Kevin,' Floyd said, and gestured to Luana that it really was time to go. She took his hand and they cast one last sweeping look at the impossible Arcadian sky, before stepping back into the gateway and disappearing.

The Arcadia Series

— Twenty-Eight —

The instant they emerged from the gateway, they knew something was terribly wrong. Still disoriented from the mind-reeling trip through the wormhole that wasn't a wormhole, it took them a few seconds to assimilate what their senses were telling them.

Dust hung in the air, and rubble was strewn over the causeway that led to the exit.

For a moment, Floyd thought that something had gone wrong with the gateway, and that they had been returned to the right place, but millions or billions of years too late.

That theory was soon dispelled as the cavern was rocked by a huge explosion, somewhere far above. A fresh slab of rock dropped from above them and crashed onto the causeway, splitting in half and the two enormous pieces dropping either side to crash to the cavern floor deep beneath them.

Eden's Gate

Luana stumbled and fell to her knees, Floyd falling against the gateway's stone frame, but miraculously staying upright.

'What the hell?' he shouted above the booming crashes above them.

A loud klaxon blared from some unseen speaker. Its insistent wail cut through the air, jarring the pair's senses. But above this, they heard an agitated voice.

'Team three to section nine. Repair detail to main hangar.'

'Is that Lieutenant Casey?' Luana shouted.

'I think so.' Floyd stumbled over to a monitoring console to the side of the gateway.

'The Black Star attack force must have gotten here early.'

'Impossible,' Floyd said, perplexed. 'We're the only ones around here who can bend the laws of physics.'

Another eruption detonated overhead and more debris rained down around them, from the tiniest pebbles to massive boulders that themselves shattered as they hit the causeway.

Luana keyed her radio. 'Lee to Calvert. Lee to Calvert. Are you receiving?'

There was a beep, followed by a crackle.

'Lee? What the hell? We thought you were dead. Where have you—'

Yet another explosion rocked the asteroid, tearing at the crust and splitting it.

'Where have you been?' Calvert yelled. 'Never mind. We're under attack. Is Floyd with you?'

'Like a bad smell; couldn't get rid of him.'

'Then get up to the command centre. A lot has happened in the last three days. Calvert out.'

A beep signalled that the line had been cut off.

'Getting to the command centre might be easier said than done,' Luana said, staring around at the debris that surrounded them.

'We'll find a way,' Floyd said. 'Luana, three days?'

'It seems we've been away a little more than an hour or so. Some weird kind of time dilation. I don't know how far we travelled, but who knows what effects it might cause.'

Floyd looked up at the roof of the cavern, splintered rocks hanging precariously. Sandy dust sprinkled down like water from a fountain.

'I don't think we should hang around here any longer,' he said, grabbing her hand.

'I don't think so either. Come on.'

They ran for the double doors and out into one of the myriad tunnels. The base was like a rabbit warren, with numerous dead ends, stairwells and circuitous passages. Fortunately, Luana had memorized most of the route. If it had been left to Floyd, the Black Star assault troops would have been and gone before he found his way to the command centre.

They were three levels below when the final missile hit the base. Floyd had the sudden unpleasant sensation of being picked up and slammed against a wall, before, mercifully, the world went dark.

The Nemesis swooped over Shadow Base, unleashing another salvo of fiery death as it passed. A dozen laser turrets strafed the base's defences, carving white hot furrows in the dust and rock. And in the wake of the lasers followed the missiles, pummelling the area and creating scores of new craters in the asteroid's surface.

Only a few of the base's defences were still intact, but their crews fired wildly at the great cruiser as it thundered past, ignoring the scything lasers and the missiles that rained down around them.

On the bridge of the Nemesis, Blade watched the carnage unfolding just a few hundred meters below. Each time one of the base's gun emplacements began blasting, it was met with a stream of fire from the cruiser and blasted into oblivion.

'Report,' she ordered.

'Just two more defence posts left, Commander. We'll get them on the next pass.'

'Good,' she said without emotion, neither pleased nor disappointed. She had been surprised at the level of resistance from the base. They were not about to simply surrender to be executed; that much was not a surprise. But the ferocity of the defence was unexpected. They had to know that they had no chance, and that even if by some miracle they survived the assault by the Nemesis, the Retribution or the Vengeance would follow to finish the job. Rye Calvert was many things, but he was surely not stupid.

The Nemesis swung about and, with a surge of energy from its main engines, soared back toward the base, peppering the area with lethal laser fire.

The two remaining gun emplacements opened up again, clearly hoping for some kind of lucky shot, exploiting some freak weakness in the cruiser. But the Nemesis had been designed well, and there were no such weaknesses.

Every gun on the ship was trained on the two defending positions, and the stream of laser fire was swiftly, brutally cut off.

Shadow Base was now completely undefended from aerial assault. If the target weren't so damned valuable to Black Star Command, she would have happily nuked the base. She liked nukes. They were so wonderfully unequivocal. There was no ambiguity with a nuclear missile. One moment, a target existed, the next it didn't. All that would remain was a cloud of radioactive dust.

But her orders were quite specific on this point: 349 Dembowska Anomaly One had to be taken intact. That meant it would be a vicious, bloody battle to take the base without destroying the anomaly. She would lose a lot of good men and women in this battle, she was sure. If

Calvert had gone this far to defend himself, then he would not surrender now.

'Commander,' her X-O said. 'That's the last of the defences knocked out.'

Below, dust hung in the sky over the target, and through the dust she could make out the charred remains of multiple gun emplacements.

'Good, prepare for a ground assault.'

'Aye, Commander.'

It was time to see what other cards Calvert had up his sleeve.

Ben Floyd slowly, ever so slowly, opened his eyes and peered out from beneath heavy eyelids. The world was bathed in a red glow and rain was pouring down. No, it wasn't rain. It was a sprinkler – a fire suppression system. And there was a face in front of him. A woman's face, her black hair saturated, a stream of blood running down one side of her face. She was shouting. Shouting at him. But the sound was muffled, as if his ears were stuffed with cotton wool.

And then he remembered the dazzling flash of light, and the shock wave, like a giant fist slamming him the length of the corridor. And that was the last thing he remembered. But that muffled yelling was not becoming any less insistent.

'Move your ass!' Luana shouted.

Floyd blinked a few times and shook his head, water spiralling out in all directions.

'Floyd, can you get up? Can you stand?'

He leaned over, got onto his knees, then staggered unsteadily to his feet.

'It would seem so. Are you okay?'

'More or less. It looks like you took the brunt of that.'

He wiggled his fingers, checked his arms and legs. Amazingly, there didn't seem to be any broken bones. But his hearing had suffered. The world sounded oddly muffled.

'Floyd, what are we going to do? I've checked the elevator. I think that's where the explosion came from.'

'An elevator?'

'Yes, and it took out the stairwell too.'

She went quiet for a few moments. He shook his head again, trying to push aside the cobwebs.

There was a sudden sound of metal and rock being ripped apart, and the ceiling above them dropped several centimetres. They stared up at it, waiting for the whole thing to come down on top of them.

'Oh, you have got to be kidding me,' Floyd said, staring with loathing at that ceiling.

But as the seconds ticked by, it held in place. Just.

'Come on!' Floyd shouted, glancing nervously upwards. As he watched, it shuddered again and dropped a few centimetres more. 'Now!' he yelled, grabbing Luana by the arm and yanking her along.

'Where are we going,' she shouted as they charged down the hallway.

'That elevator.'

Behind them they heard a section of the roof collapse, and debris cascaded down behind them. A cloud of dust billowed out, catching up with them and engulfing the pair.

They stopped, coughing violently, and Floyd wished they had had the foresight to bring the helmets with them.

'Floyd, the elevator's gone. We can't get out.'

He dragged her along once again.

'The shaft will still be there.' He *hoped* it still was, but did not add that part.

There was another cave-in behind them and more rubble came down. Floyd was sure that it was just a matter of seconds before the whole place was buried in tonnes of rock and metal.

And he was right.

They ran headlong down the corridor. Either side of them, doorways exploded outward. The ceiling was collapsing. With horror, Floyd realised this was it. The whole place was finally coming down, right on top of them. Giant stone beams smashed down from above and they hurdled one, ducked under another, stumbling but miraculously never falling.

Through the dust, Floyd could just make out the mangled doors to the elevator.

The floor vibrated as if this were an earthquake.

Fifteen meters to go, Floyd thought.

Ten meters.

A glimmer of hope flickered in his mind. The doors to the elevator had been completely blown out. And inside were the wrecked remains of the elevator car, its roof destroyed but floor intact.

With five meters to go and the roof coming down on top of them, the pair made a desperate, lunging dive for the elevator doorway.

They hit the far side of the car hard, and turned in time to see the metal and rock ceiling drop and hit the ground where they had been running scant moments before.

But almost immediately they were engulfed in another choking cloud of dust.

After a minute or so, it had cleared enough for them to make out their surroundings. The walls of the car had been effectively destroyed by the missile from space, and now a ten-tonne slab of stone covered the doorway. But, looking up, Floyd saw that the roof of the car had been ripped clean off and there was a clear view up the elevator shaft.

'Oh, you beauty,' he whispered. A meter and a half above them was the bottom rung of a service ladder. The bottom was twisted, but still looked strong enough to take their weight.

'You see that ladder?' he said, pointing up. 'That's our way out. Can you lift me up so I can grab it?

'Not a chance, you chunky bastard!'

'Okay,' he grinned. I'll lift you and once you have a firm grip, I'll climb up you and we can both go up the ladder to the top. Okay?'

She nodded without enthusiasm.

'Right,' he said, squatting down on his haunches, 'climb on my shoulders.'

She did so, sitting on his shoulders like a toddler, and he slowly, agonizingly, lifted himself up while keeping as level as he could. It probably wouldn't endear him to Luana if he accidentally pitched her off and back onto the floor.

She reached up, but the bottom rung of the ladder was still half a meter beyond her reach. So, very, very carefully, she lifted her legs until she was crouching on his shoulders. And slowly, she raised herself up until she was standing, and could lock her arms into the bottom rung of the ladder.

Floyd, feeling her take her own weight, stepped out from beneath and looked up at her, dangling precariously.

'Well done. You secure up there?'

'About as good as it's going to get.'

'Okay, if I climb up you, do you think you can take my weight?'

'One way to find out, but hurry. I'm not sure how long I can stay like this.'

'Here goes nothing,' he said, and grabbed her feet, as gently as possible hoisting himself up. He clambered up her taut body, hearing her groans as her arms endured the weight of them both until he too gripped the ladder and she could relax.

'Come on, you first,' he said, gesturing with a flick of his head upwards. 'I'll be right behind you.'

She nodded, too exhausted to reply, but began to drag herself up the ladder.

The next level also seemed to be severely damaged, and Floyd doubted that the stairway would be passable, so they carried on up, their aching muscles protesting with every rung of the ladder. At one point, Luana slipped, and was left dangling for a few seconds by just one hand. But Quinn guided her feet back to the ladder and they made it to the next level – just a single floor below the command centre.

The elevator doors had fared better here, but annoyingly were closed and wouldn't budge. So, reluctantly, they continued up until they reached the command centre level. The doors were open here and the bedraggled pair scrambled out of the shaft and into a corridor that led directly to the command centre.

Floyd wanted to just lay there and go to sleep, but forced himself to his feet and helped Luana up.

'Thanks,' she said, gasping for breath.

'My pleasure. Let's go see if Calvert is still with us. He'll be thinking we're dead. Again.'

— Twenty-Nine —

They took a few seconds to compose themselves before entering the command centre. Luana combed her hair down with her fingertips into something that made her look a little less deranged. Both were breathless and virtually incapable of speech; both needed a few seconds to calm their frazzled nerves. The attack had been so sudden for them. One instant they had been travelling through the gateway from that wondrous, mind-bendingly beautiful world, and the next they were in the midst of a vicious aerial bombardment. There was no transition time. No period to acclimatize to this new reality.

Floyd raised his eyebrows and Luana nodded. At this stage in their relationship, it was the only communication they needed.

He tapped the entry button to the command centre. A few seconds later the doors slid aside and they walked through as normally as possible, and not quite so out of breath.

The room was impressive, with three large screens at the front, and three control stations facing them. Toward the rear of the room was a raised command chair, which looked suitably imposing, befitting the base commander who stood behind it, leaning on the chair back. Lieutenant Casey was sat at one of the consoles, continuing to issue instructions to personnel around the base. Two others were sat at the other desks.

At the sound of them entering, Calvert glanced round briefly, before turning his attention back to the main screen. 'What kept you?' he asked.

'Sorry we're late,' Floyd said. 'Had a little issue with a tunnel collapsing and having to climb up an elevator shaft.'

'Hmmf,' came the less than erudite reply. 'Is that all?'

'The elevator to the command centre was destroyed, Colonel. I think we're trapped up here.'

'There's a stand-by elevator on the other side of the room,' Calvert said, gesturing toward a red-lit door off to the left. 'But that's our real problem,' he said gesturing at the screen.

The image flickered for a moment, before stabilizing. It showed a large, particularly ugly attack cruiser hanging in space a couple of kilometres above them. It bristled with weaponry, from simple lasers, which were just scaled up versions of their own hand lasers, all the way up to asteroid smashing contraterrene missile launchers. Fortunately, the assault force had not deemed it necessary to resort to them yet. If they had, there

Eden's Gate

wouldn't have been anything left by now but atoms.

'That's what a Black Star heavy cruiser looks like,' Calvert said. 'It's the Nemesis. They've been laying down blanket fire, softening us up, eliminating our defences. Done a pretty comprehensive job as well. It was their last missile that penetrated Shadow Base and took out the elevator and several corridors on multiple floors.'

'But they've stopped now?'

'Yep, no point continuing once they destroyed our surface defences. What took you so long? I mean, how come you were gone three whole days?'

'It didn't seem long to us, Colonel,' Luana said. 'Less than an hour I'd say. We never considered relativistic effects. There must have been some kind of time dilation, but I couldn't tell you why or how.'

'Well at least you're both safe. At least, for now. Find anything there that could help us?'

Floyd spoke up. 'A way out. Maybe.'

Calvert turned to look at him sharply, his piercing eyes narrowed in a stare that could cut granite.

'He's right,' Luana said. 'There is a way out.'

'Colonel?' Lieutenant Casey's voice cut in from in front of them. 'You need to see this.'

Calvert strode up to the console where the young officer sat. 'Let's have it.'

'The aerial bombardment has definitely ended, sir. Weapons bays are closing and assault ships are powering up. They're preparing a ground attack now.'

'At least the bombing has stopped. Thank God,' Luana said, not relishing the thought of a repeat of their experience in the corridor and elevator shaft.

'There,' Casey said, pointing at the main screen.

The display was showing a live image of the attack cruiser as it hung suspended over the base. As they watched, two objects detached themselves from the ship.

'Not more missiles?' Luana said.

'No, troop carrying ground attack ships.'

Calvert's face remained impassive, but beneath that façade, Luana could see that he was furiously calculating all the variables, estimating their chances, considering how to get all of his people out of this safely. And agonizing over the fact that he would most probably lose people.

'How long do you estimate until they get here?' he asked.

Casey blew air through his teeth. 'To drop from the mothership, detach the APC units, drive to the main hangar and force entry through the side access airlock, I'd say... fifteen minutes? Maybe as little as ten.'

Calvert turned to Floyd. 'A way out, you say?'

'Yeah, but it'll be a one-way trip.'

'Kevin never said we wouldn't be able to come back,' Luana pointed out.

'Who the hell is Kevin?' growled Calvert.

'If we all go through,' Floyd said, 'there'll be nothing to stop the Black Star Force from following us. Colonel, we need to destroy the gateway after we go through.'

'Through to where?'

'Another world,' Luana said. 'We don't know where, but we've been told its habitable.'

Calvert considered this. He wasn't enjoying not having all the information. It made strategic planning an ever-evolving scenario. As he burned valuable seconds, the awesome implications of this revealed themselves to him.

'None of my people could go home again,' he said flatly.

'Nor ours,' said Floyd. 'But at least they'll live.'

'This is all academic. Even if we all go through, we don't have any weapons powerful enough to destroy the anomaly.'

'*We* might,' Floyd said. 'Is the lifepod still intact?'

'Casey?' Calvert asked.

'Checking.'

Casey tapped out some new instructions to the base surveillance system and the image changed to show the battered lifepod, half buried in dust. It looked like every single panel had been buckled or twisted. But despite the damage, the sturdy little ship was still intact.

'Good,' said Floyd. 'Get me Dane Jefferson on the radio.'

'Do it,' Calvert ordered,

'Dane, are you there?'

'Floydy? Jeez, are you okay? We thought you were dead, for sure. What about Luana?'

'I'm here, Dane. We're both fine.' Luana couldn't believe how thrilled she was to hear his voice, and how much she suddenly missed the others.

'Well that's a relief. Is the attack over?'

'No,' Floyd said. 'This is where it gets ugly. They're beginning a ground assault. In a few minutes they're going to be blasting their way into the main hangar. Do you still have the controller I gave you?'

'No, I swapped it for a better room and a box of donuts. Yes, of course I still have it.'

'Good. Get as much stuff together as you can. We're leaving. Floyd out.'

'What've you got, Floyd?' Calvert asked.

'Stowed safely inside an airlock on the lifepod, we have a high-yield contraterrene device.'

'Oh my. A big one?'

'Big enough to blow this asteroid apart.'

'How in the name of hell did you get hold of—'

'Long story. I'll tell you later, if we live that long.'

'And I'm guessing Mr. Jefferson has a remote detonator for it in his possession?'

'He does,' Luana said. 'Floyd, how do we know the blast won't propagate through the gateway? Wherever we end up, we won't have time to get clear.'

He shrugged. 'We don't know. But it's all we've got. I'm not sure the Arcadians would've considered the possibility that someone would be stupid enough to explode a matter/antimatter bomb right next to one of their gateways. Or maybe they did. Kevin said some races declined the opportunity. Some of them may have tried to destroy their gateway.'

'That kind of makes sense,' she said, following his line of reasoning. 'But like you say, it's all we've got.'

'It'll have to do,' Calvert said, trying to hurry things along. 'If we're wrong, we won't know anything about it anyway. Lieutenant Lee, get down to the anom— er, gateway, and start preparing to leave.'

'I'm already on my way.'

'Sir, I'm sorry to interrupt,' Casey said. 'The first of the Black Star ships has landed. Its APC is disembarking now. They'll be at the hangar entrance in under three minutes.'

Calvert cursed. The attack was progressing too quickly for his liking. 'Send teams one and two to the hangar entrance. Their orders are to hold it as long as they can.'

'Yes sir.'

'Mr. Floyd, make your way down to the crew quarters and get your people to the gateway. I'll join the defence teams at the main hangar and try to buy you some time.'

Floyd turned to Luana, wanting to say something, but had no idea what. She saved him the bother and grabbed his head and forced her lips against his. The kiss was raw and desperate. They both knew that this may be the last time they see each other, and threw a thousand sexual encounters of passion into it.

But all too soon it was over, and Luana was heading for the stand-by elevator.

'Don't wait too long, flyboy. I want you back in one piece.'

'I'll be there.

A second later, the doors slid shut and she was gone.

— Thirty —

Six floors below the command centre, the elevator doors glided open with a swish and Ben Floyd stepped out. A pair of armed defence troops were jogging past and both automatically raised their laser rifles, but stopped when they saw who it was. Floyd recognized one of them as being one of the nameless figures who had captured he and Luana on the surface.

'You two,' Floyd said, which way to the lifepod survivors?'

'That way, sir,' one of the men said, gesturing down the corridor with his gun. 'Down to the end and turn left.'

'Thanks, good luck.'

The two men trotted off one way, while he ran the other. He wondered if they were on their way to the hangar to defend it. That, he knew, would be a bloodbath for both sides.

He got to the door he sought and punched the buzzer. A couple of seconds later, a shirtless and extremely nervous looking Dane Jefferson appeared. Floyd had never realised it before, but the self-confessed techno-nerd had a surprisingly lean physique.

'Floydy! That's a relief. Thought you might be the goon squad. Jeez, pal, you look rough. What's happening?'

'Good to see you too, Dane. The Black Star assault force will be at the hangar by now, and these guys aren't taking any prisoners.'

'So, I'm assuming you got a plan, bro. You have got a plan? Please tell me you have a plan.'

'Kind of. We're all going through that anomaly and blowing this base. There's a new planet waiting for us. We don't know where it is, or anything about it. It could be a thousand light years away. But there'll be no going back. Once we're on the other side, that's it.'

'No coming back at all?' came Suzy's voice. 'Ever?'

Floyd looked past Dane at the young woman. She was only dressed in her underwear and, Floyd acknowledged, there wasn't a lot of that.

'You two at it? Again?'

'What can I say, bro? No strings attached sex is my specialty.'

'Such a charmer,' Suzy said. 'Not to mention delusional. That lieutenant is quite cute, you know?'

'You're lucky to have me and you know it.'

'Yeah, whatever,' Floyd said. 'Get yourselves together. We don't know where we're going, or what we'll find when we get there, but it's our only chance. We've been told it's habitable but the Namibian desert is habitable, though I wouldn't want to live there. Just be ready for anything.'

'You got it, boss.'

'Oh, and Suzy's right. You are delusional.'

Floyd glanced around and saw Max Landry, leaning against the corridor wall.

'How long have we got?' Landry asked.

'As long as the defence teams can hold them at the hangar entrance. Once they break through, it won't take them long to overwhelm the base.'

'Then we'd best get a bleeding move on. Suzy, put some threads on, darlin'. Not that I'm complaining about the view, but it might be cold on Planet X.'

'Ugh,' Dane said. 'I don't know if any of you realise this, but I'm not exactly the outdoorsy type.'

'We know,' Floyd, Landry and Suzy said in unison.

Floyd held out his hand. 'Dane, have you got that detonator?'

Dane felt in one pocket, then another, then another. Finally, with a look of profoundest relief, he found it and gladly handed the device over, more than happy to be relieved of the burden.

'Max,' Floyd said as he checked the detonator to make sure it was still working, 'get our people down to the anomaly. Luana is already there.'

'Where are you going?'

'To slow them down. If I don't make it, get everyone through.'

'Don't you worry, Mr. Floyd, you can rely on me.'

Floyd could hardly believe how desperate he must be, to entrust the safety of his people to the gangster. But times were changing, and relationships evolving. Six weeks before, trusting Max Landry would have been as unthinkable as trusting a king cobra. Now he didn't have any choice, and that fact scared him more than the execution squad that were about to invade the base.

'Good luck,' Floyd said, and ran back toward the elevator.

Shadow Base's main hangar was a war zone. The dust-crawler was in its place, acting as a barrier between the two opposing groups, laser fire ricocheting off its bodywork. The Black Star troops were entering through the smaller airlock off to one side of the main entrance.

The hangar rocked as small explosions detonated on both sides, the attackers fighting as fiercely as the defenders. Lined up against the side wall were dozens of storage containers, piled high and gleaming in scarlet and gold as they were rocked by laser fire.

Calvert and his defenders were pinned down behind a small tractor, its trailer laden with stout cargo containers. Every few seconds, one of them would peek out and loose a volley of searing death at the invaders, and then duck out of sight once more.

Eden's Gate

This was not a great strategy, Calvert knew, and the attrition rate would be high.

As if to emphasize this point, one of his marines leapt up and began to fire, but a laser cut straight through his head, carving a line through his brain. The soldier dropped to the ground, already dead, like a puppet that had suddenly had its strings cut.

Calvert cursed. In a blind rage he, and two of the others, leapt up and began firing, cutting one of the invaders clean in half before they ducked back out of sight. The problem was that there were a lot more of *them* than he had at his disposal.

Enemy troops scurried between the massive wheels of the crawler, slowly, inexorably pushing forward. There were too many of them, and no way to stem the tide of black suited marines entering the hangar.

A figure dropped in next to Calvert and crouched down.

'Not very friendly, are they?' Ben Floyd said, taking the laser rifle from the dead soldier next to him and launching a blast toward the enemy.

'I don't know how long we can hold them. When will your people be clear and through the anomaly?'

'They're on their way down—'

A laser blast must have hit something critical, as the wall behind them suddenly erupted, sending debris and shrapnel in all directions. Floyd and Calvert were shielded from the worst of it, the wheels of the tractor being peppered with smaller splinters.

Two of the defending marines were not so lucky.

Razor sharp shards of burning metal were flung out in all directions. The two soldiers – one man and one woman – were directly in the path of this flying debris. The female let out one brief, tortured scream as her body was slashed into fresh meat, her throat slit by the indiscriminate flailing. Mercifully, she lived for just a few seconds. Her comrade lasted a little longer, just long enough to stare at the four useless stumps that had been his arms and legs, before his eyes rolled up into his head.

Floyd looked away in disgust. Not because of the hideous state of the two corpses, but because of the stupid, senseless waste of life.

'Your people, Floyd?' Calvert shouted, dragging him back to their situation.

'They're on their way down there now. I figure another five minutes and they'll be through. You should start moving these guys down there,' he said, cocking his head toward the fifteen or twenty troops.

'Not a chance. We're barely holding them as it is.'

Floyd looked wildly around, searching for anything that might give them a chance, or at least a tiny advantage. Smoke hung in the air like fog, the sparks of laser blasts appearing diffused in the mist of battle.

But then his eyes fell on the side wall, and he had an idea.

'Can you give me covering fire?' he yelled at Calvert.

'Why? What're you going to…?'

Floyd didn't wait to hear the rest, vaulting over the barrier. He ran, dropped, rolled, and a second later was on his feet again, clinging to the hope that the enemy were too surprised by the move to respond.

He was wrong.

The air suddenly came alive with piercing, deadly fire.

'Oh hell!' Calvert said, wide eyed. 'Give him some cover!'

Every single defender leapt up and started firing, the air filled with burning lasers coming from both sides.

Floyd made it to the cover of one great crawler wheel, taking a second to watch the spray of laser fire flying past him and slicing into the enemy. There were screams as some shots found their marks, slicing through flesh and bone with hideous efficiency.

A second was all he could afford. The attackers had not expected such a concentrated level of fire, and ducked back behind the huge wheels on the other side, taking what cover they could.

Three more were a little tardy, and were cut down easily. Another elected to stand his ground and fight, and was rewarded by half a dozen deadly blasts that cut him into multiple pieces, his head parting company with his shoulders and bouncing to the floor.

Floyd hurled himself up the ladder at the side of the crawler's cabin and yanked the door open. He threw himself inside and slammed the door shut behind him.

The windows immediately lit up as multiple lasers struck them, but the toughened plexiglass was too strong to be penetrated by hand weapons.

Floyd took a moment to stare at the controls. They looked complicated.

'Just like driving the tractor on the farm,' he muttered, recalling his first job as a farm hand when he was little more than a boy. He found the power button and the crawler roared into life. He gunned the power a couple of times, feeling the rumble of pent-up energy. It felt good. He tried one of the levers, yanking it backwards.

Outside, the crane swung upwards and its head smashed into the roof, the hook swinging back and forth wildly, debris raining down around the crawler.

'Whoops.'

He pushed the lever back and the crane descended once again. Another lever swung it left and right. He was finally getting the hang of this.

There was another explosion outside, bigger than a laser blast. He looked round in time to see a cherry bomb land next to the cabin and twirl for a couple of seconds before detonating. The blast was incredibly bright and for a moment, Floyd thought it had penetrated the cabin and blinded him, but after some frantic blinking, his vision started to return.

Floyd couldn't ignore his attackers any longer and decided to give them something else to think about. Revving the powerful electric engine, he gently pressed a pedal. The dust-crawler lurched forward and he whipped his foot away. It stopped suddenly, just in front of the smaller tractor where Calvert and the other troops were shielding themselves.

He tried another pedal and this time the crawler rolled backwards.

'That's more like it,' he said.

Floyd slammed his foot down and the crawler was launched back at breakneck speed. He marvelled at just how much torque and acceleration this thing had.

Clearly, the attackers were equally amazed, several of whom suddenly caught out in the open. The defenders took this as their cue and jumped up, blasting the hapless would-be invaders before they could dive for cover.

He had been right when he had thought this battle would be a bloodbath.

The crawler continued backwards until it smashed into the hangar doors with a clanging crash. Several more troops were trapped and crushed, their screams lasting just an instant.

Floyd pulled forward again and stopped the crawler in the middle of the bay. As soon as it had stopped, lasers started hitting the cabin again. He had one more thing to try. With laser fire from both directions whizzing by, he lifted the crane again. It hung there immobile for a few seconds, energy weapons hitting it, before he swung it across. The tip of the boom head hit the piled-up containers hard, the hook swinging wildly. Like an avalanche, the containers came crashing down. Bedlam erupted as each crate, weighing half a tonne or more, smashed to the ground. They crushed marines and equipment indiscriminately, some bursting open as they impacted, others rolling and smashing into the side of the crawler.

The vehicle lurched and began to turn over as it was pounded by the makeshift projectiles. It stayed suspended for a few seconds, and then went all the way over. Floyd was smashed against the plexiglass, his head hitting hard. Dizzy and half blinded, he held his battered cranium in his hands, thundering pain almost knocking him out. But in a few seconds it relented, just enough for him to function.

It was quiet in the cabin. The motors had shut off, and after a couple of tries, Floyd realised that the crawler would never move again.

Dazed, he stood and reached up, throwing the door open. As the crawler was now on its side, the door was now effectively a roof hatch, and he dragged himself up through it.

There were no more lasers, no more cherry bombs to contend with. An eerie stillness had descended upon the hangar. Smoke hung heavily in the air. The floor on one side of the crawler was littered with the smashed remains of dozens of containers, and among them he could hear the cries of the dying. He couldn't do anything about that. They had chosen the wrong side. Now they were paying for that mistake.

He scrambled down until he was on the ground again and scurried over to the small tractor, and hopped over it to crouch beside Calvert.

Eden's Gate

'That ought to hold them for a couple of minutes,' he said, panting heavily.

'You're certifiable, you know that?' Calvert said, but Floyd was pleased to see a twitch at the corners of the man's mouth, and respect in his eyes.

'Probably. Don't tell Luana I did that. She'd kill me.'

Calvert grinned, and turned to his troops. 'Team one, get your butts down to that anomaly. Move, damn you, move!'

Nearly a dozen men and women shuffled past them and through the exit to the rest of the base.

'Team two, your turn. I'll follow on behind.'

'But sir—' the leader of squad two protested, her face smeared with blood.

'That's an order, Corporal Kennedy.'

'Yes sir,' she said, and chivvied her squad along. Once they were all safely away she gave the best salute she could while hunched behind the tractor, and followed her team.

Calvert keyed his mike. 'Casey. Give the evacuation order, and get yourself down to the anomaly. Hurry.'

'Yes sir. Good luck, Colonel,' came the harried response.

'You too, Mr. Floyd. Get those people to safety.'

A fresh burst of weapons fire came from the airlock. More enemy troops were beginning to break through the mountain of debris that the dust-crawler had caused.

Floyd shook his head. 'Not without you, Colonel.' He popped his head above the trailer and loosed half a dozen rounds in the general direction of the airlock.

'I'm giving you an order,' Calvert said sternly, in the tone he used when he wanted to make sure no one argued.

'And I'm disobeying it. Come on, we'll set up a defensive position at the gateway until everyone's through.'

Almost no one argued.

'Goddamn civilians,' Calvert cursed, and launched another volley at the enemy, a couple of shots waywardly hitting the crawler that lay on its side.

The two men edged out of the hangar and continued firing until the doors slid shut.

And then they ran.

— Thirty-One —

Colonel Rye Calvert did not like running. Running was a coward's solution, and he was no coward. He had proven himself in battle often enough, had demonstrated his heroism, his courage and his loyalty, which is what made this retreat all the more galling. These people were not an enemy force to be defeated. These were his own people. Hell, he had probably fought alongside some of them. Had probably trained some of them. He had certainly fought alongside Katherine Blaize. She was the most natural warrior he had ever encountered, either as a comrade-in-arms or as an enemy. And now she wanted to kill him. She had a duty to fulfil, just as he had done on numerous occasions. The difference was that she enjoyed it. She took no pleasure in unnecessary cruelty, but she would kill with ruthless, machine-like efficiency.

Even more than any of that, running was undignified.

But he ran now. He ran for his life. He could imagine Blade laughing at him for it, cackling at his cowardice. She would never run like this. No matter what the cost, she would always stand and fight. But running with Ben Floyd didn't feel so cowardly. He'd rarely seen such an act of heroics as Floyd had displayed in the hangar. If this man was running, it could not be cowardly.

They reached one of the base's myriad junctions where two corridors intersected and Floyd skidded to a halt. 'Where to now, Colonel?'

Even Calvert had to take a second to think. It wasn't just a case of knowing which way to go. He had to factor in the damage that had been caused by the aerial bombardment. A lot of tunnels and at least one elevator shaft were out of commission. He took a second, but only a single second.

'To the right,' he said with a certainty that he didn't quite feel.

So again they ran until they reached a stairwell. They barely had time to acknowledge that there were figures at the bottom of these stairs before a hail of laser fire filled the air around them. Floyd fired back wildly and scrambled to get clear.

'How the hell did they get down there?' he asked.

'They doubled around us,' Calvert shot back. 'Come on!'

Eden's Gate

Blade strode down the corridor, a dozen Black Star troops surrounding her, weapons drawn and pointed at the far end. Behind were two dozen more. They weren't bothering to delay the advance by securing the myriad other corridors and dead ends. That could be done later. For now, the Black Star Force concentrated on their main objective: eliminate the defenders. More than that, Blade wanted Calvert. If possible, she wanted to kill him herself. She owed him that much.

A barrage of laser fire erupted from ahead, cutting down two of the Black Star troops. The others ducked down, doing what they could to evade the shower of laser blasts. All except Blade, who stood there in defiance of death, teasing it. She was the first to return fire, concentrating a stream of laser pulses at the junction ahead.

The rest joined her, and the entire corridor was ablaze with shimmering light from a dozen high powered laser rifles.

Blade held up a hand and within a second, all weapons fire had ceased. Ahead, the corridor was quiet, the smoke of battle giving it a hazy, otherworldly look. Four troops scurried ahead, rifles ready to cut anyone down.

A few moments later, one of the men ran back and breathlessly gave his report.

'Commander, we have them.'

The Arcadia Series

Floyd and Calvert pelted down the corridor from where they had just come, firing behind them, keeping the enemy at bay. They got to another stairwell and hurried down it, Floyd taking four steps at a time and risked breaking his neck, which would save the invading troops the bother of killing him.

At the bottom was another junction. Why did this bloody base have so many goddamned junctions?

'To the left,' Calvert shouted.

More laser fire skirted past them and they ducked.

'Okay, scratch that. Right!'

The Black Star troops seemed to be everywhere, systematically cutting off escape routes. Floyd and Calvert were getting closer, but more and more avenues were being blocked by indiscriminate barrages of deadly laser fire.

Another stairwell, this one clear.

'This level,' Calvert gasped as he fired behind him.

Another junction. No, Floyd thought. Just a sharp right-hand bend. As he reached it, more fire exploded around him.

He cursed furiously. The path ahead seemed filled with enemy marines, and at the top of the stairwell behind, the bulk of the troops were amassing. 'Is there any other way round?' he shouted as he hurled repeated volleys of laser blasts down the corridor.

Eden's Gate

'No, this is the only way to the anomaly,' Calvert shouted back, firing behind them at marines emerging from the stairwell.

'So that's it then,' Floyd said. 'Damn it.' He fumbled with his radio. 'Luana?'

There was a delay of three or four seconds before she answered, sounding flustered and anxious. He made use of those seconds by blasting a salvo down the corridor ahead as Calvert tried to keep troops at bay in the stairwell behind them. They were caught in a classic crossfire. Nowhere to hide; nowhere to run and nothing to shield them.

'Floyd?' she shouted.

'We're pinned down and can't get to you.'

'I can hear the gunfire from here.'

'Yeah, no kidding. Luana, is everyone through?'

The invaders at the stairwell launched a fresh attack, two marines diving out into the open and firing as they went. Laser fire exploded around Floyd and Calvert, and one round found its target. It blasted into Calvert's side and he went down with a roar of agonized fury. He fired back and Floyd joined him. Two seconds later, both invaders were riddled with laser hits, blood spurting from one particularly brutal neck wound as the man's heart pumped its last.

'Colonel,' Floyd said, dropping to his knees to tend to the injured man.

'I'm all right,' Calvert shouted through teeth clenched tightly shut. 'Keep firing, man!'

Floyd did as he was told and the stairwell was once again lit up with laser fire. He took Calvert's rifle and fired that as well: one weapon at the stairwell and the other down the corridor, holding those attackers at bay.

'This is pointless, Rye,' came the sound of a woman's voice.

Floyd looked round. It came from the stairwell. 'Who the hell is that?' he shouted, and fired three more shots in both directions.

'Blade,' Calvert croaked, trying to drag himself upright. His face was red, sweat pouring from his forehead. 'She's commander of the Nemesis.'

The radio squawked into life again.

'Floyd, did you hear me?' came Luana's frantic voice.

'Yeah, is everyone through?'

'Almost. Floyd, what are you going to do?'

He knew what he wanted to do. He wanted to miraculously find another doorway so he could get to Luana and they could both escape. He wanted every one of the invading troops to suddenly drop dead.

He knew what he wanted to do, but also knew what he *had* to do.

'Let me know when everyone's gone, then you'll have five seconds to get yourself through before I detonate the bomb.'

'Floyd, there's got to be another—'

'Do it, Luana!'

Eden's Gate

He really had thought that they might have a chance, that they might just make it to the gateway and then they would be free. But life isn't like that, he reminded himself. Just when hope would shine a light along the path, life would come along and snuff it out.

'Rye, I'll make it easy for you and your troops,' Blade's voice came again. 'Quick and painless.'

Luana hadn't answered. Floyd fired again at the stairwell and heard a satisfying scream as a laser rifle, with half an arm still attached, clattered to the floor.

'Luana?' he shouted, firing again.

'Stand-by,' she said.

Calvert growled in agony as he reached for his hand laser. Blood was spilling from the open wound in his side, trickling onto the floor and forming a slippery pool. He fired several shots wildly at the stairwell.

One soldier was bold enough to leap out into the open, presumably hoping to catch the two men off guard. It didn't quite work. He managed to loose two wild shots at the exact moment a blast went cleanly through his head. The corpse dropped onto the other two bodies.

Floyd shouted into the radio. 'Luana, you've got to go now! We can't hold them any longer.'

Silence. Where was she? Had something happened to her?

A new round of shots came from the corridor ahead, lasers being spat toward them. Floyd ducked away and saw three more men at the stairs.

They fired. He fired. Calvert fired.

Lasers lanced their way into walls and flesh, smoke billowing. One of the three was killed outright, a lucky shot piercing his heart. Another received a slicing wound to the leg, almost severing it and cutting clean through the tibia. He went down with a scream, and a moment later was silenced as another shot pierced his eye and fried his brain.

A shot from the third man hit Floyd in the fleshy part of his arm and he grimaced, grunting at the pain. He fired a sustained barrage and heard the last of the marines cry out and hit the floor.

'Luana!' he screamed.

Nothing.

He felt in his pocket for the detonator. He pulled it out and clicked on the power, then released the safety. All it would take was one press of the switch.

He hoped she had gone through. He couldn't wait any longer. This was it.

He started to press down on the firing switch.

Another barrage of weapons fire came from the corridor. Lasers were released and flew wildly in random directions.

And then…

Silence.

He expected another round of shots, but heard nothing.

Another shot came from the stairwell and he fired back.

Two more shots and he returned the favour, hearing a scream and a figure fell to the foot of the stairs, writhing in anguished torment.

He fired several more shots, one of which ended the soldier's suffering.

A figure appeared behind him, from the corridor. He swung around, finger squeezing the trigger.

But then he stopped.

'Taxi for Mr. Floyd?' Max Landry said with a grin, and fired several pulses of laser fire toward the stairwell.

'Max, I never thought I'd be pleased to see you.'

The two men quickly dragged Calvert around the corner and out of sight of the stairwell, the colonel cursing with eyes screwed tightly shut.

'Didn't I tell you, Mr. Floyd?'

'Tell me what?' he said, firing several shots at the stairs and keeping the invaders holed up there.

'I said you'd need me again. And I'm here to help.'

'Yeah, whatever. Now help me get Calvert back to the gateway.'

'Right you are, guv.'

'And keep blasting down that hall.'

Landry let his laser rifle do the talking and showered anything and everything with laser fire.

'Oh, and Max?'

'Yeah?'

'Thanks. Now let's get out of here.'

— Thirty-Two —

With the limp, barely conscious form of Rye Calvert draped over their shoulders, Floyd and Landry staggered through the doorway and into the cavern.

'Bloody hell, would you look at that thing?' Landry said, staring with rapturous eyes at the gateway, its shimmering incandescence undiminished since they had last been here.

Luana was at the door to greet them, and fired a dozen shots into the corridor. Three times that amount were returned, blasting the frame, rocks, even the gateway itself. She punched the control for the door and quickly locked it.

'That won't hold them for long,' she said, helping Floyd to extricate himself from Calvert.

The colonel sagged onto one of the rocks, one arm pressed hard into his side. His face was ashen, skin seeming to hang loosely from his eyes.

Eden's Gate

A second later, the bedlam of the corridor erupted through the doorway, the twin doors exploding outwards and being accompanied by yet more vicious laser blasts.

Landry and Luana both dropped, grabbing Calvert and dragging him to the ground. He let out and anguished shriek, his side erupting in sheer, uncontrolled agony.

Floyd spun and dropped to one knee, firing both his rifle and hand laser, twin columns of fire finding targets. The screams of the dying didn't bother him now. He hated everyone on that side of the doorway. Let them feel pain and torment and terror in their last moments.

He fired and fired and fired.

Beyond the doorway, smoke billowed and all he could see were the blasts from his guns disappearing into it.

More screams came. There must have been a dozen of them in the corridor, in the open and unprotected as a constant stream of white-hot death cut through them.

Floyd kept firing until no more shots came his way.

He swung around and said urgently: 'Max, take Calvert through.'

'No,' protested Calvert weakly, but with some of his iron resolve still intact. 'You go. I'll stay and blow this place.'

'Not necessary, Colonel,' Landry said in that oddly upbeat voice of his. 'There's a five second delay before the CTD explodes. Plenty of time to send the signal and get through the… well, that thing.'

'Take him, Max,' Floyd yelled. 'Move.'

Landry took one of the injured Man's arms and threw it around his neck, dragging him toward the gateway. They staggered together like a pair of drunks, and just before entering, Landry looked around.

'Thy kingdom come, Thy will be done,' he said uncertainly, and without another word, took the two of them through, disappearing like a dry leaf tossed into a fire.

More shots came from the corridor.

'Luana, you're next,' Floyd said as he returned fire.

She dropped to the ground, scrabbling in the dirt as she reached for Calvert's discarded rifle and started blasting.

'We go together,' she shouted back.

Floyd shook his head. If she could just do as he asked. Just once.

'Okay,' he said. 'On three. One—'

An odd sound came from the doorway. The sound of metal rolling along the floor. With a suddenly sick lump in his stomach, he realised what it probably was. What it had to be.

The object dropped the few centimetres from the corridor floor onto the uneven ground in the cavern.

There was barely time to react at all. All he could do was shout.

'Hit the deck!'

Luana was quick to respond, but perhaps not quick enough.

Eden's Gate

The cherry bomb exploded, sending out a violent, penetrating shockwave.

Floyd felt himself hurled through the air and hit the loose gravelly floor hard, sliding to a stop right next to the precipitous edge of the causeway.

Everything was a swirling blur, his brain jarred as if wrenched from his skull and slammed against a wall a few times. At this moment, death didn't seem a bad option. He'd given it his best, but now he had nothing else to give. Let them kill him. He just didn't have anything left.

Except…

Luana. He had to get her to safety. After that, it didn't matter what happened to him.

He lifted his swimming head, and could blurrily make out a number of dark figures cautiously entering the cavern, weapons raised and ready to kill anything that moved. On the other side of the cavern was the unmoving form of Luana.

Was she dead?

Eight troops were just inside the doorway. One of them looked across at Floyd, saw that he was alive, saw that he was still a threat, and swung his weapon round.

Something stirred in the back of Floyd's mind in that instant. A recollection. A recent recollection. He remembered when he and Luana had returned here earlier from Arcadia. He remembered how surprised they had been when the first explosion from above had rocked the cavern. He recalled how the roof had split and huge chunks of rock had come crashing down, almost crushing them. And he recalled looking up and seeing a massive splinter of stone poised, hanging precariously and ready to drop.

Looking up now, he saw that that slab still hung there. His fingers closed on the rifle and swung it upwards, just as the other soldier prepared to fire.

Floyd blasted into the roof – a sustained, high energy blast that cut away at ancient stone.

With a grinding wrench it was cleaved from the roof and dropped.

He turned over, curling into a tight ball and closed his eyes.

And hoped.

The massive block hit the ground. Several of the marines had looked up at the last instant, but it was too late. It came down like a hammer, smearing their bodies over the floor, grinding them to molecules.

As it hit, it broke into a hundred separate boulders, sealing the doorway.

Floyd stared in shock at what had just happened. He had done that. It was so brutal, so violent. And oh so satisfying.

Somehow, and he would never question his good fortune, he was still alive.

He dragged himself up onto all fours and crawled across to where Luana lay. Touching two fingers to her neck, he could feel a pulse and leaning over, felt her breath on his cheek. He was too exhausted to appreciate the wave of sheer joy that swept over him.

Eden's Gate

Very gently, with as much tenderness as time would allow, he lifted her head.

'Come on, honey. Time to wake up.'

From the area of the doorway, behind a small mountain of debris, some rocks began to fall away and a shaft of light penetrated the cavern, illuminating the dust that hung in the air. There was the sound of shouting: the unmistakable voice of Lieutenant Commander Katherine Blaize furiously screaming orders.

'Luana, come on, I need you to wake up.'

He gave her a light shake, and something inside her began to stir. Luana's eyelids opened, just a crack. Just enough for her to make out his face.

'Floyd?' she asked, and blinked her eyes open. 'What happened?'

'Cherry bomb. Somehow, we're both here to tell the tale.'

'Did we make it?' she asked, glancing around at the unrecognizable cavern.

'Not yet. I sealed the doorway, but they're breaking through.'

At that moment, a laser blast flew from a crack at the top of the doorway and hit the far wall.

'Can you stand?' Floyd asked. 'I need you to go through. Then I can blow this place.'

'We go together,' Luana said groggily as he dragged her upright. She stood there on swaying legs, held upright by Floyd.

Another shot hit the stone frame of the gateway, and another couple of boulders fell away from the doorway. Floyd looked up, but it didn't look like any more large rocks could be persuaded to cleave themselves from the roof.

'It's time to go now, sweetheart,' he said as he guided her to the gateway.

A blast hit a rock not a meter from them.

'Wait,' she said. 'We go…'

'Yeah, whatever.'

Floyd pushed her through the threshold and in an instant, she was gone.

He turned in time to see a pile of rocks crumble and fall away. Three heads immediately filled the space, with rifles at the ready. The middle head was female, with shoulder length hair and a look of cold malevolence in her eyes. He didn't need Calvert around to tell him that this was Blade.

Floyd fired and the three heads had to flinch away.

The reprieve gave him enough time to fish the detonator out of his pocket.

A laser blast whizzed past his cheek. He fired again, and powered up the device.

Then the safety was disengaged.

Another shot as the marines scrambled and fought to get at him.

Floyd looked at them and smiled. The men froze. They recognized that smile. It was the smile of a man who knew he'd won. But Blade did not recognize the look. She

Eden's Gate

had never seen the victory of another. She had never known defeat.

Ben Floyd pressed down hard on the firing switch.

Around twenty kilometres away, the contraterrene device hummed into life, its display board acknowledging that the countdown had started.

Floyd stepped through the threshold, waving as he went amid a petulant barrage of furious fire. To Blade's fearsome rage, he disappeared, enveloped by that field of impossible colour, more precious than the finest jewel.

Blade pushed one of the boulders aside, the chunk of rock rolling over the debris. She scrambled through, firing her laser into the anomaly.

At this point, she didn't care for its value, didn't care that her superiors would have her rank stripped until she was somewhere around the level of assistant cook. No, now she just wanted blood. She wanted to inflict death on anyone in her way.

She scrambled over the loose rocks, slipping and skating as if on roller skates. Behind her, three others followed, hurling rocks away.

Blade got to her feet and ran for the gateway, not knowing when death would come, but sure that its icy fingers would touch her flesh at any moment.

From two meters away, she flung herself at the shimmering ball of light that was the gateway. Either side, two others joined her, all three flying through into the swirling mass of kaleidoscope colours.

The Arcadia Series

When the countdown reached zero, the instruction was sent from the active command subset to the magnetic containment management system. Five separate sets of codes had to be received and authenticated, before the management computer would process the command.

All of this took a fraction over one microsecond.

The next stage was technically a lot simpler, however took almost a full second to accomplish. Once the command was given, the magnetic buffers needed to be shut down one by one until all five had been removed. Now there was nothing that could prevent the detonation. The two chambers, one containing deuterium, the other containing antimatter, were free to come into contact.

As matter and antimatter collided, a reaction occurred that would make the largest hydrogen fusion bomb ever detonated look like the flare of a match.

All the energy from every single atom was suddenly liberated, the device disappearing in a brilliant sphere of expanding energy.

One-point-one seconds after the command had been received, the wave had engulfed the lifepod, and was in the process of vaporizing every rock, indeed, every atom of matter in the area.

Inside the base, the invading force had no conception of what had happened. In the space of a millisecond, they went from healthy, functioning human beings, to white hot vapours.

Blade and two of her marines had entered the gateway scant milliseconds ahead of the wave of all-consuming energy. The third man was not so lucky. His head, shoulders and arms entered the swirling vortex. The rest of him was vaporized.

The Black Star cruiser hanging over the base was just far enough out of range to evade the initial matter/antimatter explosion. Unfortunately, that still meant that millions of tonnes of rock and debris were flung out at relativistic speeds.

As the Nemesis tried to turn away, molten rock pummelled the great ship. As soon as her reactor was ripped in half, she too erupted in her own fireball in a pyrotechnic display that would rival the initial explosion.

She carried two of her own contraterrene reaction missiles. When the ship tore itself apart, the missiles were also ruptured, power to the magnetic containment fields cut off.

The two missiles were vaporized within a quarter of a second of each other, the resulting flash briefly lighting up the sky on Earth, a hundred and fifty million kilometres away.

Nothing survived. The destruction was absolute. From the most senior human officer, down to the humblest tardigrade, every single living thing in a thousand-kilometre radius was killed.

There was no time for even the briefest of distress calls.

But in around a minute, the military leaders on the neighbouring asteroid of Ceres would find out.

Commander-in-Chief Commodore Viktor Barkov would have a lot of explaining to do when he was summoned by his own superiors on Earth.

Three days after that, the Black Star cruiser, Retribution, which was sent to investigate, would report back that the asteroid 349 Dembowska had been destroyed.

Almost.

What had been left behind was a giant, crystalline structure beyond the wildest imaginings of anyone in the Solar System.

The 349 Dembowska anomaly was secret no longer.

Eden's Gate

— Thirty-Three —

Ben Floyd stumbled from the gateway, half blinded and his head ringing with the sound of laser fire. As soon as he had been released from the gateway's clutches he fell forward and landed on his hands and knees.

With a splash.

He blinked away the flashing lights that seemed to have burned his retinas. It was water. Muddy water, yes, but water.

Floyd had, it seemed, landed in a puddle.

He wondered for a second whether this was one of Kevin's little jokes. He wouldn't put it past the strange alien of multiple false masks.

He raised his head slowly, wishing to savour every moment of this experience. There were others around him. His people. His friends. There were his fellow survivors from the Aurora, shocked, scared and confused. Except Max Landry. He didn't think anything would ever phase him. There was Calvert, his comrade in arms, half sat/half sprawled against a rock. Two of his marines were tending to him. Another thirty or so men and women were around, weary, battle worn. They had managed to bring quite a lot of equipment and supplies through the gateway, which was good. They would need everything they could get their hands on if they were going to survive in this new and strange land.

The gateway, he thought.

Floyd spun around, raising his weary arms and pointing his laser directly at the churning, pulsating wall of colours.

What if the antimatter weapon hadn't worked? What if it had worked, but the gateway had survived? What if the annihilating blast followed them through as easily as they had stepped.

Though if that happened, then in a few moments all their worries would be over. He was ready to deal with what he could affect, and wouldn't worry about anything else.

Floyd waited. And waited, sweat beading on his forehead and trickling down his temples. If they came through, he was ready to hack them to pieces with a laser machete.

The gateway seemed to glow brighter, its incandescence too brilliant to look at directly. Floyd looked away, expecting to be vaporized at any moment.

But that didn't happen. The light dimmed, and in a few seconds disappeared completely. All that was left was a ring of stone, with nothing filling it but warm, humid air.

Floyd felt a hand on his shoulder and looked up, blinking in the sunlight. His mouth dropped open in wonder. Silhouetted against the sky was Luana. He could just make out the smile on her face. It was a face he had come to know very well, and he would be happy to grow old looking at that face.

But beyond that he stared at the sky, and the three suns that shone down on the surface of this new planet.

Luana helped him to his feet. Landry gave him a friendly thumbs up, which was frankly a little unnerving.

'Did we all make it through?' he asked.

Luana's face clouded, her expression a look of concern mixed with sadness. 'Most of us did. We took some casualties, but the death toll was not too bad, considering. There's just one thing.'

'What?' A feeling of dread swept over him.

'Tamara didn't make it,' she said, her eyes glistening and a single tear rolling down her cheek, carving a channel through the grime.

'She didn't make it off the asteroid?'

'No, she entered the gateway with Conor. He arrived here; she didn't.'

He looked away, unable at that moment to meet anybody's gaze. Least of all, Conor's.

'The defenders lost eight people in all,' Luana said. 'But everyone else is here and safe.'

'Thanks to you, sir,' a uniformed woman said to him. He recognized her as the leader of one of the squads that had defended the hangar. Corporal… Kennedy? Yes, that was it.

He waved the compliment away and the young woman smiled, going back to her team and starting to get them organized.

Looking around, Floyd took in their immediate surroundings. They seemed to be in a clearing. Squelching mud and chocolatey puddles stretched for twenty meters all around. Beyond this were trees, but they weren't quite like any trees he had seen before. The closest analogy he could think of was the monkey puzzle tree, but even that wasn't quite right.

'Floyd,' a weak, croaking voice said, and he looked round to see Calvert beckoning him over.

He traipsed through muddy water and knelt down next to the wounded soldier.

'How're you feeling?' he asked.

'Damned stupid question,' Calvert grumbled, before erupting into a fit of coughs that looked extremely painful, but the man was doing an admirable job of downplaying it. 'Listen Floyd, if I don't make it through this, these people are going to need some leadership. I need you to do that job. You understand me?' Another fit of coughs ensued.

'You'll be fine, Colonel,' he said firmly, although he could see the prognosis was by no means promising.

Eden's Gate

'Maybe, maybe. Maybe not. But even if I am, it'll take me time to get back on my feet. Casey is a good man, and a fine officer. But you're a proven leader. My people will respect you. They saw what you did in the hangar. They saw the sacrifices you were willing to make. Where you lead, they'll follow. You hear?' He started coughing again, clutching his side fiercely with one hand, angrily swatting away the medics with the other.

'He's right, sir,' Floyd heard a voice behind him and looked round to see the young corporal who had complimented him a few moments before. 'Mr. Floyd, can I speak with you a moment?'

Floyd nodded to the medics and went over to speak to the corporal.

'Sir, Lieutenant Casey has gone up to that high ground over there.' She pointed to some high rocks that protruded through the tree line. 'He just sent back this recording.'

Floyd took the comm-pad from her and shielded it from the sunlight. It was a low quality, ten-second segment of video. It showed the trees coming to an end a few hundred meters away, and then ocean as far as the eye – or, in this case, camera – could see.

But what grabbed his attention was not the vastness of this ocean, but the island on the horizon. It shimmered in the heat haze, but one thing was for sure: the island was almost completely covered by the gleaming towers of what was unmistakably a city.

He handed the comm-pad over to Luana, who stared at the image for a full minute, watching the island appear again and again and again, those golden minarets and obelisks glimmering in the sunlight.

'It doesn't look like we're alone here after all,' she said.

'Let's hope the natives are friendly,' Floyd replied. 'Because this is the only home we've got now. Let's hope we don't have to fight for it.'

Eden's Gate

THE FIRST HARVEST

A THRILLING, NAIL-BITING ACCOMPANIMENT TO THE ARCADIA SERIES

IN THE FARTHEST REACHES OF THE SOLAR SYSTEM, IN ITS COLDEST, DARKEST PLACE…

…SOMETHING IS STIRRING

IAN FRASER

The Arcadia Series

Eden's Gate

— One —

Knock-knock-knock.

The sound was so mundane, so commonplace and so innocuous that in any other situation it would barely be noticed, like a shuttle rumbling overhead, or birds singing in the trees. But this wasn't any ordinary situation, and nothing about this place *could* be described as 'ordinary'.

This was Triton: largest moon of Neptune and humanity's farthest outpost.

Natasha glanced across at Dmitri, who gave her a beats-the-hell-out-of-me shrug. After three years of marriage – the previous nine months of which had been spent on the icy moon – they could read each other's feelings as easily as reading the pages in a book.

He was just easing from his chair when Terrell, the outpost's chemistry specialist, slipped into the lounge. 'You guys hear that?' he asked, tucking his shirt into his waistband. He and Kalisa had been working in the chemistry lab, and had probably been enjoying each other's company a little more than their superiors on Earth would have liked.

'It was neither of you?' Dmitri said.

'No, we've been running tholin sample analysis.'

'What about Craig and Amber?' Dmitri asked as he leaned over his workstation and brought up the external camera feed.

'In the Gym,' Terrell said. 'I heard them arguing.'

'That is not unusual,' the Russian said absently as he checked every external camera, but none showed any movement, except the constantly shifting dust and gentle swaying of the antenna.

Craig and Amber's marital problems were no secret, and tempers would flare up at least once a day, the entire habitat being treated to the sound of abuse being hurled back and forth. The arguments rarely lingered, the couple usually quick to make up. The passion they displayed while arguing was frequently matched by the passion of their make-up sex afterwards. Craig was as stubborn and obstinate as the most intransigent mule, while Amber took the moniker 'fiery redhead' almost to the point of cliché. Natasha could never grasp how the relationship could endure this never-ending cycle of furious vitriol and passionate reconciliation, but endure it did, and they seemed as devoted as when the group first left Earth.

Knock-knock-knock.

This time all three jumped, and kept perfectly still. There was no other sound, aside from the never-ending howl of the wind that never stopped on this lonely, frigid world.

'What the hell is that?' Terrell said to no one in particular.

Dmitri quickly flicked through all the external cameras, searching for something, or *anything* to explain the sound.

'There must be something knocking against the outer skin in the wind,' Natasha said, but even she could hear the scepticism in her voice.

Two more figures appeared from the direction of the science labs.

'Who the hell is making all the goddamn noise?' Amber shouted as soon as she was in the room, and Natasha was certain that they probably heard her on Ganymede. Kalisa merely winced at the profanity.

'We are trying to ascertain what it is now,' Dmitri said, holding up a hand to silence her. To everyone's amazement, it worked, and once again, all that could be heard was the howling of the wind outside.

'Something must have become detached from the antenna,' Natasha persisted, hoping that if she said it enough times it would become true.

'I don't know,' Terrell said as he stroked the stubble that permanently covered his chin. 'Sounds like someone knocking to me.'

'Yeah, no kidding,' Amber said. 'We all heard someone knocking. But we're all here, and it ain't none of us.'

'Except Craig,' Dmitri pointed out. 'Are you sure it wasn't him playing a practical joke?'

'Well it ain't Craig, I can tell you that for nothing. He's been too busy trying to get himself murdered by me.'

Everything went quiet again. Even the wind seemed to have died down, and was now just a low, mournful howl. They waited, listening for any noise, any hint of movement outside.

The sound, when it came, originated from an unexpected direction.

'So, I'm guessing it's not one of you banging on the front door?' Craig said, emerging from the direction of the science section. 'Anyone got any theories?'

'It is probably just a loose cable hitting the outer wall,' Dmitri said. 'What else could it be?'

Amber was not noted as being the most patient in the group. 'I'm going outside to check it out.'

'No, I'll go,' her husband Craig said, and Natasha could immediately see where this would lead. 'This is an operations matter, which is my department.'

'Like hell it is!' Amber blurted. 'If something has come loose and is banging on the outer wall, then that's an engineering issue. My department.'

'Quiet, both of you,' Dmitri said sternly. 'I am the base commander and I decide who is to go out. Is that understood?'

Craig said nothing, and Amber just stood there, seething quietly.

'You can both go, but be careful. If something has come loose, then it constitutes a danger, so stay alert.'

The outer hatch slid closed behind them, the sound of metal bumping metal muffled in the faint atmosphere. The echoes lingered for a few moments, until they were lost to the ceaseless wind.

It was only from the outside that the base's design could be appreciated. The central hub contained the living area, kitchen and stores. Radiating out from this were corridors leading to sleeping quarters and gymnasium, the various science sections, fusion reactor and engineering section.

'Right, I'll go this way,' Craig said, gesturing toward the fusion reactor. 'You go that way. We'll meet on the other side of the base. And be careful.'

'What, are you afraid some big space monster is out here, waiting to grab me?' Amber replied, her electronically modified voice dripping with sarcasm.

Craig turned to face her, his expression a peculiar mix of dull weariness mixed with contempt. 'No, I mean something is loose and could puncture your suit. But, whatever.'

He turned away with a dismissive wave of the hand and did his best to stomp, which was not easy to achieve in one seventh of a gravity. Amber merely sashayed off in the opposite direction, which was an equally difficult feat to achieve.

She was furious with him. Again. She always seemed to be furious with him these days. She wondered whether it was a deliberate, calculated strategy to coerce her into a little energetic make-up sex. Somehow, that didn't sound like Craig's style. He was more straightforward. If he wanted it, he would just ask. Or worm his way into her affections the way he usually did. He knew her weaknesses so well. He knew all the things that would melt her cool veneer and encourage her to open up – both metaphorically and physically.

There was a swift, but annoying burst of static in her ear.

'Found anything yet,' Craig asked.

'If I had, don't you think I would've told you?'

'The way you've been acting lately, who knows? Out.'

There was another crackle of static, and the line went dead. Her anger with him wasn't about to abate any time soon. She was sure now that he was just playing her. Well, he wasn't going to screw his way back into her affections this time. No, she would leave him to stew for a few days. She was fairly sure that his need was more urgent.

There was another burst of static in her earphones, and she waited for whatever asinine comment would follow. But the line remained silent. She waited a few more seconds. Was Craig giving her the silent treatment?

Eden's Gate

Really? Well, this was a new tactic, and it just wasn't like him.

'Craig? You there?' She wasn't about to familiarize the comment with a 'honey' or 'babe'. It was his turn to do some grovelling.

Amber turned a full 360 degrees. Craig had this habit of sneaking up behind her and making her jump, but there was no sign of him.

'Craig, are you hearing me? This is not funny. Respond now, or else.'

Amber waited for a full minute before continuing around the base. She passed the ice-hopper that was parked outside the science modules, which marked the halfway point. There was still no sign of him. Where the hell *was* he?

Amber keyed her mike again, changing frequencies. 'Dmitri, it's Amber. Can you raise Craig? I've lost contact. Or the loser just won't acknowledge me.'

'Just a minute,' came Dmitri's reply.

So she continued around the base, but more attentively now. There were no tracks to follow on this side; the incessant winds had scoured the ice clean and dust was piled up against the sides of the structure in frozen drifts. When she made it round to the lee side, she came across his footprints. There was no sign that he had circled back, no hint as to which direction he might have gone in.

The Arcadia Series

Her earpiece crackled again and she let out a breath she didn't realise she had been holding. 'Craig, is that you? I've been—'

'No, it is Dmitri. I have not been able to reach Craig. He may be hurt. I am coming outside to help you look.'

'Roger that,' came her whispered response. She changed frequencies again. 'Craig, can you hear me? Talk to me now, or I ain't letting you touch me for a month. Goddammit Craig, do you hear me?'

Amber felt a tear escape her eye and roll languidly down her cheek. She shook her head, flicking the droplet away. She didn't know whether to be angry, sad, worried or wallowing in despair. But she knew that she didn't want anyone else to see her as a wretched mess.

She froze. Someone was watching her. She didn't know how, but she felt eyes behind her, regarding her with curiosity. Very, very slowly, she turned around. Hovering just two meters away was one of the base's maintenance bots. Six lenses stared unblinkingly at her, its eight legs curled up into its body and making it look like a dead spider, coated in shining chrome.

'Hello Amber,' the robot's voice said into her earphones.

'Vincent, if you ever sneak up behind me like that again, I'll tear your goddamn robotic heart out. You hear me?'

'I hear you perfectly, Amber, and I apologize for startling you. Dmitri ordered Bob and I to search for Craig.'

Eden's Gate

'Then get on with it.'

'Thank you, Amber.'

The bot descended to the ground, its legs opening out. As soon as its feet touched the rocky surface, it scampered off in search of her husband. Some genius back in Pasadena had worked out that a spider was the most efficient design for a maintenance robot. It didn't seem to have occurred to them that it would spook the hell out of the research team. This was probably the same 'genius' who decided that sending three childless married couples would offer the most harmonious group dynamic.

Almost the instant the bot disappeared from sight, she saw a figure come into view. For a fleeting moment, she thought it was Craig, but almost immediately recognized it as Dmitri.

'I take it you have had no luck,' he said, sounding slightly out of breath.

'No, the bots are scouring the base now. Dmitri, why won't he answer?' She could hear the quaver in her voice, but by this stage, didn't care. She was now sure that Craig was dead. All that remained now was to find the body and ascertain the cause.

'We will find him, Amber.'

They searched the base for almost an hour, hunting underneath every pipe, in every equipment locker. It was only when Vincent, the spider bot, ascended a hundred meters into the wispy atmosphere, that they found Craig.

And everyone on Trident Base heard Amber's horrified, anguished scream.

— Two —

The body had lain a full four hundred meters from the base. How Craig had gotten that far away was a mystery, but what was a bigger mystery was the state of the corpse.

The body was mostly undamaged, but what was immediately apparent was that he had had his neck broken. However, this did not do justice to the level of damage. His neck had been crushed so violently and so completely, his head was barely attached to his body. Only skin and splintered bone were left, barely a couple of millimetres thick.

Amber was too distraught to walk back to the base, so Dmitri had half carried her back. He left the two bots to bring the body back a few minutes later. He didn't want Amber to have to witness her husband's head hanging by barely a string of flesh.

Once back inside, Natasha had insisted that Amber take a sedative. She was in shock, and the best thing for her right now was sleep. She hadn't objected, and didn't seem to have the energy to offer any resistance to anything.

'What happened out there?' Natasha asked Dmitri quietly when they were safely in their own quarters and away from the others.

'I have no idea.' He replied as he peeled off the environment suit. 'There were two of them out there, and one of them is dead.'

'You don't think Amber could have done *that*?' The bots were still carrying the corpse back to the base, but she had seen the video images, and the horrific damage that had been caused.

'No. No human would be strong enough to cause that kind of damage.'

'Then what? You think there's a monster loose on this moon?'

He laughed, but quickly stopped himself as he realised how inappropriate that was in this situation. 'No, I mean one of the robots would be physically capable.'

'What? But they can't. Preservation of human life fundamental to their programming.'

'Who knows,' he said, throwing his hands into the air. 'All I know is that a man is dead and that the only possible suspect is a robot. Perhaps one or both has had its program altered. But that would suggest that someone here has done that, so is a murderer.'

Natasha went quiet for several moments as she digested this. She knew it wasn't her or Dmitri. That left

Amber herself, Terrell or his wife, Kalisa. She couldn't imagine it would be either of those two. Terrell was one of the kindest, most placid men she had ever met. And Kalisa was one of the sweetest women. It was impossible to conceive that either would do such a thing, and she doubted that either would have the technical abilities to reprogram the bots.

That left Amber, but considering her reaction to the sight of her dead husband, it just didn't add up.

Dmitri tossed the environment suit aside, and slipped into the pants and sweatshirt he habitually wore around the base.

'I need to inform Trident Command,' he said, and the two of them returned to the lounge hub.

By now, the bots had returned the body of Craig Parker to the base and Natasha had put it in a cold store in the medical section.

When she returned to the lounge, she found a sombre scene, Terrell and Kalisa sitting quietly on one of the couches. She could see that Kalisa's eyes were reddened from tears.

From his workstation, Dmitri ordered the two maintenance bots to shut down. If they were responsible, he didn't want them loose on the surface.

He brought the comms system online. It normally stood idle, unless activated manually as Dmitri just had, or to receive the four prearranged messages from Trident Command in Pasadena. Once activated, the transmitter/receiver dish above the engineering section would align itself with Earth to get a clear signal through.

But there was a problem; the dish was not aligning. Dmitri ran a full diagnostic of the system, and everything checked out, except for the dish itself. No signals from his console were reaching the dish mechanism. It was with reluctance that he reactivated one of the maintenance bots.

'Vincent, can you hear me?' he asked, glancing over at Natasha. She was sat huddled with Terrell and Kalisa.

'I can hear you, Dmitri. How may I help you?'

Well, at least that was something. 'Vincent, switch on your camera systems.'

His screen suddenly sprang to life, showing the other robot, Bob, and a section of the habitat wall.

'I want you to give us a visual inspection of the primary communications array. Can you do that for me?'

'Certainly, sir.'

The image on the screen wobbled for a moment, and a small cloud of dust was blown away as the jets fired, lifting the bot into the air. It rose above the main hub and pointed toward the dish antenna.

'What the hell…?' Terrell said.

The dish hung limply, most of the retaining struts severed. Those that were still attached, had been crushed, squeezed flat in a chilling reproduction of the injuries to Craig.

'Vincent,' Dmitri said slowly, deliberately, 'do you know what happened to the communications array?'

'It would appear, sir, that the communications array has been deliberately sabotaged. I know of no way that this damage could be caused by accident or naturally. Say, by a meteorite impact.'

'Vincent, I am now giving you a direct order: command override alpha one: epsilon delta 6-6-9-4-2-7 omicron alpha omega theta. Did you cause this damage?'

'Command code accepted. Thank you. No sir, I have no knowledge of how the communications array came to be in this state.'

That seemed unequivocal, but Dmitri was still not convinced.

'Vincent,' he continued, 'command override alpha one: epsilon delta 6-6-9-4-2-7 omicron alpha omega theta. Did Bob cause this damage?'

'I do not believe so, sir, however I have not been in a position to observe Bob for all elapsed time since the array was last used.'

That was fair comment, Dmitri had to admit, but one of the bots had to have been responsible for the damage. Not to mention the murder of Craig Parker.

'Thank you, Vincent. Is the communications array repairable?'

'I believe so, Dmitri, but I would estimate that it will take four days to fabricate new components and repair all remaining systems.'

'Four days with no contact with Earth?' Natasha said. That's a long time to be out of contact with Trident Command.'

Eden's Gate

'Sure is,' Terrell said. 'They'll think we're all dead.'

Dmitri held up a hand to quieten the others. 'Vincent, please return to your station and shut down.'

There was a delay of a heartbeat. 'Are you sure you want me to do that, Dmitri? I really think I should start work repairing the antenna array.'

'No Vincent, please do as I ask, for now. We will address the communications issue later.'

'As you wish, Dmitri.'

The bot returned to its station and shut down as ordered. For some reason, everyone sagged a little, as if the tension was all that had been keeping them upright.

'So, do we believe him?' Terrell asked.

Dmitri shrugged. 'It does beat me.'

Terrell and Kalisa both smiled at Dmitri's precise way of speaking.

'There's not a lot more we can do tonight,' Natasha said. 'I think we could all use some sleep. We can decide on a course of action tomorrow when we have clearer heads.'

'Quite right,' Dmitri said. 'We will decide what to do tomorrow.'

The Arcadia Series

— Three —

Kalisa lay awake, contemplating, analysing, thinking. That was ninety percent of her job. Field geological research was largely a case of studying ice strata, rock types, mineral deposition and so on and so forth.

But tonight, geology could not be further from her mind. She had seen the two bots carry the lifeless form of Craig into the habitat, had seen Natasha take it through to her medical lab, which was not difficult in one seventh of a gravity.

What was most distressing, though, was the head, and the way it just hung listlessly by a thin sliver of flesh and mashed bone.

She had looked accusingly at the two bots as they scuttled back through the main hatch and thanked God that they were locked outside.

She kept going through the events of the night over and over and over again, and could not get the image of

Eden's Gate

Craig's lolling, listless head out of her mind. The eyes had stared unblinkingly ahead, and specks of blood had splattered onto the lower half of his face.

It was no good, she thought. She was not going to get any sleep tonight. She had been ensnared by busy brain syndrome, and the only cure was to put that brain to better use.

Kalisa quietly slipped from the bed as Terrell continued to snore quietly, threw a robe around her shoulders and tiptoed out of their sleeping quarters and out to the science section.

The geology lab was, as expected, just as she had left it. It wasn't a tidy lab. She didn't want it to be. Tidy labs were for people who spent more time cleaning than carrying out research. She didn't trust scientists with tidy labs.

Samples had been catalogued and were stored in racks on either side. Ahead was a window. It was only a forty-centimetre circle of plexiglass, but she could spend hours staring out across the moon's smooth, icy surface and beyond, to the great, azure blue disc of Neptune itself. Even when Triton was in its shadow, lightning from the storms that raged in those swirling cloud systems lit the surface of the moon.

Her workbench was strewn with a variety of samples. Rocks were few and far between on Triton, almost the entire surface consisting of frozen nitrogen and water ice. But this did not mean that there was not a great deal to interest her, as a geologist. Two hundred years earlier, a wandering dwarf planet had struck Triton, the two massive bodies merging to form what was now one of the largest moons in the Solar System. Cryovolcanoes spewed out an exotically diverse range of minerals, and the team had already amassed enough data to keep a small army of geologists busy for fifty years.

Kalisa picked up a beaker of cloudy water and held it up to the window, lightning flashes in Neptune's cloud systems briefly illuminating the liquid. Sometimes she could make out the fleeting sparkles of microscopic precious gems.

Something caught her eye. It was not in the cup, but beyond the window. It was only for an instant, but she thought she saw something out there. It had moved so quickly that it was gone in well under a second, but she was sure there had been something. It almost seemed to be running, a figure sprinting across the surface.

Kalisa shook her head, as if trying to flick the memory away. It was impossible. Nothing could be running around out there. Although she didn't feel tired, she was self-aware enough to realise that fatigue could well be causing her mind to play tricks on her. That, coupled with the horrors of earlier. Yes, that was what it was.

She slipped the beaker into the spectrometer, the contents displayed on a screen in front of her. There was nothing special in this sample. Nothing special for Triton. On Earth, the sheer wealth of minerals contained within would have staggered a geologist. But not here on this remarkable little world.

She popped the beaker out and replaced it with another. This sample was from four kilometres south of the last, but its contents were wildly different. The cup swarmed with hydrocarbons and amino acids. If the surface were a couple of hundred degrees Celsius warmer, this little cocktail might develop into single celled lifeforms, given enough time. But Triton was doomed to forever be a frigid, lifeless world of eternal twilight.

She caught a movement again. She was certain of it this time. She *had* seen it. She was sure.

Kalisa leaned closer to the window, so close that her breath momentarily fogged the plexiglass.

There was another movement, but this time she thought it was a reflection. A reflection in the glass. The reflection of something right behind her.

She had no time to move; no time to scream. It came at her from behind, its unyielding, cold body pressed against her back while a solid arm swung around and squeezed her throat.

She flailed, her arms swinging uselessly, legs kicking at whatever it was. The pressure on her throat increased, throttling her, squeezing the life from her.

'Ple… Plea…' she croaked weakly, and the pressure increased. With horror, she had a vision of Craig's throat, his neck crushed.

Her fingers clawed uselessly at the frigid arm, her strength deserting her. She stopped kicking, stopped fighting it.

A final, agonized gurgle escaped her lips, bulging eyes rolling up into their sockets.

In one swift, violent movement, Kalisa's neck was crushed until it was no thicker than a leather strap.

Her body went limp and, its life extinguished, was tossed aside.

※

Natasha stared at the body in wide-eyed horror. Whatever had done this had crushed Kalisa's neck as completely and brutally as it had Craig's. Her lifeless corpse had then been cast aside to land, draped across her chair, her limbs splayed out and hanging limply. Her head had been all but severed, cadaverous eyes staring off into the distance, mouth open and her tongue lolling.

It was Dmitri who had found her as he went through his habitual routine of powering up the various sections of Trident Base, as he did every morning. His first thought had been to check on Natasha, but she had been sleeping peacefully. He had then burst into Amber's room. With the body of her husband lying in cold storage, she had slept alone and would have been the most vulnerable, but he had found her sitting up in bed, staring absently at the ceiling.

Eden's Gate

'What the hell are you doing, Dmitri?' she had shouted angrily. She had, at least, been wearing a vest top, which spared both of their blushes.

'It's Kalisa,' he had said simply, and she instantly knew what must have happened.

The three of them stood in the doorway to the geology lab, saying nothing, simply staring.

'What's going on?' came a male voice from behind them.

'Don't come in here,' Dmitri warned, and turned to physically hold back the chemist.

The two men stared at each other for a moment, silently communicating what had happened.

'Out of my way,' Terrell said, pushing Dmitri aside. 'Kalisa? Kalisa, what's happ...' The words died in his throat as he caught sight of the grotesque image of his wife, legs and arms hanging limply, head virtually severed. 'Oh my God, no!'

He stood there, his eyes wide and staring as he pulled at his short hair with both hands.

'I am so sorry, my friend,' Dmitri said, holding Terrell in an embrace of shared woe. He eased him back, away from the abomination that had been his beautiful wife.

'Hey,' Amber said. 'Come on, Terrell. I'll take you back to your room.'

Dmitri released him and Amber took his place as she guided him back to his quarters. She turned just long enough to give Dmitri and Natasha a weak and uncertain smile.

'We must get her into storage,' Dmitri said, looking at the body once more. 'Natasha, who can have done this? Why would they?'

'I don't know,' Natasha replied as she gently lifted the body. 'Craig had a tendency to rub people up the wrong way, so if anyone was going to be murdered, I wouldn't have been surprised it was him. But Kalisa? She was just the sweetest thing.'

'I know. I was thinking the same. I did not want to see Craig dead, but in a way it was understandable.'

They delivered the body to the medical lab, and sealed it in a cold store. They only had two units. The mission planners had not envisaged that more than two people would realistically die while on the surface.

Dmitri stalked stiffly back to the lounge in the central hub and fired up his workstation. When the screen hummed into life, it showed the maintenance bots both sitting right where they had been the previous night.

'This was my fault,' he said. 'I caused this to happen.'

'No, you didn't,' Natasha reassured him. 'How could it be your fault?'

'I told the bots to shut down. I thought that would be enough. I should have gone out there and ripped their power units out!' Dmitri slammed his fist onto the desk, the noise thundering through the habitat.

Natasha rested a comforting hand on his shoulder, and bent down to kiss the top of his head. 'None of us thought they would reactivate themselves, or come inside the base in the middle of the night.'

'We can make sure we do it properly now,' came Amber's resolute voice.

She appeared in the doorway, with Terrell right behind her. His eyes were red and he looked wretched, but there was also a stone-faced resolve to him now that was almost intimidating.

'I will go outside and disable the bots,' Dmitri said, rousing himself from the desk.

'And I'll go with you,' Amber said.

'It is a job that only requires one person to be outside.'

'Wrong. It'll need two. One to disable the bots, and another armed to the teeth and ready to blow those things straight to hell if they try anything.'

Dmitri considered this for a moment and then nodded, recognizing the logic of the suggestion. 'Very well. You and I shall go outside and do this.'

He walked over to a sealed cabinet in the wall and punched in a six-digit code. The door slid open, revealing two M130 laser rifles and four Glock SS9 hand lasers. Taking up arms was not something he had thought he would have to do when he was first appointed mission commander, although he had been trained in when and how they should be used. He handed one of the rifles to Natasha, and the other to Terrell.

'You both remember how to use these weapons?'

'Of course,' Natasha said. 'But we're not the ones—'

'I need you to watch those bots on the monitor while Amber and I get suited up. If they move just one centimetre, let me know. If they try to gain entry to the base, they will probably come through this hatch, but remember there is the emergency hatch in the science section. Just stay alert.'

'But you've sealed all the doors,' Terrell said. 'You don't think that will hold them?'

'The seal is a six-digit combination. They could have that bypassed in under twenty seconds.'

'That's always assuming,' Amber cut in, 'that they don't decide to cut their way through first. Then we really would have a problem.'

Dmitri handed one hand laser to Natasha, and the other to Terrell, who took it with a shaking hand.

'Remember,' Dmitri said as he and Amber headed for the environment suit store, 'do not take your eyes off those bots.'

— Four —

Ten minutes later, Dmitri and Amber were inside the airlock, awaiting the atmosphere to be pumped out.

'Are you all right doing this?' he asked.

'Of course. Why wouldn't I be?'

'You saw your husband murdered by one of these things yesterday. I need you to be focused on the job.'

'Just shut up, Dmitri, and let's get on with this.'

When the pressure matched external conditions, they heard a clank and the outer hatch slid aside. Amber already had her rifle up and ready, just in case the robots tried to jump them, but it didn't seem to be necessary.

They spent a moment to stare out at the twilight world at the edge of the Solar System. Neptune hung in the sky above them, a shimmering quarter crescent of impossibly beautiful blue. The night side of the planet crackled with lightning, each flash illuminating the icy vista before them.

'Remember Amber, we need to disable the bots, not destroy them.'

'What difference does it make?'

'The difference is that we need them as evidence,' he said as they left the airlock and walked in that slow, plodding gait that was the most efficient way to move on this moon. 'I do not believe that any one of us is responsible for these murders. Which means the bots were sabotaged before we left Earth.'

'You think this is some grand plan? To kill us all off? For what purpose?'

'I believe someone wants this mission to fail, and fail so badly that no one comes back to try again.'

They rounded the accommodation section and came to the maintenance bots, sitting quietly where they seemed to have stayed all night. Dmitri raised his own rifle and pointed it at Bob, the closest of the robots.

'Remember, only fire if they attack,' he said, and heard a tut and a sigh as a response. Dmitri keyed his mike and flicked to the bots' frequency. 'Bob: initialize.'

The bot's operating lights immediately sprang to life and despite himself, Dmitri's trigger finger twitched involuntarily.

'Good morning, Dmitri,' Bob said in his usual, amiable and polite tone.'

'Good morning. Bob, we believe you may have an internal fault, and need you to power down so we can remove your battery pack for inspection.'

Eden's Gate

There was the faintest of pauses before the robot responded. 'I have just run an internal self-diagnostic and can find no fault, Dmitri. All systems appear to be nominal.'

'I know, Bob. The fault may not show up in a standard diagnostic, but we have it on good authority that it is there.'

'Very well. If there is a fault, perhaps I should remain operational until the fault develops.'

There was a crackle of static in his ear as Amber cut in on a different frequency. 'He's not going for it, Dmitri.'

In response, he held up a hand, and addressed the robot again. 'No Bob, we believe that if left, the damage to your systems could be irreparable.'

'I really think I should remain active until the fault develops, Dmitri. If I am damaged, then there is every probability that Vincent will be able to repair me.'

'No, and I am afraid I will have to order you to shut down. Command override alpha one: epsilon delta 6-6-9-4-2-7 omicron alpha omega theta.'

There was an even longer pause this time, and Amber's eyes darted from the robot to Dmitri, and back again.

'Very well, Dmitri,' Bob said. 'Shutting down now.'

The lights on the robot suddenly went dark and it sat, immobile and apparently shut down.

Both humans sighed, but did not relax for an instant. The robots were supposed to have been shut down the previous night, but if that were the case, why was Kalisa lying in a cold store with her slender neck crushed flat?

'I will need to retrieve the battery pack from Bob's underside, which means climbing under him.'

'Okay, but you be careful. If I had my way, I'd blast him into a million pieces and that'd end our problem.'

'Indeed, but I think this is why they made me mission commander and not you,' Dmitri said as he squatted down and reached under the robot's belly. Removing the batteries was not, alas, simply a case of flipping a catch and pulling them out. There were six retaining screws that held the cover in place, and he carefully, methodically, unscrewed each one. When the last screw was released, the cover pivoted down and the battery pack slid halfway out. It was then just a case of removing the couplings.

And that was it. One robot was completely disabled. Dmitri was almost disappointed. After all the build-up, all the trepidation and preparations, it had been remarkably easy. But this still left one more unit to go.

Dmitri extricated himself from underneath the bot and got to his feet, brushing mineral dust off himself. He handed the battery pack to Amber.

'There's a storage locker behind you,' he said.

She turned and saw the locker he had gestured to.

The scream was so abrupt, so sudden to come, and so sudden to be extinguished. Amber shot back round to see a cloud of swirling, billowing dust surrounding Dmitri.

As she watched, she saw his head suddenly fall back, as if on a hinge. The body crumpled to the ground, as lifeless as the ice on which it lay.

Amber started to scream, scream like she never had before, blasting the thin air with vicious, searing laser fire.

Natasha's hands came up to stifle a silent scream. In a literal blink of an eye, the scene went from placid calm to a vision of hell. Her hell. Her nightmare.

In an instant, Dmitri was engulfed in a whirl of dust, an arm swinging round and crushing his neck as easily as she could crush a paper cup.

And then she saw that awful sight, the most awful thing she had ever seen. Dmitri's head had swung back in a hideous pivot, and his body collapsed beneath him.

'Ye gods,' Terrell breathed.

Amber's screams erupted from the speakers, and she began to fire wildly, blasting the disabled robot until all eight of its legs had been severed.

Outside, Amber was in a blind panic. It was out there. It had killed Dmitri and it was now after her.

She ran, her legs feeling like rubber as she was a scintilla away from giving in to her terror. But running on this world wasn't easy. It was more akin to running in waist deep water. She tried to propel herself away from the nightmare, but stayed almost in the same place, her feet scuffing and skidding on the ground.

She crawled and clawed at the ice with one hand, the other firing the rifle around her in a spray of blazing, white-hot rain. Amber tried to look round, but her helmet remained resolutely facing forward. She was certain that at any moment, she would feel that arm snake around her neck and crush the life from her.

There was a crackle in her ear. 'Amber, get back here. Hurry!' screamed Natasha.

'What d'ya think I'm trying to do?'

She started to gain a little momentum, using a pipe to drag herself along. A little further, she thought. Twenty meters. She could do that.

Something touched her leg. Something hard and deadly.

Amber leapt into the sky, her body carving a parabolic arc through the thin atmosphere. Twisting round, she fired into the ice cloud that followed her, laser blasts cutting through it and slicing into the thick ice of the surface.

One blast hit something else, and she heard the furious roar of something crying out in pain. The noise was unlike anything that she had ever heard before, the primeval bellow of a wounded hunter.

Amber crashed to the ground and rolled several times before coming to a stop. Dust swirled in the air around her in extravagant eddies. She expected to see some monstrous beast appear, surging through the cloud to grab her and crush her in a savage rage.

She waited. And waited.

'Move your ass, you dumb bitch,' she cursed, and pushed herself upright, staggering over to the hatch and punching the door release. It slid open and she backed inside, watching that menacing cloud as it churned and billowed.

Not taking her eyes off the swirling veil, her free hand fumbled for the hatch controls, her fingers probing, feeling, searching. She daren't take her eyes off the icy blanket that broiled in front of her. She was certain that if she did, whatever was concealed within it would reach out and grab her.

She found the control and punched it. But as the door began to slide closed, she finally saw it.

It was more monstrous, more terrifying than anything she could have conceived. It was huge, the size of a grizzly bear. Its body, as large as it was, was dwarfed by disproportionately large and powerful arms. The limbs seemed segmented, like those of an insect, and the face was a mass of vicious-looking mandibles and razor teeth.

And then it was gone. The door slammed shut and she could hear air being pumped into the airlock. She stood there, hyperventilating, transfixed by the memory. It was her worst nightmare made manifest. Poor Craig had never stood a chance against that. He had been tough, with an uncompromising attitude that was both infuriating and sexy as hell. If he were going to die, he deserved a fair fight of it. But this thing didn't fight fair. It skulked in the shadows, waiting to ambush its hapless prey. Like Dmitri. It must have been concealed right there, but neither of them could see it.

The inner hatch slid aside and Amber stumbled backwards into the habitat, Terrell catching her before she could topple over completely.

She unclasped her helmet and was instantly bombarded with questions as she gasped for air.

'Are you all right?' Natasha asked. 'We just saw the whole area erupt in a dust storm.'

'What happened?' Terrell said.

Amber threw both hands up in the air. 'Quiet!'

For half a second, it worked, and then Natasha continued. 'I saw Dmitri die. It was…'

Amber pulled her close and hugged her, her squeeze tight enough to elicit a tiny squeal of pain. But she needed this human contact for now. She needed to feel the warmth of a human body. All too soon, it came to an end.

'I'm so sorry about Dmitri,' Amber said.

'It just happened so fast. We didn't even see the robots move—'

'It wasn't the robots.'

'What?' said Terrell.

'There's something else out there. Some kind of… animal.'

Natasha's mouth dropped open a fraction. 'An animal? Some kind of creature lives on this moon? But that's not possible.'

'I saw it, Natasha. I saw it right outside that hatch.' She gestured with a flick of her head toward the door. 'It's out there, and I'm sure it won't stop until we are all dead.'

The three of them stared at one another as they assimilated the implications of this.

'Kalisa was killed inside the habitat,' Terrell said, and the other two looked at him. 'Either it let itself in to kill her and then let itself out again, or…'

'Or there is more than one of them,' Amber finished for him, 'and one of them is still in here with us.'

Slowly, they tore their eyes away from each other and cast their collective gaze over the room.

'Just suppose,' Natasha said, 'that it is invisible.'

'Not invisible,' Terrell answered slowly as his bulging eyes scanned the room, his hand laser following close behind. 'Amber saw the creature outside.'

'Not quite true,' Amber said. 'I saw its shape as it emerged from the dust cloud. It may have some form of active camouflage.'

'That begs the question: why would it need active camouflage on a dead moon?'

'We don't know for sure that Triton is completely dead. There's an entire subsurface ocean under our feet. Who knows what could be living down there.'

Natasha butted in. 'That's all very fascinating, but do either of you have a plan for killing them?'

'We don't know how many there are,' he said. 'There could be dozens of them out there.'

'There's a way to find out,' Amber said, lowering her rifle and going over to the workstation. She fired up the external cameras and multiple feeds were split over the screen. 'Can either of you see anything?'

'No,' Terrell said, 'but we couldn't see anything before.'

'It's negative 235 degrees C out there. You think these things might have a heat signature?'

She adjusted the view to infrared. The screen flared for a moment, and when it settled down, their worst fears were realised. Just outside the hatch, no fewer than eighteen forms waited, some moving around, others stationary.

They also saw their own heat signatures in the lounge.

One, two, three, four.

'Amber,' Natasha said, her voice brittle with terror. 'There are only three of us.'

— Five —

They spun around and as one, blasted the area where the fourth heat signature was. Natasha and Terrell both missed. Amber's laser found its mark.

The creature roared into life, agonizing, white fire drilling into its hide. Its camouflage flickered for a moment, then died. They could finally see one of the creatures in full, terrible clarity.

Once they had a clear target to shoot at, Natasha and Terrell's lasers joined Amber's, the creature roaring and thrashing. Thick, brown blood spurted from its belly, entrails and organs spilling out. Natasha focused her fire on its head, the lancing beam of incandescent death cutting into its mouth and slicing the tender tissue of its throat. More gloopy blood erupted and the roar turned to a gurgle.

The beast crumpled to the floor, but the three of them kept firing until it moved no more.

They stood there, panting, and waited for the monster to suddenly rear up and attack. They had all seen horror vids where the heroes had relaxed too soon, and weren't going to make the same mistake.

'Is it dead?' Natasha asked.

'I damn well hope so,' Amber said, edging forward and kicking what was left of the creature's head. She was impressed. Natasha had done a pretty comprehensive job of destroying it. 'One down, eighteen more out there. Maybe more.'

'We only just managed to kill this one,' Terrell said. 'How are we supposed to kill them all?'

'We don't,' Natasha said, glancing at Amber who nodded, clearly thinking the same thing.

'No, we get the hell off this godforsaken ball of ice and head for home, as fast as we can and never come back.'

The shuttle rested on its landing/launch pad five kilometres from the base, just beyond a low hill. Its chemical rockets would quickly get them up to the main ship that was in orbit above them.

Natasha knelt down next to the creature and prodded at it with the barrel of her hand laser. 'Oh my God,' she breathed.

'Oh for mercy's sake, what now?' Amber shouted. She had had more than enough surprises from this world for one morning.

'This armour,' Natasha said, peeling a section away. 'It's not a natural part of the creature's anatomy.'

'What?'

'At a wild guess, I would say it's more like an armoured environment suit.'

'Are you kidding me?' Amber said with both eyebrows raised way above her eyeline. 'You mean these freaking monsters have made their own suits to live on this stinking walrus' butt of a moon?'

'All I'm saying is that this skin...' She tapped the shell-like plating, '...is artificial. It's no more a part of them than our environment suits are a part of us.'

'There's another thing,' Terrell said. 'They've not been hunting us for food. All they've done is kill us quickly and efficiently.'

'Unless they're storing the bodies to take back to a hive or nest later,' Natasha said. 'Maybe human is a favourite for the baby Tritonians.'

'Or they're hunting us for sport,' Amber finished for her. 'Either way, I don't want to be around when they come to break the door down. I mean it's not going to take them long to figure out we just wasted one of their buddies.'

Knock-knock-knock.

'Oh Jesus!' Amber shouted. 'Both of you: get into your environment suits. I'll hold them here.'

'Okay,' Terrell said, 'but just you keep an eye on that monitor, and make sure none try to circle around the back to ambush us.'

The Arcadia Series

The trio of scared, watchful humans moved uneasily through the base, their eyes and weapons darting this way and that. There were multiple heat signatures within the habitat. Each piece of equipment they possessed generated heat, and their infrared cameras were not sensitive enough to differentiate between innocuous machine and murderous alien. Amber had adjusted their suits' head-up displays to show an infrared overlay, which went a small way to evening the odds. At least now they would *see* the rampaging monster that was about to kill them.

'Do we have a plan?' Natasha asked.

'The ice-hopper is parked quite close to the emergency exit hatch in the science section,' Terrell said. 'As long as we can get it fired up before they attack, I think we could be away before they can respond. I'm betting the hopper can move faster than they can.'

'I wouldn't bet my mission fee on it,' Amber said grimly. 'You have no idea just how fast they are. I literally just blinked and Dmitri had a pancake for a neck.' She glanced across at Natasha, realising that the comment wasn't quite as sensitively put as it might have been. 'Sorry Nat.'

'Don't worry about it. I'll take out my pent-up aggression on one of those things, when I see one.'

'You and me both, honey. The next one will be for Craig.'

Terrell nodded. 'The next one I kill will be for Kalisa.'

'And I'm saving one up for Dmitri.'

'Okay, here we are,' Amber said, dragging some piled up equipment away from the emergency hatch.

'What if they're waiting for us on the other side?' Natasha asked.

Amber just shrugged. 'Then we'll have a lot more targets to shoot at. Right, here we—'

'Kill it!' screamed Terrell. He managed to fire two shots, both of which went wide.

Amber and Natasha turned, their eyes going wide as they saw the immense form of a creature behind them. With unbelievable agility, it shot out one of its immense arms and snatched Terrell, giant pincers clutching his waist. His scream of pain and terror echoed around the base as his pelvis was crushed, crimson blood spurting out.

Amber was the first to start firing at the beast, doing her best not to hit Terrell as he was swung around in the air.

Another arm darted out and closed around his stomach, and its vicious pincer squeezed.

Blood erupted from Terrell's mouth as he screamed and choked. His legs flailed limply, arms pathetically hammering at the pincers that held him tight.

And then the beast yanked its two arms apart, tearing Terrell in two. He lived for a few more terrified, tortured seconds, before it smashed his head against the wall. It exploded in a violent spatter of blood and brain and bone.

The monster roared in fury, the whole base shaking.

Natasha cut through its head, slicing it in two, yet still it fought and lumbered toward them. She shifted her aim and concentrated her fire on its abdomen. It was sliced open, a ribcage of bone as thick as a man's forearm opening up.

An enormous arm swung out to try and grab her, but Natasha dodged out of the way of the beast's pincers as they snapped shut, missing her leg by scant centimetres.

'Fire into its chest!' Natasha yelled, and the pair of them fired into that grotesque, gaping hole in its abdomen.

The creature spasmed for several seconds, its limbs thrashing and quivering in a violent frenzy. It reared up, the bloodied remains of its head smashing into the ceiling before it collapsed and crashed to the floor.

They stared at it, and at the bloodied remains of Terrell.

'What the hell?' Amber said, not really sure of what question she wanted to ask. 'You blew its head off and it still kept coming.'

Natasha had sunk to the floor, wallowing in the creature's sticky brown blood. 'I suddenly realised that its brain must be in the most protected part of its body: its chest. The head isn't really a head as we understand it. It's just an appendage designed to accommodate a mouth.'

'Well screw me sideways.'

'Yes, ingenious design. There's nothing like it in any terrestrial animals that I know of.'

'Yeah, very fascinating, professor. But we need to get the hell out of here before any more of those things show up.'

Amber checked the gauge on the airlock. It was pressurized to 1,013 millibars, which she found a little reassuring. At least they hadn't opened it from the outside.

She opened the inner hatch and held her breath, half expecting one of the monsters to be in there. But the airlock was, mercifully, clear. The two women edged inside, dragging a mixture of brown and red blood into the chamber with them.

Once inside, neither was inclined to open the outer hatch and face whatever was out there, but both knew they had to.

When the chamber had finished depressurizing, Amber held her hand over the outer hatch control. 'Are you ready?'

'No. The last thing I want to do is go out there. But if we must.' Natasha gave her a weak smile, closed her eyes as she took a deep breath.

Amber did the same, and punched the switch that would open the outer hatch.

— Six —

They both jumped as they saw an infrared flare on the body of the ice-hopper, before they realised that it came from the power unit in the rear of the machine. The hopper consisted of a large, domed cockpit at the front, a pair of variable vector jets on the sides and six spindly legs. Carrying on the same design philosophy that had created the maintenance robots, it looked disturbingly like a giant white ant.

But that giant ant was the most welcome sight they had seen that day.

'Okay,' Amber whispered, even though she doubted her words would be audible in the thin atmosphere, 'move slowly toward the hopper. No sudden movements until we're inside, then we floor it. Got it?'

Natasha nodded, and the two of them crept out into the open, almost keeping their backs to each other as they went. They had both seen how swiftly the attack on Dmitri had come, and took no chances.

Eden's Gate

The hopper was just a few meters from the hatch, and to the amazement of both, they reached it without being crushed, eviscerated, slashed or disembowelled. As quietly and unobtrusively as they could, they opened the hatch and slipped inside.

Amber really didn't want to say "phew". That would imply that they were safe – that they had made it. She knew how tenuous their chances really were, and did not want to invite fate's capricious wrath.

'Ready?' she whispered.

'Go for it.'

Amber flicked the power switch and the craft thrummed into life. It sounded like the roar of a lion in the confines of the cabin, and she silently cursed its mechanics.

Amber and Natasha shared a look, then both looked outside.

Hurtling towards them, around and over the top of the habitat, was a blurred mass of infrared heat signatures.

'Aww hell!' Amber shouted, giving up any pretence of stealth. 'Hang on!'

She wrenched the control column back and the hopper reared into the air, leaving a trail of hydrogen gas in its wake. It soared into the sky, a hundred meters up, and then began a gentle descent.

This was the hopper's most unusual design characteristic, and was the reason it had been given its name. Engineers on Earth's Moon had calculated that the most efficient form of locomotion was for the craft to 'hop' across the surface, coming to within a few meters of the ground before the jets would once again propel it skyward.

Fuel efficient, it was. Safe, when fleeing a marauding pack of vicious alien killers, it was not.

Its closest point to the ground on its first hop was just fifty meters from Trident Base, and they could see the horde charging to intercept them. The creatures were now not bothering to conceal themselves behind active camouflage, and the two women were treated to the sight of thirty or more enraged monsters scurrying and clawing their way over the ice.

'Take us up!' Natasha cried.

'I can't. Brace yourself,' Amber said, pushing herself back into the seat, as if this might put a little more distance between her and the monsters.

They cringed as the craft reached its nadir, and the leading wave of creatures launched themselves at them. They flew into the air, huge clawed arms reaching for them. One creature smashed into the plexiglass cockpit full on, fracture lines snaking away from the point of impact. Another beast would have succeeded in its attack, but was deflected by the first.

A third creature did manage to cling on.

It clamped one pincer onto one of the hopper's forward legs, hanging there suspended for a moment, before wrenching itself up and punching one arm into the cockpit, shattered plexiglass exploding and showering the two women.

Eden's Gate

The craft's flight management computer went crazy, trying to find a way to compensate for the sudden extra mass on one side.

'Kill it!' Amber screamed as she fought with the controls.

Natasha fired wildly at the arm that swung back and forth, its pincer snapping again and again. It swung close to Amber's helmet, grazing the visor, before the pendulum motion took it back toward Natasha. It hit her shoulder hard, and her body was smashed against the cockpit's side. The door, not designed for such abuse, swung open and Natasha was flung out through the gaping hole in the craft's side.

'Tasha!' Amber screamed as she saw her friend flung outside, but there was nothing she could do. Natasha was gone, and any moment now the horde of monsters would be on top of her, tearing her to pieces.

Amber had her own problems. The arm swung back toward her and she felt it smash into her helmet, which in turn hit the other door. Mercifully, this one held and she wasn't propelled out into the void as Natasha had been.

The pincer snapped at her. Crack-crack-crack.

The computer feverishly sought a solution to the hopper's handling issues, firing the attitude jets in various combinations, none of which helped. As the craft began another descent, it calculated there was just one option left.

Instead of fighting the burden on the port side, it did the opposite.

The ice-hopper rolled a full 360 degrees, a manoeuvre that caught the creature off guard. The snapping pincer disappeared back through the forward screen and the beast once again clung to just the forward leg, its body swinging wildly.

The barrel roll had surprised Amber, but what happened next surprised her even more.

From nowhere, she saw a series of laser blasts crackle through the thin air, hitting the beast.

It roared in fury.

'What the *hell* is going on?' she cried, reason rapidly deserting her.

Another blast hit it, more sustained than the first barrage, slicing through its arm.

The monster howled in pain as its arm was sliced clean off, and it went tumbling away toward the ground.

A hand appeared in the open doorway on the opposite side of the cockpit, followed by another. Amber reached across and dragged Natasha back inside.

'Good to see you,' Amber grinned. 'Have to admit, I thought you were a goner there.'

'Not just yet,' Natasha panted breathlessly. 'Nice move with the roll thing. Caught it completely off guard.'

'Don't mention it.' If they survived the next hour, she would tell Natasha then that it was the ship's doing, and not hers.

The hopper reached its lowest point again, but this time there were no creatures anywhere near close enough to pose a threat.

'Where are we going?' Natasha asked. 'The shuttle is in completely the opposite direction, isn't it?'

'Yeah, I'm hoping to lead them away and give us some time. I don't want to be powering up the shuttle while fighting off our new friends.'

'Good thinking.'

The hopper went through another half dozen cycles of hops before Amber turned them around and headed straight for the shuttle.

Most of the creatures followed them.

Three did not.

Ψ

Amber ignored the landing pad a full one hundred meters from the shuttle. The mission planners had thought it a prudent measure, putting it so far away, and assumed that the science team would not mind traversing this small distance on foot.

However, the mission planners had not factored in the possibility that the team would be pursued by hideous, Tritonion monsters. So, on balance, Amber decided to say screw the regs; she would put this thing down practically on top of the shuttle, the hopper coming to rest barely ten meters away.

They quickly leapt from the cockpit and turned for the shuttle but stopped.

Appearing from behind the rocket were one, two, three of the monsters. They lumbered forwards, almost swaggering as they knew they had the hapless Earthlings now. The middle creature roared into the air, a triumphant, thundering roar.

The two women stood there, unable to move; barely able to breathe. There wasn't time to get back in the battered ice-hopper and lift off. The creatures would be on them in seconds.

Underfoot, they could feel the rumble of something heavy approaching. A lot of heavy somethings. The horde of monsters would be over the low hill in a minute. Perhaps less than that, and they had no doubt that they would be swiftly torn apart.

Amber slowly raised her rifle. 'How much charge on your laser?'

'Not enough. I'm down to under five percent. Enough for three good, sustained blasts.'

'Mine's not much better. But we might as well fight. It's better than just giving in. We'll be dead either way.'

Natasha smiled, despite the hopelessness of the situation. 'Sounds good to me. Aim for the belly of the middle one.'

'You got it. On three. One, two—'

There was a sudden flash of gleaming silver. It was so unexpected that both women took a full second to respond.

A chrome spider, as big as a man and ten times as strong, dropped onto the creature on the right.

Eden's Gate

'Vincent?' Amber shouted, completely astonished.

With one of the creatures being kept occupied, Amber and Natasha both fired at the centre beast, which reared up, roaring in anger as it prepared to attack.

Natasha fired one sustained shot into its vulnerable underside, carving open its chest just as her hand laser fizzled and died.

But Amber was ready, and fired a powerful blast of her own straight into the open cavity.

The animal screamed, the shrill, plaintive wail cutting through the air. But the sound was cut off, the beast already dead before it hit the ground.

'The chest, Vincent,' Amber shouted. 'That's where it's vulnerable. That's its brain.'

'I understand, Amber,' came the strangely calm response.

The monster reared and bucked, flinging the robot from side-to-side, but Vincent tenaciously clung on with seven of its chrome legs. The eighth, with a high-powered drill bit attached, slammed into the creature's chest, boring deep inside. Thick, brown blood spurted from the wound, instantly freezing as it hit the $-235°$ C air, dropping to the ground in solid lumps to shatter like glass.

The third creature leapt onto its embattled comrade, its heavy arms slamming down onto the robot's back with a reverberating clang. Vincent doggedly pushed the drill into the other beast's chest as it convulsed in spasm, thrashing its hefty arms wildly.

The other monster pounded the bot again, and when this had no obvious effect, began to cut it metal legs away, one by one.

Amber dived for the cockpit of the hopper.

'Where are you going?' Natasha cried.

'To finish this,' Amber yelled back as she brought the craft's systems back online. Numerous red lights indicated multiple system failures, but she hoped she could still get the ship airborne. 'Get to the shuttle and fire up the engines!'

'I'm already on my way,' Natasha shouted back.

The creature had hacked four of Vincent's legs off when the robot was satisfied that the other beast would not move again. It then proceeded to do battle with this new threat, although with four legs now gone, the odds were not in its favour.

Natasha skirted the battle, hoping and praying that Vincent could keep the beast occupied just long enough for her to get into the shuttle.

Just a meter in front of her, Vincent was slammed to the ground, the monster holding one of his legs. It lifted him again and Natasha took that moment to scurry past, her boots sliding on the ice. She half ran/half scrambled toward the ship's access ladder.

Just behind her, Vincent was slammed to the ground again and bounced off toward the edge of the launch pad. It had lost another leg, and didn't move for several seconds.

The creature used this time to turn its attention toward Natasha, who was backing away up the ladder. It moved slowly, its pincers snapping.

She felt the shuttle's hatch at her back and, daring not to take her eyes from the beast, fumbled for the door release.

The creature reared up, roaring, its claws raised and ready to come crashing down.

Natasha had nowhere to run, nowhere to hide, and crouched down, awaiting the inevitable.

— Seven —

Vincent stumbled unsteadily to his three legs, his battered data processing centre desperately trying to make some sense of the scene. Four of his cameras had also been knocked out, but he still had two working. Just. He would run diagnostics later.

But what he did see was one of the creatures. His systems had not succeeded in identifying these lifeforms, merely assigning them as a threat to human life, and as such were a priority and were to be eliminated.

The shuttle appeared to be undamaged, and he could see the cowering form of Natasha, defenceless and under attack.

He staggered toward the creature, analysing his systems and calculating probabilities as he moved. One of his jets was still working, but stable flight would be impossible. He tried anyway, and was surprised that he had some control.

He had only one option, if he was to be of assistance to Natasha.

Eden's Gate

Vincent brought the jet up to full power and surged toward the creature.

The monster reared up in front of her, and Natasha could see it in all its terrible magnificence. The arms were held high, ready to smash down and end her life. At least that would be quick. She didn't relish the thought of being conscious as her arms and legs were ripped from their sockets.

But then something unexpected happened. Something silver flashed into view, and a heartbeat later she realised that it must be the valiant robot, Vincent. He crashed into the side of the beast, knocking it aside.

It shrieked in pain, lashing out at the bot and swiping it hard. Vincent was sent flying off to crash into the side of the shuttle. It tried to move, wobbling back and forth several times, sparks coming from smashed circuits.

The beast turned its attention back to Natasha.

But it hadn't taken the other human into account.

Natasha had watched the hopper unsteadily ascend into the sky before Vincent's attack.

And now it came back down.

The hopper smashed into the monster at a little over fifty kilometres per hour, its legs impaling the beast. It screamed in an agonized frenzy, bucking and spasming.

Amber was dazed for several seconds, not sure if she were dead or alive. Amazingly, she seemed to have survived the impact without serious injury. She staggered from the cockpit, the hopper rocking back and forth as the wounded creature writhed beneath it.

'Get inside the shuttle,' she said wearily to Natasha, who simply waved and finally managed to open the hatch, scooting up the ladder to the flight deck.

Amber could feel the rumble of creatures thundering toward them through her boots. They must be just seconds away, she thought. She bent over and retrieved the remains of Vincent, his three chrome legs hanging limply, and lurched back toward the shuttle.

Inside, she joined Natasha in the cockpit.

'What kept you?' the Russian asked.

'Just picking up what's left of Vincent. Least I could do for the poor guy.'

'Okay, bringing the engines up to full…'

Natasha and Amber peered out of the screen at the hilltop that dominated the view.

'Oh dear, this could be bad,' Amber whispered.

An army of the creatures thundered over the crest, leaping into the air at the shuttle.

'Get us in the air!' Natasha screamed, and Amber slammed the throttles forward.

The shuttle shook with the energy being released, and began to rise into the air.

But not fast enough.

A dozen creatures hurled themselves at the craft, landing on top. A dozen more followed.

The shuttle wobbled in the air, the sudden extra mass more than its lift off engines could tolerate. It began to drift sideways, but not upwards. More creatures leapt at them, pincers clinging on to the landing struts.

'More power!' Natasha shouted.

'That's all we've got. And it's not enough.'

The craft gained speed, sliding further and further to starboard.

And the ground seemed awfully close.

'This is it,' Amber said. 'Dammit, sorry Tash.'

'Let's hope it's quick,' Natasha replied, a second before they smashed into the ice at a hundred and fifty kilometres per hour.

— Eight —

Knock-knock-knock.
The noise was familiar. She had heard it somewhere before. It was quite recent as well. But she couldn't quite place it. Maybe Craig could…

And then the memories started to return. At first, just a trickle, but then in a cascade of horrific images and terror. Craig was dead. She had seen his discarded body, tossed aside four hundred meters from the base.

And the others. All those others.

Dead.

Amber twitched, feeling pain in her shoulders, her forearms and wrists. She opened her eyes, just a crack at first. Bright lights. That was all her mind could think. She blinked several times, the image blurred beyond recognition to begin with, but rapidly resolving into something, if not recognizable, then relatable.

She was in a room four or five meters square. It was bright, strong lighting coming from the floor. There appeared to be no furniture in the room and no decoration.

Eden's Gate

This wasn't where she had been. What was her last memory? The shuttle. They had been trying to lift off, but those monsters had brought them down. She had a blurry recollection of the icy surface of Triton rushing toward them.

Them? She remembered that she had not been alone. Natasha. Natasha was with her.

Amber suddenly realised that her wrists were manacled together and she was suspended from the ceiling a meter above the floor. Her helmet was gone, and her hands and feet were now bare, but she was, at least, still wearing the environment suit.

She looked across and saw that Natasha was there, and hung from the ceiling just as she was. Like two pieces of meat in an abattoir. She hoped the analogy didn't turn out to be quite that accurate.

'Tash,' she croaked, and coughed several times, spitting out bile. 'Tasha, you alive, honey?'

Natasha's head suddenly jerked, her hair swishing back and forth.

'I'm alive,' she said groggily, sounding like Amber felt. Natasha looked around, squinting in the dazzling light, moving her head back and forth to loosen her neck muscles. 'Where are we?'

'I have absolutely no idea. But from the gravity, I'm guessing we're no longer on Triton.'

'Maybe we should just play dead and hope—'

With a clanking crash, a large double door swung open in the opposite wall. First one, then two of the monstrous creatures lumbered inside.

'Oh great,' Amber said, glancing across at Natasha. 'You reckon it's feeding time for the crab monsters?'

Natasha said nothing, but the colour drained from her face as she stared fearfully at the two gigantic creatures that now seemed to fill the room.

'Noo challa groopla kampakla doe,' it rumbled, its voice an impossibly deep baritone.

'Yeah, yeah,' Amber said, 'and your momma does it with lobsters.'

It looked at her, its head cocked as if considering her words, but then moved over to Natasha and spun her round roughly so she faced the wall. She shrieked once, her body quivering as she expected the thing to rip her apart as had happened to poor Terrell.

'Hey, hey ugly,' Amber shouted. 'Eat me! Eat me. I'm way tastier. Come on, you fat piece of filth!'

It ignored her and, with surprising dexterity, used one of its pincers to pull the material of Natasha's environment suit away from her neck. She sobbed as she shook uncontrollably.

The beast used the pincer of its other arm to slice the organic polyamide from neck to halfway down her back. Her vest was cut in the same way, leaving the flesh over her spine bare.

The other creature handed it something. It was a tool of some kind, which looked ludicrously puny in its giant pincer. It held the instrument against Natasha's back and... it hissed.

It turned her back around and grunted in her face. Natasha looked stunned, her head lolling.

The creature moved over to Amber and began to repeat the operation.

'Keep your stinking paws off me!' she yelled, and was about to scream even more colourful invective at the creature when she heard Natasha speak softly.

'It's all right, Amber. I'm fine.'

She didn't look fine, but how much of that was a result of the procedure and how much was shock and fatigue, was impossible to tell.

Amber didn't struggle as she felt the back of her suit cut open just as Natasha's had been. The instrument, whatever it was, was metal and felt cold when pressed against her spine. There was a hiss, a brief burst of pain, and then it just tingled like a two-day old nettle sting.

'Noo chora kloo,' the creature said. 'Palla kroo delar heard a female complain as much as her.'

It swung Amber back around.

'I heard that in English,' she said, utterly confounded. 'Did you—'

'I did,' Natasha replied.

'And my mother does not do it with lobsters,' the creature finished.

Both monsters backed away and waited.

They heard footsteps. Not the lumbering footfalls of the huge beasts, but the light deliberate steps of a human. A human female.

She stepped through the doorway and stared up at the two women suspended above her. She was average height with blond hair that bordered on light brown, and had an aristocratic air about her.

'You haven't cut them down yet?' she asked the larger of the two creatures that towered above her, her face taut with suppressed anger.

'I haven't been ordered to,' it replied grumpily, shifting its weight and stomping its feet.

'Well I'm ordering you to do it now.'

It pulled a device from its belt and pressed one of the oversized buttons. Immediately, the manacles on Amber and Natasha's wrists sprung open and they dropped to the floor where they both instantly collapsed. The woman stepped forward and crouched down with them.

'I'm terribly sorry about this. They were ordered to find the greatest and most resourceful warrior on that world, but couldn't decide which of you qualified as such, so kept you both alive.'

'Kept us...' Amber said. 'They killed our husbands. Murdered them without remorse. Plus another couple. An innocent couple. All for—'

'Don't blame the Drakani. They were just following the orders of the Arcadians.'

'Is that supposed to make some kind of sense?' Natasha asked, rubbing her sore wrists as blood flowed back toward her fingertips.

The woman shook her head. 'It will. Listen, there's been a complication. My name is Tamara Jax, and I need your help if we're going to have any hope of saving humanity.'

The Arcadia Series

THE NEXT BOOK IN THE EPIC ARCADIA SERIES

TRINARY CODE

**MAROONED ON A FAR-OFF WORLD
A TRIBE OF HUMANS BATTLE TO SURVIVE**

DID YOU ENJOY EDEN'S GATE?

I WOULD BE HUGELY GRATEFUL IF YOU COULD LEAVE AN HONEST REVIEW ON AMAZON.

☆☆☆☆☆

EITHER COPY THE LINK BELOW TO BE TAKEN TO THE EDEN'S GATE PAGE, OR CHECK YOUR RECENT ORDERS.

AND THANK YOU.

amazon.co.uk/dp/B08BYYVY8N

The Arcadia Series

Printed in Great Britain
by Amazon